Please return this item to any Sandwell Library on or before the return date.

You may renew the item unless it has been reserved by another borrower.

You can renew your library items by using the 24/7 renewal hotline number - 0121 569 4949
or FREE online at opac-lib.sandwell.gov.uk

THANK YOU FOR USING YOUR LIBRARY

BY THE SAME AUTHOR

NOVELS
Bridles Lane (West Country Trilogy #1)
Hills of Silver (West Country Trilogy #2)
Wild Light (West Country Trilogy #3)
Forgotten Places
The Devil and the Deep Blue Sea

SHORT STORIES
Moonshine (West Country Trilogy Prequel)
Goldfields: A Ghost Story
The Dutchman
Afterlife

ONE OF US BURIED

A NOVEL

JOHANNA CRAVEN

Copyright ©2021 Johanna Craven

All rights reserved. This book or any portion thereof may not be reproduced or used in any manner whatsoever without the express written permission of the author except for the use of brief quotations in line with copyright law.

www.johannacraven.com

ISBN: 978-0-9945364-1-9

PART ONE

I imagine I can still see the blood on my hands. Perhaps my fingers are forever stained.

I hide my hands in the folds of my skirts. Focus on the rhythmic clack of footsteps against stone.

I am surrounded by men, as I was the day I arrived in this place. And just like that day, there are soldiers in red coats, convicts, settlers. Englishmen, Irishmen and me, the lone woman. We all step into the courtroom together, though we are anything but equals.

My mind is on the distant sigh of the sea, on the pearly afternoon light, on the wall of birdsong that comes before evening. These things have been part of my world for the past two years, but only now, with my end approaching, am I coming to see their beauty.

They sent me to this place; this sun-bleached colony at the end of the world, to pay for my crimes; to weave cloth, to populate this land with my descendants.

But there will be no descendants. No more cloth, no more birdsong, no more light.

For there can be only one verdict. My bloodstained hands will see me to the gallows. How can I pretend to be surprised? I knew from the start I would never leave this place alive.

CHAPTER ONE

Penal Colony of New South Wales
1806

The land was a shadow breaking the horizon. An illusion, surely. I'd begun to believe the sea was without end.

Creaks and groans and rattles of the ship. I felt the shoulders of the other convict women bump up against mine.

The water came at me before I'd readied myself. Seamen upended buckets over our heads, to a grizzled chorus of cursing. I wrapped my arms around my chest as the water turned my thin shift transparent.

"That's it," laughed one of the sailors, as we tried to clean our grime-caked bodies with grime-caked hands. "Make yourselves presentable." And then more laughter, as though he, like the rest of us, knew any chance we had of making ourselves presentable was long gone.

I shivered. Here, on the outskirts of our new life, the

wind was cold, though the air held a lingering warmth. The scratches Hannah Clapton had made on the bulkheads told us it was mid-April; autumn, apparently, here at the bottom of the earth.

I looked out across the sun-streaked water, watching the edges of that land sharpen. My lips parted and I tasted salt on my tongue.

Dire as conditions were on the *Norfolk*, they had become familiar. The fortnightly wash was not unexpected, nor was the speed with which we'd be shunted back into the convicts' quarters, or the beads of hot, black pitch that seeped through the deck and dotted our bunks like remnants of plague. But the land awaiting us was utterly unknown.

Back down below, the stench swung at me; a soupy haze of bodies, and filth, and inescapable damp. The few minutes on deck had given me a chance to breathe. The iron grille slammed behind us, padlock closed tight. We elbowed and shoved our way to the pile of trunks against the bulkheads, hunting for our belongings amidst the dark roll of the sea. This was our chance, we knew, to escape the mythical factory for women and serve our time as housemaids, or cooks. Perhaps a settler's wife.

We'd been permitted to bring one small trunk on the voyage. And while many of the women had brought nothing but the clothes on their backs, I'd carted along my best worsted gown, along with woollen stockings and a pair of gloves I'd lost just days out of England.

On the ship we'd been given clothing for our new life: two sets of shifts and petticoats, a linen cap and apron each, matching gowns – one blue striped, the other the colour of milky tea.

I pulled my trunk out from the bottom of the pile. There was my apron, my striped dress, a shift that had become sweat-stained and worn.

My worsted gown was gone. I stared blankly into the trunk, as though I might will it to reappear.

"All right, Nell?" Hannah Clapton asked from behind me.

I nodded stiffly, though I felt anything but all right. The ship was lurching violently, and the world was lurching with it. The unknown land was approaching and I couldn't find my gown. I'd convinced myself it would be my ticket out of the factory. My way of making myself presentable. I felt a wave of deep panic.

Hannah gave me a wry smile. "We'll be off this cursed ship soon at least." She tucked lank, grey-streaked hair beneath her cap and tried to bash the creases from her skirts.

"And then what?" I asked, still staring into the trunk. The unfamiliarity of what was next was tying my stomach in knots. Somehow, having to face it without my gown made it worse.

Hannah had no answer for me. Not that I'd expected one.

I took the striped flannel dress and petticoats from the trunk and tied my underskirts over my wet shift, fighting the elbows of the other women. Like all the clothing the Navy Board had issued, the skirts only reached halfway down my shins. I was unsure if it was a deliberate attempt to shame us, or ignorance on the part of the Navy Board. I buttoned my dress with unsteady fingers.

In the pale, hatched light of the convicts' quarters, we were identical creatures; long, loose hair and striped skirts; skin so thick with dirt the seawater had done little to clean us.

"Would you look at us?" I said to Hannah. "No man could ever tell us apart. What does it matter which one of us they choose?"

A faint smile curved in Hannah's round cheeks. "They'll be able to tell you apart, Nell. Ain't no worry about that."

I smiled wryly. She was right, of course. My fiery hair had never allowed me to hide, nor had the inches of height I had on most women. Perhaps blending into a crowd was a little wishful thinking.

I shoved on my cloth bonnet. Seawater trickled down my neck, but my skin was still velvety with grime, hair stiff as tarred rope.

I could feel the ship slowing, turning, groaning. Heard the roar as the anchor slid from its hawser and rattled down to the sea floor.

Movement in the men's quarters on the other side of the bulkheads. Shouted orders from the sailors. And a barrage of footsteps as the male prisoners were corralled onto deck.

I stood bedside Hannah at the foot of the ladder, staring up at the thin streams of sunlight outlining the hatch. My gaze darted around for anyone wearing my gown. In spite of everything, I couldn't let the damn thing go.

And then I was on deck, my new home folded out before me, and all thoughts of the gown gone. New South Wales was vast and bright; cracked mud flats straining for the water beneath high clouds and a sky almost violently blue. The sea swept in between jagged nuggets of land, tiny islands dotting the bay. The harbour swarmed with movement; bodies darting in and out of harbour taverns, women in coloured gowns who looked like they'd been plucked directly from Mayfair. Men chained at the ankles to one another hauled wood along the mudflats, the scarlet coats of the soldiers stark against the prisoners' bleakness. Behind it all, untameable forest; brown and green and thick with shadow. Eighteen years of colonisation, it seemed, had made little more than a dent on the place. Warm wind blew my hair across my cheek, bringing with it peals of laughter, shouts of men. A scent of sea, of sweat, of a land that felt raw and rugged, caught halfway between horror and inescapable beauty.

A crowd of men was waiting on the docks; settlers, emancipists, soldiers. At the midshipman's signal they charged up the gangway onto the deck of the *Norfolk*; seeking cooks, seeking housemaids, seeking wives.

We stood in line, blue-striped skirts after blue-striped skirts, silently awaiting inspection.

"Officers first," barked the naval lieutenant who had overseen the fortnightly dunking. And the soldiers were upon us. *Click click* went their boots. Their eyes raked over us like we were stock in a shop window.

I understood. We were a precious commodity here. Precious and vital. Despite our grimy skin and light fingers, the colony would die out without us.

"Right here, sir," Hannah belted out, as a pink-cheeked soldier strode past her. "Whatever it is you're looking for, I got it, you'll see."

One of the sailors clipped the back of her head to silence her.

The men took their cooks, their housemaids, their wives. They did not take me.

Though I did not want to be dragged from the ship and turned into a stranger's wife, I couldn't help a pang of bitterness. What was wrong with me? Was it my too-short skirts, or the crude colour of my hair? The freckles on my cheeks my governess had always urged me to cover with powder? Would things have been different if my gown had not been stolen? Perhaps.

Or perhaps somehow these men knew I was not well suited to being a housemaid. Even less suited to being a wife.

Us left-behind women were led from the ship and herded along the wharf that rose from the murky plane of the mudflats. Six months at sea and the ground was lurching beneath me. I felt unsteady on my legs as though I were a child just learning to walk.

We were led to a long log barge that knocked against the dock with each inhalation of the sea. A crooked shelter rose from the middle of the vessel like a misplaced turret.

I watched the waves spill over the edges of the barge. Such a thing was not seaworthy, surely. I had seen, had felt the power of the ocean; had witnessed the way it could toss ships and make men disappear. It would swallow a raft like that in one mouthful.

Hannah stopped at the front of the line, the rest of us dominoing into the back of her. "No," she said. "I ain't getting on that. I ain't. Not a chance."

The soldier at her side jabbed her in the shoulder with his rifle and she stumbled forward, landing on her knees on the barge. It seesawed on the surface, a swell of water gusting over it. One by one, we stepped on behind her. And before I could reconcile myself with the feel of solid earth beneath me, we were back on the water.

The barge, thankfully, did not take us to sea. Instead, the

waterman guided it down a wide, dark river, where the water became coppery and trees hung above us like ghosts. Bronze light shafted through the branches, banks of thick wilderness swallowing the specks of civilisation scarring Sydney Cove.

I hugged my knees, watching coloured birds swoop down and ripple the river. The sound from the forest was unending; musical trills and discordant birdcalls, within the constant sighing of trees and water. My senses felt overloaded.

There were fifteen women crammed onto the raft, watched over by two marines and the burly, bearded waterman. But our humanity seemed insignificant. I felt as though we were the only people left on earth.

We were to be taken to the factory for women in Parramatta, I knew, but what was that but a name? It seemed impossible there could be any civilisation among this endless wild.

For the first time, I began to truly appreciate the abrupt turn my life had taken. Somehow, tucked away within the confines of the ship, I had managed to block out the reality of it. Perhaps a part of me had believed that when I finally set foot on solid ground again, I would be back at the docks in Woolwich. I'd never known any home but London, so how could my mind fathom this boundless forest and this quicksilver river and the impossible stretch of the sky?

When the last of the light was sliding away, the waterman tied the barge to a chalky tree trunk at the river's edge. He disappeared into the shelter in the middle of the vessel and returned carrying a flask of water and a loaf of bread. He passed them among us.

Surely we weren't to stay here the night. Not with trees

all around us and nothing overhead by sky. The meagre shelter was barely big enough for a single person to stand.

In the corner of the barge, two women sat bundled in the thin grey blankets we had slept under on the *Norfolk*.

"Would you look at that?" Hannah said, jabbing a finger in their direction. "Don't I wish I were smart enough to have done the same."

I hugged my knees. The thought of bringing my blankets with me had never even crossed my mind. What kind of savage place was this, where we were not even to be given bedclothes? I forced down a mouthful of bread, the anxiety in my stomach leaving me with little appetite.

The waterman leaned back against the shelter, blowing a line of pipe smoke up into the darkening sky. The soldiers sat side by side on the riverbank, chuckling between themselves. One crunched on an apple and flung the core into the trees. The baby born on the voyage mewled in his mother's arms.

I wondered distantly at the time. The sun was slipping below the horizon, but in this strange place, I had no thought of whether that made it ten in the evening or three in the afternoon. Time seemed insignificant. A construct of men trying to tame an untameable world.

As the darkness thickened, a chaos of shrieking pressed against us. Birdsong, I told myself, but in this violent wall of sound, there was not the barest hint of musicality. The river lapped up against trees that seemed to grow within the water; their gnarled, bare branches eerie in the twilight.

And then there were stars; an endless brilliance lighting up a deep black and purple sky. I lay on my back with my spare clothing in a cloth bag beneath my head, staring up at the crescent moon that hung above the treetops. Lying there in the cradle of the river, I could give no form to the shape my life was to take. It hardly seemed to matter. Against the vastness of this place, what was I but an insignificant scrap? And with each minute I spent here, I was coming to see that, as a discarded woman bound for the factory, the shape my life would take mattered less than anything.

CHAPTER TWO

'It will readily be admitted by every impartial observer ... that there is no class of the community [that] calls more earnestly for the attention of the state than these unhappy objects, who have from various causes and temptations, departed from the paths of virtue and forfeited their civil liberty."

Rev. Samuel Marsden
A Few Observations on the Situation of the Female Convict in New South Wales
1808-1817

By dawn, the barge was carrying us back down the river. My back was aching from a night on the uneven logs, my skin a mosaic of insect bites. I'd managed a few hours of broken sleep, punctuated by images of creatures in the dark. I couldn't tell if they had come from my dreams or reality.

Bend after bend, the river swept onwards, the

waterman's oar rising and falling, rising and falling. Just as I was beginning to believe it would go on forever, the wilderness broke.

A riverside tavern. A sailboat tied to a narrow jetty. And then a cluster of mud huts and farmland.

Parramatta.

A row of redcoats was waiting on the riverbank to meet us, rifles held across their chests. How many? Six? Eight? Ten soldiers with their weapons out, ready to greet a barge full of women. Their message was clear; we were prisoners. Step into line or come to regret it. But there was something oddly defensive about the soldiers' gesture. I couldn't help but feel as though those rifles offered them a little protection against everything that raft of women represented. Protection against allure, desire, temptation.

The redcoats peered at us as the raft bumped against the wharf, sizing us up like the men had when they'd climbed aboard the *Norfolk*. The look in their eyes told us we were both nothing and everything. A commodity to be coveted, bartered, perhaps even feared.

The tallest of the soldiers stepped up to the waterman, exchanging words I couldn't hear. He looked out across the barge at the new arrivals. I lowered my head, cowed by his presence, shame tugging my shoulders forward. I held my breath as I stepped past him onto the narrow wooden jetty.

I had not been expecting London, of course. But this place; what was this? Rusty plains of farmland pushed up against a tangled, grey-green forest, intercepted by a wide, dusty road that cut through the middle of the settlement. Huts dotted the farmland, presided over by the twin spires of the church. The morning sun was searing the tops of the trees, and I squinted in the brassy light.

Two of the soldiers strode past and I found myself taking a step closer to Hannah. She gave my wrist a squeeze as we followed the marines down the main street.

"Just keeping walking," she murmured.

And so I kept walking. For what else was there to do?

We were led to the government food store, a sandstone warehouse on the edge of the settlement. Soldiers turned through our indentation documents and scrawled our names on their ledgers. And here was our food for the week, wrapped into packages as small as our fists. I looked down at the bundle in my hand. I had little thought of what was inside it. But one look at its miserable size and my stomach was already rolling with hunger.

The factory was nothing more than two long warehouses above what I would later learn was the men's jail. Up the stairs we went, herded by the soldiers who had lavished us with food.

It was the stench of the place that hit me first; the same filth and damp, and unbreathable air we had languished in on the prison ship. The floorboards were misshapen and dark, the blackened bricks above an unlit grate marking all there was of a kitchen. The place was a chaos of rattling looms and whirring wheels, punctuated by the shrieks of young children. Women hunched over spinning wheels, their babies in baskets, strapped to their backs, tottering across the muck and straw that carpeted the floor. The carding machines and looms sighed and thudded steadily, my muscles tensing as the jagged rhythm moved inside me.

Here came the superintendent, with his beak of a nose

and cloud of white hair. Waistcoat straining against a puffed-out chest. He looked over us, clustered at the top of the stairs like lost sheep.

"Plenty of them," he said to the soldiers in a thick Scottish accent. "The men not like what they saw?"

One of the marines chuckled. "A bad bunch perhaps."

The superintendent led us into the second warehouse through a sea of blue-striped dresses. Some of the women peered at us, as though inspecting, calculating. Others kept their eyes on their spinning, seemingly oblivious to our arrival. What were we to these other women, I wondered? Potential friends? Rivals? Nothing more than an inconvenience?

The bad bunch of us was divided; some to the carding machines at the far side of the warehouse, others to the looms. I was shunted by the superintendent to an empty stool in front of a large spinning wheel, a sack of colourless wool dumped at my feet. I watched some beastly black insect crawl through the mass of it.

"See she knows what she's doing," the superintendent said to the woman next to me. Then his heavy footsteps clomped off towards the other new arrivals. I gave the young woman next to me little more than a glance.

"I know how to spin," I mumbled.

In truth, I'd had little cause to do such a thing in the past, but I didn't want to speak, or sit by that mangy sack of wool and be taught the ways of my new life. Tears were stabbing my throat, and I knew if I spoke again they would spill. For all its chaos, there was an empty, hollow feeling to this factory above the jail. A sadness that pressed down upon the place, wrought by the regret and grief of these striped-skirted women. I felt an ache deep within my chest that I was to exist in a place filled with such sorry creatures. And at the realisation that I was now one of them.

I shot a quick glance at the woman beside me, watching as she sat rolls of carded fleece on her lap and teased it onto the yarn that was gathering on her wheel. Yes, I thought, I remembered this from some long ago, barely accessible part of my childhood. An aunt's house. A spinning wheel in the parlour. I let the memory in my hands take over.

Slowly, I pedalled, then faster, eyes on the wheel to avoid even a glance at this horror that was now my life. At the feel of the wool sliding through my fingers, and the mesmerising cycle of the spokes before me, I felt my tears sink back below the surface.

An hour, perhaps two, and heavy footsteps sounded up the stairs, the rhythm a counterpoint to the clattering of the looms. Here was the soldier I had seen at the river. He strode across the factory floor towards the superintendent. Bent his head and spoke in a murmur.

His presence seemed to suck the air from the room. I felt my eyes pull towards him.

"No," hissed a voice beside me. "Don't even look at him."

The woman next to me at the spinning wheels was sharp-eyed and slender. A few years from thirty, I guessed; close to my own age. Strands of brown hair hung out the sides of her cap, the lines of her face precise and angular.

I frowned, taken aback by her brusqueness. "Who is he?"

"That's Lieutenant Blackwell." The woman's voice was dark, despite the gentle Irish contours of her speech. "He's the worst of all them lobster bastards. Full of hate."

Heat prickled my neck. But curiosity had me glancing back over my shoulder.

The lieutenant was somewhere between thirty and forty, I guessed. His hair was coffee-coloured and straight, slightly overgrown. A sculpted, faintly handsome face, but one that held neither kindness nor malice. There was a blankness to him. An emotionlessness. He looked too empty to be capable of hate.

His pale eyes shifted, catching mine. I looked away, my heart jolting. I pedalled the spinning wheel harder, focusing on the steady rhythm of the thing until the soldier's footsteps disappeared back down the stairs.

"I saw the raft come in this morning," the woman beside me said once my chaotic spinning had slowed. "Were your journey all right then? Did the most of you survive?"

I nodded. "The most of us, yes." We'd lost just four women on the journey; a number I knew enough to be grateful for. Their deaths had not been announced to us, nor were we allowed on deck for their burials. We'd just assumed them dead when they'd never returned from the surgeon's cabin.

"You're English," said the woman, making it sound like something of an insult. "Your ship come in from London then?"

I nodded.

She made a noise from the back of her throat. "What's your name?"

"It's Nell," I told her. "Nell Marling."

Her hazel eyes shifted, as though debating whether to trust me. "Lottie Byrne," she said finally, giving me a ghost of a smile. The warmth of the gesture filled me with relief. I hadn't realised how much I was craving kindness.

"You'll be all right, Nell," Lottie said, her eyes back on the wheel. "We do our best to look out for each other. There's no one else going to do that for us."

When dusk fell over the factory, bells rang and spinning wheels slowed. Women climbed from their stools and spread out around the edges of the room, claiming their belongings, their squares of floor, their children. Some, I saw, had brought their threadbare blankets from the prison ships. Others upended sacks of oily wool and curled up on them between the spinning wheels.

No beds in the factory, but room on the floor for perhaps thirty. Room for less than half the women whose hands were red and raw from weaving Parramatta cloth. No space for any of us who had just climbed off the barge. The superintendent herded us towards the stairwell.

"Where are we to go?" Hannah asked.

"I don't care. Find yourself lodgings somewhere in town."

A humourless laugh escaped me. This was a joke, surely. Find lodgings? With what money? All I had to my name were my shin-length skirts and a pair of old stockings.

I stepped blankly out of the factory, flanked by the other women from the *Norfolk*. I followed them over a rickety wooden bridge, back towards the main street. After the stench of the factory, the air smelled fragrant and clean. Birds shrieked, swooping and zigzagging through a pink and lilac sky.

I had been expecting bars and locked gates, like the cell I had languished in at Newgate. But my incarceration here was disguised as freedom. I saw then that there was little point in restraining us. In the fading daylight, the surrounding forest was a shadow. But I could see there was no end to it. The land was so vast it was dizzying. Only a madwoman would turn her back on the meagre security offered by the settlement.

I heard Lottie call my name. I spun around, achingly glad to see her.

"How do we go about finding lodgings?" I wrapped my arms around myself, wishing for a cloak or shawl.

She nodded to the street ahead of us. "They have lodgings."

Word of our arrival, it seemed, had reached the men of Parramatta. They stood on the edge of the street in clusters, reminding me of the men who had come trawling through the *Norfolk* in search of wives. But these were no well-dressed settlers, or soldiers with polished buttons. These men were grime-streaked and ragged, with scruffy beards and unwashed skin. Men, I knew with certainty, who had been sent here on His Majesty's pleasure. I recognised the dejected slope of their shoulders, the dulled anger in their eyes.

They called out to us. *Shelter and fire. Four shillings a week. Come on lass, you can do no better.*

"We're to lodge with these men?" I coughed.

"Four shillings a week," Lottie said flatly. "For shelter and fire."

"Four shillings a week?" I repeated. "How am I to pay

that?"

Lottie said nothing. My jaw tightened as the reality of the situation swung at me. We were that precious commodity of soft skin and curves. A novelty here in this land of men.

"They're willing to bargain," she said finally. "They'll give you a little coin as well as extra food and lodgings." She gave me a wry smile. "A fine deal."

"You do this?" I asked. "Sell yourself for a bed?"

She pressed her lips into a thin white line. I wondered if I had offended her with my sharpness.

I swallowed the sickness in my throat. "I'll sleep on the street."

"Don't be mad. You want to be torn to pieces by the savages?"

A hot ribbon of fear ran through me, but I pushed it away. I'd heard talk of the savages, of course; wild warriors who could throw four spears in the time it took to load a flintlock pistol. I'd convinced myself they were little more than a myth. The savages hiding in the dark was a fear I didn't have room for.

Head down, I began to walk. Away from the factory, away from the men. I had no thought of where I was going. There was nothing in this place. I just needed to keep moving.

"Do as you like," Lottie called after me.

I closed my eyes, feeling a cold wind up against my cheeks. This place had taken my freedom. But it would not take my dignity. Not any more than it had already.

Huts of mud and bark lined the road, stretches of farmland behind them. I knew well I'd find nothing beyond the rim of the town but more of the trees and dark that had flanked us down the river.

"Where you off to, lass?"

I spun around to see a tall, dark-haired man standing a few yards behind me. His cheeks were pock-marked and leathery, thick stubble across his square jaw.

"You'll not find much out that way." His voice was rough and Irish. "Two hours to Toongabbie." He chuckled. "That's if the dragons don't get you."

I kept walking. "Leave me alone."

"I've a bed if you need it."

"No. I'm not interested."

He reached suddenly for my wrist and yanked me back towards him. "You think you're too good for us?" Breath stale against my cheek. "Look at yourself, lass. Just look where you are."

Fear shot through me and I pulled away. "Get away from me." I changed direction abruptly and strode towards the dark spires of the church. I heard the man's laughter behind me.

"You think a factory lass is welcome in a house of God?"

I began to walk faster. My cloth bag swung on one shoulder, carrying the creased mess of my spare dress. Animal sounds rose from the darkness; screeches, rasps, and the blessedly familiar lowing of cows.

In the falling dark, the church was empty. Through the narrow windows, I could see nothing but shadow. I pushed against the door, but it refused to move. Perhaps the man was right. Perhaps the factory lasses weren't welcome here. A locked door to keep out the lags.

I made my way around the back of the building, where shadows lay thick and allowed me to hide. The roof was slightly overhanging; perhaps half a foot of shelter. I leant wearily against the wall. Laughter floated out of a crooked hut I assumed was a tavern. The women from the *Norfolk* had disappeared, lured into houses for four shillings a week. I glanced into the street for the dark-haired man. Was glad to find him gone.

The sudden stillness struck me. When was the last time I had been alone? On the *Norfolk,* there had been not a scrap of privacy. In seven months, I'd not done so much as relieve myself without another woman watching. This sudden isolation felt disorienting.

My legs were aching, and my fingers stung from hours at the spinning wheel. Exhausted, I let myself sink to the ground.

The acrid stench of my food package hit me the moment I opened my cloth bag. I pulled it out warily, unwrapping the brown paper. The sliver of salt pork was discoloured and gnarled, the smell of it turning my stomach. I hurled it into the darkness. At the bottom of the package was a small cup of flour. Unspoiled, as far as I could tell. And what, I wondered, staring blankly down at my food rations, was I to do with a cup of flour and not so much as a candle flame to bake it into bread?

I wrapped up the package and set it back inside my bag. Curled up on my side and tried to find a little sleep.

CHAPTER THREE

"During the night these women spread themselves through all the town and neighbourhood of Parramatta, and [some] are glad to cohabit with any poor, wretched man who can give them shelter for the night."

Rev. Samuel Marsden
An Answer to Certain Calumnies
1826

At the spinning wheels the next morning, Lottie asked questions. Where did I go last night? Did I sleep? Who took me?

After rolling around in the dirt all night, I was too tired to speak. But her last question sparked something inside me. "No one took me," I said sharply. "I slept on the street is all."

"On the street?" she demanded. "What about the savages?"

"I didn't see any savages." I turned back to the spinning wheel. My eyes were stinging with exhaustion and Lottie's questions were getting under my skin. Hunger was gnawing deep into my stomach.

"So what then?" she said, after not nearly enough silence. "You going to spend your whole sentence sleeping in the street? Seven years without a roof over your head?"

I didn't answer. I couldn't contemplate the rest of my sentence. All I could think about was what I would do that night. That morning, I'd walked back up the stairs to the factory to find the door unlocked. Perhaps, I thought, I could creep inside at dawn and manage an hour of sleep on the staircase before the bells rang for the workday to start.

"What d'you do?" Lottie asked. "Thieving?"

I kept my eyes on the wool gliding though my fingers. "Yes. Thieving."

"And me," she said. "I asked a cobbler the price of a pair of shoes. He took one look at me and told me I couldn't afford them. So I pinched them."

I flashed her a smile. "Sounds as though he deserved it."

The superintendent stopped by the spinning wheel of a dark-haired woman in the corner of the room.

"Stand up," he said sharply.

The woman stood, arms held protectively around her swollen belly. The superintendent clicked his tongue in loud disapproval.

"Took him long enough," Lottie murmured. "Poor thing's about to drop right here on the factory floor."

"Who is the father of your child?" the superintendent asked.

The woman looked at him squarely. "Reverend Samuel

Marsden."

A snort of suppressed laughter went through the room. I felt a small smile on the edge of my lips.

Lottie caught my eye and chuckled. "Never in my life have I met a man with as many children as the good Reverend Marsden."

When I stepped out of the factory that evening, three soldiers were approaching the building. I recognised the tallest as Lieutenant Blackwell.

I put my head down and quickened my pace.

"You. Stop."

My chest tightened. I froze, looking ahead for Lottie, but she had disappeared. Two of the soldiers continued into the jail, but Blackwell took a few steps towards me, boots crunching on the road. Despite the dust, his uniform was immaculate, brass buttons gleaming and the braiding on his jacket inexplicably white. My heart began to speed.

"You came in on the *Norfolk*," he said. It was not a question. His voice was deeper than I had been expecting. I could feel it in my chest. "I passed you this morning," he said. "Saw you sleeping behind the church. There's no need for that."

I felt a flush of embarrassment.

"I know the system here is not so easy for..." He hesitated. "New arrivals."

I almost laughed at that. Was he not part of the system, this polished officer in the New South Wales Corps? I kept my eyes on the ground, as though I might save myself from turning to stone by avoiding his eyes.

Somewhere between London and Parramatta, I had

trained myself to not be afraid. I'd spent months in abject terror; a tearful mess in my Newgate cell, weak legged in the courtroom dock. I had no strength, because I'd come to believe it was my place to be weak. To let the men in my life carry me; to pick me up when I fell.

But one morning, in the dark and damp bowels of the prison ship, I came to see there was no one coming to rescue me. If I was to survive in this new life, I would have to find a way through my terror.

And so I steeled myself against my fear. Found some long-hidden part of me that vaguely resembled strength. The filth of the *Norfolk,* the mountains of ocean, whatever awaited me in New South Wales; I would find a way through it. Because my only other option was to die.

But standing in front of Lieutenant Blackwell, I felt that old fear returning. I felt unsteady around him, as though those expressionless eyes were prising away the wall I'd erected around myself to keep my terror at bay.

Full of hate, Lottie had said. But when I looked at Blackwell, I didn't see hate. I didn't see anger. I didn't see anything at all. And that, I realised, was what made me feel so damn unbalanced.

"I have shelter," he said after a moment.

I shook my head. "I know the price of shelter in this place."

"Four shillings a week," he said evenly.

"And what else?"

No response.

"I don't have four shillings a week." I put my head down and walked, making it clear our discussion was over.

That night, thunder rolled in across the mountains and the air thickened with approaching rain. Black clouds drained the colour from the sky.

I crouched with my back against the wall of the church. The awnings above my head were narrow and I knew they would do little to keep out the rain.

My stomach groaned. Hunger seemed to be seeping into every part of me; weakening my legs and tangling my thoughts. Tears pricked my eyes and I blinked them away. I couldn't find the energy to cry.

It was my empty stomach that led me to the tavern. Lamps flickered in the windows, and I could hear a muffled roar of laughter coming from inside. I had never been in such a place before, and I was dimly aware that I ought to have been nervous. But things had gone too far for that. What room was there for emotions as petty as nervousness when my life had been pared down to a thing of survival?

I pushed open the door. The place was cramped and noisy, bathed in hot orange light. Men in grimy shirtsleeves were clustered at the bar, and at the crooked tables dotted around the room. I spotted a few women among them; faces I'd seen at the spinning wheels that day.

I glanced around, my heart thudding.

What was I seeking? Money? Food? A man who would use my body as payment for shelter from the rain? I wasn't sure. I only knew that staying beneath the awnings of the church tonight would nudge me towards insanity.

I saw it then, on the edge of a table; a plate of roasted meat, two chunks of potato. A man sat with his back to it, howling with laughter, far too engrossed in the woman on his lap to bother with his supper. I edged towards the plate, as calmly as I could. Eyes down, cap pulled low. With my striped skirts and fiery hair, I knew I would draw attention. And before I could think, could hesitate, could judge myself, the potatoes were in my apron pocket.

The man whirled around at my movement. "Hey!"

He tipped the woman off his lap and made a grab for my wrist, but I was already darting towards the door. I clattered my way through chairs and bodies. Raced out into the street. I turned down the narrow alley beside the tavern and hurried into the thick darkness.

"Where the hell are you?" the man called. I could see the dark shape of him at the top of the alley. I pressed myself against the wall, holding my breath.

The sky opened suddenly, sending the man hurrying back into the tavern. I lifted my face upwards, grateful for the downpour. Water pelted the road, turning it to mud in seconds. I hurried back towards the church and pressed myself against the wall, trying to find shelter beneath the narrow awnings. Rivulets of water rolled from the roof and slid down the back of my neck. With each shard of lightning, pieces of Parramatta were lit up, picked out from the enormity of the surrounding forest. Rain drummed loudly against the earth, making the bush smell fresh and clean.

And then there was a figure a few yards from the church. Between the shafts of lightning, he was little more than a silhouette, but his height left no doubt as to who it was.

I turned away. I didn't want him here, with his *I have shelter* and his ludicrous pretence that I would not have to part with a piece of myself in order to claim it.

He came towards me slowly, footsteps sucking through the wet earth.

"I don't need shelter," I said, before he could speak. I gave an empty laugh; a laugh to keep myself from screaming. Rain ran down my cheeks. Ran down his cheeks. It pooled in the mud at our feet.

"And that is a humorous thing, is it?" he asked.

I didn't answer. In spite of his authority, I felt no need, or desire, to justify myself to this man. I took a step back, my shoulders pressing hard against the wall of the church.

He stood for a moment with his head tilted. He was still wearing his coat, but his head was bare and his gorget removed. Had he returned to his hut, then thought better of it, and headed out into the storm to rescue me? Why did the thought of that make me so uncomfortable?

"What is it that stops you from trusting me?" he asked. "Is it my uniform? Or is it the man inside it?"

"I don't have money to pay for lodgings," I said. I did not want to go into issues such as trust. I just wanted him gone.

"There are other ways to pay for lodgings," he said.

I gritted my teeth, shook my head. "Please leave."

He stood motionless, eyes fixed on me. "How can you sleep out here?"

"I'll manage," I said. But I was sure he hadn't heard me. The wild weather had carried my words away. A sense of complete and utter hopelessness pressed down on me. This storm, this land, this dark, it would swallow me.

Blackwell slid a hand around the top of my arm. "Come on now. You're being foolish."

My breath caught. "You're going to force me?"

But I walked with him, because what other choice was there? Take me to shelter. Take the last scrap of dignity I have left.

It had taken me less than two nights to crumble, to succumb to this twisted game Parramatta was playing.

For the first time since I had arrived in this place, I let my tears fall.

CHAPTER FOUR

When we reached a small mud hut at the far end of the village, Blackwell let go of my arm. Beyond the building I could see nothing but darkness.

He opened the door and gestured for me to enter. I stood frozen in the doorway, wiping my eyes hurriedly with my wet sleeve. The lieutenant stepped awkwardly past me, his dark head inches from the roof.

"You're frightened," he said. "I'm sorry. I didn't mean to frighten you. I just wanted to get you inside. These storms are dangerous. They're far more wild than those in England. Last month a man was killed by a falling tree." He lit a lamp and turned to face me, his hollow cheeks darkened with stubble. Thick brown hair was plastered to his head, water dripping from the ends. The dancing light left shadows beneath his eyes.

I wondered distantly if he would chase me if I ran.

He took a step towards me, and I inhaled sharply, but he just reached over my shoulder to close the door. I stood with my back pressed against it and glanced about the hut.

The sleeping pallet was narrow, pressed up against a wall, a wash basin beside it. A crooked brick chimney climbed into the thatched roof, a blackened pot hanging from a hook above the grate. Crooked shelves jutted out from one wall, lined with jars of potted meat and a bottle of liquor. A pile of books sat on the shelf below. A table was pressed into a corner of the room, the lamp flickering in the centre.

Water drizzled in through the cloth covering the small window, rain pattering in the puddles outside the hut. Thunder rumbled distantly. The storm was moving, I realised, drifting away from us, moving out towards the ocean. I could hear the faint burble of the river behind the hut.

"Please," I said huskily, "I don't want this." Every inch of my body felt taut. "Just let me go back out." When he didn't speak, I added, "The storm is passing."

Blackwell slid off his wet jacket and hung it over the back of a chair. "What's your name?"

I swallowed. "Eleanor Marling." I didn't know why I'd introduced myself that way. No one had called me Eleanor since my father had died.

Blackwell reached for the cloth that hung on a hook beside the table. He held it out to me. "Dry yourself."

I wiped my face and squeezed the water from my hair. I sat the damp lump of fabric on the table. It was streaked with the dirt I had wiped from my cheeks. Blackwell looked down at the bulge in my apron.

"What's in your pocket?"

Panic welled up inside me. Twice I'd broken the law. And twice I'd been caught.

I brought out the potatoes and sat them on the table.

"Where did you get those?"

I looked up at him. What point was there in lying? "I stole them from the tavern." I swallowed heavily. "My meat was rotten. And I've no way of making bread."

He nodded.

I gripped the edge of the table, my legs weak beneath me. Blackwell looked down at the potatoes.

"Eat them," he said. "You must be hungry."

I hesitated. Was I walking into a trap? Would he haul me to the cells the moment I took the first bite? But then my hunger got the better of me.

The lowest point of my life, I saw then, was not the moment I'd been arrested. Or sharing a shit bucket with fifty women at Newgate. It was this moment; here, now, eating a stolen potato, about to sell my body to the redcoats, with the filth of the factory clinging to my skin. I turned my face downwards as I ate, unable to look another person in the eye.

Blackwell took a loaf from the shelf and broke off the end. Held it out to me.

I chewed slowly, the dry bread sticking in my throat. But the food in my stomach took away an ache that had begun to consume me.

I could feel Blackwell's eyes on me. Could feel the heat rising from his body. I closed my eyes. I had eaten his bread now. The thing was done. I owed him compensation, and my only way of paying was to lie on my back and lift my skirts.

He opened a wooden storage chest beside the bed and took out a thin grey blanket. Laid it on the floor in front of the empty grate. "You'll sleep here."

I watched him smooth the edges of the blanket across the uneven dirt floor. What was this? If he was going to take me, I just wanted it over with.

But I went to it, that thin little blanket by the unlit fire. My sodden skirts tangled around my legs, dampening the blanket. I was barely warmer than I had been on the street. Blackwell crouched in front of the grate and laid a fire, despite the water drizzling down the chimney. I shuffled backwards and hugged my knees to avoid his arm brushing against mine.

The fire hissed and spat before taking. I watched a line of steam rise from my clothing. I was acutely aware of Blackwell's presence as he moved slowly around the edges of the hut, rearranging things that didn't need rearranging. The silence was thick and heavy. Rain pattered dully against the window.

He took a book from the shelf and carried it to his sleeping pallet. He slid off his boots, and stretched out on his side, a blanket pulled to his waist and the book opened on the floor beside him.

A faint flicker of hope stirred inside me; perhaps he wouldn't come to me that night. But that scrap of hope felt too dangerous. I steeled myself against it.

I looked past him to the door. I could reach it without difficulty.

I could run.

But I didn't. What was keeping me there? Was it the warmth of the fire, or the roof over my head? Was it the faint flicker of curiosity I felt for this man? Perhaps I just wanted to see who would be first to break this silence.

I shivered hard and shuffled closer to the fire. Blackwell looked up from his book.

"Your clothes are wet," he said. "If you sleep in them you'll get ill."

His words were matter of fact. No threat, no lechery. But I understood them to be an order. I wrapped the blanket around myself and reached beneath it to unbutton my bodice, wriggling out of my dress and laying it beside the fire to dry.

Was he still watching me? I couldn't tell. I dared a glance over my shoulder. His eyes were on his book, but the muscles in his forearm were tense beneath his rolled-up shirtsleeves.

There were no more words. Just a thick, weighty silence and the crackle of the fire.

I see now, with painful clarity, that I should never have set foot inside that hut. I ought to have stayed beneath the awnings of the church and let the rain soak me through to my bones. But I didn't leave. Instead, I stayed with the blanket pulled to my chin, hardly daring to breathe. Waiting for footsteps to come towards me. Waiting for the moment that I lost a part of myself.

When I opened my eyes, dawn was flooding the hut and Lieutenant Blackwell's sleeping pallet was empty. I sat up, rolling the stiffness out of my shoulders.

I'd done my best to stay awake through the night, but exhaustion had finally pulled me down. It was a surprise to be woken by the morning light and not the lieutenant's breath on my skin.

I climbed to my feet and folded the blanket, hanging it over the back of a chair. My skirts were still damp and smelled of wet wool.

My eyes moved to the small wash basin sitting beside the storage chest. It was filled with clean water, a bar of soap and a washcloth resting on the rim. It was almost as though it had been placed there for me. I knew it foolish to think such a thing. I would likely be punished if Blackwell returned and discovered me splashing about in his washbin uninvited. But I didn't care. I could barely remember the last time my skin hadn't been caked in grime.

I plunged the washcloth into the water, scrubbing at my arms until they were red. I sloughed away at my face and neck, then lifted my skirts and worked the cloth up my legs, beneath my shift and across my stomach. I worked the soap suds over my body, inhaling their faintly sweet scent. Tears of gratitude overcame me. I had become so accustomed to the layer of filth on my skin, to my own stench of grime and sweat and saltwater. With soap suds gliding over my body, I felt fleetingly, preciously human again.

I looked back at the basin. I had left the water murky and brown. I carried it outside and emptied it into the vegetable patch behind the hut. Then I went to the river and refilled the basin, ready for Blackwell's return.

I stepped back out into the street, the door scraping loudly as I tugged it closed. Broken as my sleep had been, it was better than any I could remember. There was a clarity to my thoughts I'd not had for months.

I crossed the bridge and walked towards the factory, a wry smile on my lips. I tried to imagine the prisoners at Newgate walking obediently back down Giltspur Street to be let back into their cells.

As I reached the jail, I stopped abruptly. A man had a convict woman pinned up against the wall, driving into her with loud, rhythmic grunts. The woman caught my eye and I turned away hurriedly. I couldn't bear to look. Not at what was happening to her. And not at that haunted expression in her eyes.

On the *Norfolk*, I, like all the other women, had not been spared male attention.

A young ship's mate had ever so kindly chaperoned me back down below after we'd been let out to wash. Invited me to lift my skirts.

I shook my head, grabbing my dress from my bunk and holding it against my wet shift to shield myself. "Leave me alone." He could force me, yes, I knew that well. But why bother? There was nothing about me that warranted a fight. There were plenty of women who were willing. Talk rippled regularly through our quarters of girls who had earned a little extra favour by seeing to the sailors' needs. An hour of fresh air. A scrap of extra bread. A comfortable bed for the night.

"I can do things for you in return," the ship's mate said. "I'll call on your family in England. Give them news of you."

Later, I found out this ship's hand had promised to call on families from Glasgow to London with news of their wayward daughters.

I gave him a wry smile. "No one's waiting for news of me."

Foolishly, I'd imagined bartering with our bodies might end once we were back on solid ground. But I was quickly coming to learn the currency of this place. Coming to learn where the women in striped skirts fitted into the puzzle.

I hurried up the stairs, eyes down and my thoughts churning. I was acutely aware that I had not paid for my night on Blackwell's floor. Not in coin, not with my body. I couldn't fathom his intentions.

When the bells rang at the factory that night, what would I do? I'd been gifted a night of food and fire, and I knew myself lucky. Going back to that hut felt like I was tempting fate. But what was the alternative? Lottie was right; I could hardly spend my entire sentence sleeping in the street.

It was a decision for the evening, I told myself as I took my seat at the spinning wheel. I was coming to learn that the best way to survive in this place was to look no further than the moment I had in front of me.

Out the window that day I caught my first glimpse of the reverend. I'd heard talk of Samuel Marsden the day before; magistrate of Parramatta, assistant chaplain of the colony and, if the women in the factory were to be believed, father of every illegitimate child this side of Sydney.

Maggie Abbott, one of the most outspoken women in the factory, stuck up a finger as she filed past the window on her way to the carding machine. "Would you just look at that bastard? Strutting around with his chest puffed out like he were the king himself."

I glanced out the grime-streaked glass. I guessed Marsden close to forty; broad and flat-faced with pale, thinning hair. He swept past the factory, dark robes billowing, without a glance in our direction.

I took a sack of carded fleece from the corner of the room and carried it to my spinning wheel.

"Off he goes," Maggie sang as she made her way to the wheel beside me. "Potato on legs. And with all the mind of one too."

On the other side of her, Hannah gave a snort of

laughter.

"Quiet, all of you," barked the superintendent. I hid a smile and tucked myself onto my stool.

Soft sobbing was coming from the woman behind me. I tried not to look at her. I wondered if Maggie's jabbering had been intended to block out the sound of the woman's grief.

I had become adept at ignoring another woman's tears. I'd been surrounded by crying women for the past year; tears in the cells at Newgate, in the convicts' quarters of the *Norfolk*, and now here at the factory.

Once, I had been empathetic by nature. Another's tears had tugged inside me. But here there was no place for empathy. Every one of us who'd been shipped out here was grieving; grieving for husbands, for children, for lovers left behind. Grieving for England, for Ireland, for the lives we'd had before. My own grief was striking enough, without taking on others' as well.

But this woman's tears were impossible to ignore. They turned into racking sobs I could feel deep inside my chest. When she got up to relieve herself, I turned to Maggie. "What happened to her?" I asked.

Maggie kept her eyes on her spinning. "Her little one got taken away today. Sent to the Orphan School in Sydney Town."

"A school? Is that so bad?"

Maggie looked at me as though I were half-witted. Her eyes were a brilliant blue, set deep in tanned, leathery cheeks. Dark corkscrew curls sprung out from beneath her cap. "Once a little one gets sent away, they got next to no chance of their mamas ever seeing them again." Her brassy voice dropped a little. I wondered if she were speaking from experience.

"Oh," I mumbled, not wanting to dig further. I felt an ache in my chest for the crying woman. Her plight reminded me why I had taught myself not to take on other people's pain. "How dreadful."

"Would you listen to you," Maggie crowed, "talking like a princess."

I said nothing. I could hear it, of course, the smoothed edges of my own speech up against the ragged phrases of the other women. I'd spent the six months of the voyage trying to roughen my words, but Maggie's comments reminded me I hadn't succeeded.

But I didn't want to stand out. Nor did I want to face the questions I knew would follow.

The woman's tears had dried by the time dark fell over the factory and we were sent back down the stairs. The air was thick and humid, and smelled of fragrant, passing rain.

I stiffened at the sight of Blackwell in the street outside the jail. Had he been waiting for me?

"You didn't eat this morning," he said, his voice low. "There was food for you on the table."

"I've no way of paying for food," I told him stiffly.

"You must be hungry."

I began to walk. My stomach was groaning with hunger, yes, but that was no business of his. I didn't want Lottie to see me talking to him. I couldn't bear for her to find out I had slept on his floor. I was surprised she'd not asked questions after I'd appeared at the factory with my skin scrubbed clean.

I could hear his footsteps behind me, sighing through the mud. "There's a bed for you, Eleanor."

I bristled at the sound of my name on his lips. Back in London, no man beside my husband would have dared called me by my Christian name. It was a cold reminder that I had sunk to the bottom of the pile. *Eleanor*, like some ash-streaked scullery maid.

I stopped walking. "What do you want for it?" I kept my head down, bracing myself for his answer.

"Housekeeping," he said after a moment.

A laugh escaped me. "Housekeeping?"

"Is that not to your liking?"

I swallowed, my gaze drifting over his shoulder to the crooked silhouette of his hut. Perhaps it was foolish to trust him. But how desperately I needed to believe I might earn myself a bed and fire just by sweeping a man's floor.

I hesitated. Blackwell stood beside me, silent and patient. I managed a faint nod.

"Good," he said shortly.

Inside the hut, the broom was resting beside the front door. I didn't remember it being there the previous night. Had he put it there in anticipation of my arrival? Had he known he could convince me to crawl back through his door? The thought made me inexplicably angry. But he had been right. Here I was.

Blackwell nodded towards the broom. "The floor needs sweeping. And then please empty the grate."

I swept with my eyes down, losing myself in the rhythm of it. Sweeping an earth floor felt like a losing battle, but I was glad for something to put my mind to. Rainwater had seeped beneath the door, turning the floor at the front of the cottage to mud.

Blackwell hovered awkwardly in the corner for a few

moments, his eyes following the rhythmic strokes of the broom. Then he stepped out into the night, giving me the space I craved.

Housekeeping, Nell? I imagined Lottie saying as I swept. *You believe he wants you for housekeeping?*

I was aware of my naivety, so perhaps that erased it. It was not blind optimism that had brought me to Blackwell's door, but desperation.

I swept that dirt floor, then scooped every last speck of ash from the grate. There was a part of me that believed if I worked hard enough, it might convince him that my shelter and fire had been duly paid for. Might prevent him from demanding more.

The dark was thick when the lieutenant returned. I wondered distantly where he had been. He looked at the swept floor, then at the empty grate.

"That's enough," he said. "You've been working all day." He nodded to the loaf of bread on the shelf. A monstrous ant was traversing the crust. "Take a little. Rest."

I broke off a small chunk of bread and hovered in front of the unlit fire, unsure what else to do. The hut felt too small for strangers. I chewed slowly, the bread coarse on my tongue. The crust was crisp and warm where I had sat it too close to the lamp.

I dared a glance at Blackwell. He was opening the jar of potted meat, his back to me. Would he come to my bed tonight, I wondered? There had to be more for him in this than a swept earthen floor that would become thick with dirt again before morning. The lid of the jar popped noisily.

I looked up at the sound of voices coming towards the hut. And then a sudden screech of fabric as a rock came flying through the cloth window. It thudded loudly against the bookshelf.

Blackwell snatched his rifle. "Get down."

I scrambled beneath the table.

"Did they hit you?" he asked.

"No." My voice came out breathless. "Who is it? The savages?"

"It's not the savages."

I heard yelling; mostly men, some women. Incoherent voices. English words? I couldn't tell.

Blackwell charged from the hut with the rifle poised. "Get the hell away from here," he hissed. His voice was taut and controlled, as though his anger, along with all his other emotions, was kept behind bars. I realised he'd not loaded the rifle.

"What'll you do, you *sasanaigh* murderer?" spat a gravelly Irish voice. "Shoot us in the street?"

A cold laugh. Terse, unintelligible words from Blackwell. He marched back inside and bolted the door.

I stepped out from beneath the table. "Who was that?" I asked shakily.

He leant the rifle up against the wall. Used his wrist to push a swathe of dark hair from his eyes. There was a moment of silence, as though he was debating whether to speak to me. "The rebels," he said finally.

"Who?"

He sighed heavily. "The Irish rebels. They rose up at Castle Hill in the north a few years ago. Tried to take Parramatta and Sydney Town. Overthrow the government and bring in Irish rule."

I wrapped my arms around myself, suddenly cold. "What

was that they called you?"

Blackwell didn't look at me. "*Sasanaigh*," he repeated. "Englishman."

I nodded stiffly. But it was the other word that rang more heavily in my ears.

Murderer.

I looked down at the rock that lay beneath the shelf. "Why did they do this?"

Blackwell stared at it for several moments. "They're angry," he said. "They feel oppressed and abused. And I represent everything they hate." He picked up the rock and flung it out the torn window.

The muscles in my shoulders felt taut. It wasn't just Lottie who despised the lieutenant, I realised. Perhaps in my desperation I had been too dismissive of her warning. Perhaps I ought to have stayed beneath the awnings of the church.

"You can't leave," Blackwell said as I edged towards the door. "Not now. It's dangerous out there. The rebels are agitated. They'll likely go after you."

"Because of my English blood, or the fact I'm lodging with you?"

"Both."

I looked up at him, taking in his face up close for the first time. He was younger than I had first guessed. Little more than thirty, perhaps. I imagined that in England, his hair had been cut to his collar, trimmed within an inch of its life. But in this place, a raggedness had begun to creep over him, the way it had done to all of us. His hair tickled the top of his eyebrows, reached past his collar. His pale blue eyes were sharp and clear, but I couldn't see behind them. It made trusting him a difficult thing.

Outside, I heard loud laughter. I took a step away from the door. "And I'll be safer here with you?"

Blackwell held my gaze. "Do you think you won't be?"

I said nothing. Truly, I had no idea.

CHAPTER FIVE

"It would be a wise and prudent measure to bring up the rising generation in the Protestant religion, in order to remove that extreme ignorance and barbarism which constitute the natural character of all the lowest class of Irish Catholic convicts."

Rev. Samuel Marsden
A Few Observations on the Toleration of the Catholic Religion in New South Wales
1808-1817

I knew little of the atrocities taking place in Ireland, like I knew little of so many other things. My father had done his best to provide me with a sheltered upbringing; one in which I would be married to a gentleman and keep my eyes and ears closed to anything that might upturn my polished existence. Politics, my father liked to say, was no domain for a lady.

Nonetheless, I had caught word of the rebellion in

Ireland some years back. I knew the Irish had allied with the French to overthrow the Englishmen who ruled their land. As an impressionable nineteen-year-old, I had panicked, sure the United Irishmen would gallivant across the seas and turn London upside down.

Father had laughed off my concerns. "This is why young ladies should not involve themselves in politics," he said, reaching across the supper table and topping up his glass with an enormous glug of wine. "Those witless fools have no mind to take London. I daresay their minds couldn't even fathom such a notion."

In London, I'd not known any Irish men or women. But sitting beside Lottie at the spinning wheels, I did not see a witless fool.

"I heard the rebels in the street last night," I said, careful to sidestep any mention of Blackwell.

Lottie made a noise in her throat, but she didn't look at me. I could tell she didn't want to discuss the matter.

"Do you know them?" I asked.

She shrugged, not taking her eyes off the spinning wheel. "Some of them."

"They want freedom," I said. "Is that it?"

Lottie looked at me then, her hazel eyes shining. "Aye," she said, with more sharpness than I had been expecting. "That's it. Freedom and respect."

"We all want those things," I said.

She snorted. "Your people have it."

I'd had no thought there might be an 'us' and 'them' between two lags sitting side by side at the factory. "Does I look like I have freedom?" I asked bitterly.

Lottie gave me a dismissive look that stung more than

her sharpness. A look that said I wouldn't understand. A look that said I had no right to argue, or to have an opinion on the matter.

"They've taken everything from us," she said. "Even our God. You think we like spending our Sundays listening to your Protestant poison?"

"I'm sorry," I murmured, unsure of what else to say.

A part of me ached to ask her about the lieutenant. Ask her if she knew why the rebels had stormed his hut last night. Ask her what had happened at Castle Hill. The settlement was crawling with soldiers. Why was Blackwell the target of the rebels' rage? But then I would have to admit that I had crept through his door as his housekeeper. And that, I was becoming increasingly certain of, was something Lottie would not take well.

When dark fell and the spinning wheels stilled, we strolled out of our prison and wandered to the river. By now, I had come to understand that our punishment was transportation. Not incarceration.

There were plenty of men who came to join us at the river. Convicts, emancipists, free settlers, with liquor bottles in one hand and pipes in the other. They talked a lot, their shoulders pressed to ours and their bristly faces edging closer with each mouthful. Told us rum-scented stories about their farms and their houses and their hard-earned tickets of leave.

Just now need me a wife, they'd say.

It wasn't a difficult thing to find in this colony. Just that day, a settler had turned up at the factory with his marriage permit from Reverend Marsden. We'd lined up to be inspected, been given the chance to offer ourselves as wives.

The settler had left twenty minutes later betrothed to Sally Quinn.

Being chosen as a convict wife, I'd learnt that day, was a thing to be celebrated. Once you'd signed yourself over to your husband-to-be, it marked the end of your time at the factory. Sally Quinn's settler was a loud-mouthed drunkard from what I could tell, but he'd saved her five more years of weaving Parramatta cloth. Tomorrow he'd be whisking her off to be mistress of a grand house in Sydney Town. Filthy and ragged though these men on the riverbank were, I was beginning to see they were the way to freedom.

The evening was warm, with parrots shrieking in the trees above us and bugs swarming the surface of the river. The sloping roof of Government House peeked out between the trees.

One of the wife-hunters climbed onto a log and squinted up at the row of dark windows.

"The governor in, Ned?" called Dan Brady, the man who had followed me on my first night in Parramatta.

Ned chuckled. "I think I see him there through the window. Eating his mutton with a finger raised to the poor croppies."

Brady leapt onto the log and bared his pasty white backside in the direction of the house. An unenthused chuckle rippled through the group.

I looked away, wishing for a mouthful of rum to dull my senses.

"Did you hear?" Maggie Abbott began brassily. "Tom Evans got caught stealing from the granary last night."

Lottie snorted. "Tom Evans is a bloody fool. How many times we seen him strung up for a flogging? He'll be off to the coal mines now, just you watch." She grabbed the rum bottle from the man sitting beside her. "He's a woman from the factory staying with him," she told me. "Only thing is he's got no way of paying her keep. Half the thieving in this place is lags stealing to pay their whores."

I hugged my knees, looking out across the darkening river. How precious us factory lasses were. Precious enough to steal for. Strange how something so precious could be treated with such disdain.

Lottie held the bottle out to me. I gulped down a mouthful, coughing as it seared my throat. The rum was terrible. Tasted like the sea had gotten through the barrel.

"Careful there," said the man beside Lottie. He was sharp-eyed and too handsome, with ragged, sand-coloured hair and a smile that wasn't entirely warm. Spoke with a liquored-up Irish lilt I had trouble understanding. "I'm yet to meet a *sasanaigh* that can hold their liquor." He reached over and took the bottle from my hands, to a chorus of laughter from the men around him. I felt my cheeks flush.

Maggie had introduced the man earlier as Patrick Owen, an emancipist who was seeking to sell his land for a plot in Sydney Town. He was loud spoken and sure of himself, with a constant flotilla of Irishmen around him, laughing at his questionable jokes.

Lottie's eyes followed him as he got up and strode towards the riverbank. He flung a stone into the river and sent water fountaining upwards. He looked over his shoulder and gave her a broad smile. She grinned.

"Patrick Owen?" I said witheringly. "Really?"

She shrugged.

"Sally's new husband is a free settler," I said. "You can

do better than an emancipist."

"That's the thing, Nell," she said, watching Owen as he grabbed another stone and flung it into the water. "I'm not entirely sure I can." She gave me a wry smile. "Don't you know Irishwomen are as low as the blacks? So the good reverend says anyhow."

"Sally Quinn is Irish."

Lottie snorted. "Sally Quinn is all arse and tits. These things help." She traced a stick through the dirt. "Besides, it's not really about doing better now, is it. It's about getting out of the factory. I'd rather be an emancipist's wife than spend another four years weaving shirts for the lobsters." She looked back at Owen.

"It don't matter anyhow," she said. "Owen's got Maggie in his bed and she's got her claws in tight."

Dan Brady took his pipe out from between his teeth and blew a line of smoke down at me. "What did Blackwell want with you then?" he asked.

I stiffened. Felt Lottie's eyes pull towards me.

"I don't know what you're talking about."

"Saw you with him in the street yesterday," said Brady. "He after a bit of company was he? You tell him you're too good for him too?"

My cheeks flushed.

"If one of his kind were after my company, I'd give it to him," Maggie announced, planting a hand on her hip. "Earn myself a little sway over a powerful man. The Rum Corps controls everything in this place. Even the liquor."

I frowned. "What do you mean?"

Lottie tapped her fingernails against the side of the rum bottle. "The redcoats are the ones making all this. They got stills out behind the barracks. Their liquor's as good as coin in this place. Can buy yourself anything with it."

Maggie waved a finger at me. "That's what you want, girl. Believe me. An officer's attention. Ain't an easy thing to get. Most of them wouldn't dare let themselves be seen with our kind."

"Shut your mouth, Maggie," Lottie snapped. "She knows better than to go near that bastard Blackwell. Don't you, Nell?"

"Of course." I couldn't look at her.

Two soldiers marched past the river, heading towards the barracks.

"Fine work you're doing, lads," Owen sang, his words dripping with sarcasm.

His voice made the muscles in my neck tighten.

Sasanaigh murderer.

Suddenly I knew without a doubt that Patrick Owen had been at Blackwell's hut the previous night. Was he the one who had flung the rock through the window?

"Be quiet, Patrick," said Lottie. "We don't need you making trouble for us. Some of us still got to answer to the lobsters."

Owen chuckled, looking her up and down. "Who's making trouble?"

Lottie looked back at him for a long second. A smile flickered in the corner of his lips. And in swanned Maggie, scooping up Owen's arm and whisking him away from us in one smooth movement.

"Come on now, Patrick," she crooned. "Let's go, aye?"

For a moment, Owen kept his eyes on Lottie, despite Maggie's fingers crawling up his arm. He gave her one last hint of a smile and marched away from the water.

I stayed at the river until Lottie had disappeared into the hut of the man she was lodging with. I knew it only a matter of time before she realised I was no longer sleeping on the street. Only a matter of time before she began to ask questions.

When I stepped into the hut, Blackwell was sitting in a chair beside the crackling fire, a worn book in his hand. The scent of woodsmoke and eucalyptus was thick in the air.

He looked up as I entered.

"I'm sorry," I said. "I meant to be here before you returned, but…" I trailed off.

A faint frown creased the bridge of his nose. I could tell he was debating whether or not to reprimand me. This infant colony's idea of incarceration was hazy. Neither of us knew the rules.

"There's meat for soup," he said finally, nodding to a bloodied paper package sitting on the table.

I nodded wordlessly, thankful he had not seen fit to punish me. I unwrapped the package, and stared blankly down at the meat. I'd never cooked a thing in my life, and had little thought of how I might magic this slab of flesh into supper.

I hacked the meat into pieces and placed it in the pot with water and some limp carrots I'd discovered at the back of the shelf. I hung the pot carefully over the flames.

Blackwell stayed in his chair, reading. After the drunken chatter at the river, the wordlessness felt thick and heavy. I stirred slowly, eyes fixed on the pot, watching the meat darken as the liquid bubbled steadily. I was pleased to find it vaguely resembled soup.

"It's ready," I ventured, when much of the colour had drained from both the meat and vegetables. "May I eat some too?"

Blackwell put down his book and shifted his chair to face the table. "Of course."

I filled the bowls and set them on the table. Blackwell lowered his gaze and murmured a short prayer. I waited for him to begin eating before bringing my spoon to my lips.

The soup was watery and more than a little bland, but I felt my effort was admirable, given my complete lack of knowledge, and what I'd had to work with. I had no doubt I was eating an animal I had never even heard of.

Our wooden spoons tapped against the side of the bowls.

"There's no need to be afraid of me," Blackwell said finally.

"I'm not afraid of you." My voice came out softer than I had intended.

"Yes you are." He looked up at me for the first time. "Why? Because you fear I will come to you in the night?"

I swallowed hard, the meat sticking in my throat. That was a part of it, of course. But perhaps it was unfair to have such a fear. For three nights, he had not asked anything more of me than sweeping his floors and cooking his supper. Of that I was grateful.

"You're here as my housekeeper," he said evenly. "Nothing more."

It was the intimacy of this that frightened me, I realised then. For almost a year I had been crammed into jail cells and spinning rooms and the stinking convicts' quarters of the *Norfolk* with women on every side. These sparsely worded nights when it was just he and I alone felt foreign and hard to navigate.

But I didn't want to fear him. I wanted to believe Lottie's warning was misplaced. How much more manageable this place would seem if I had a safe haven to return to each night.

A sudden burst of wind made the cloth window drum and the roof rustle loudly.

"I ought to fix that," said Blackwell, as a triangle of bark glided down and landed in the middle of the table.

"Why do you not have convict workers?" I asked. "Men to tend to the garden and the like?"

"I prefer the solitude."

"Then why take me in?"

"Because you were sleeping in the street."

His answer made me feel strangely hollow. I didn't want him to have taken me in merely out of pity. I wanted him to see more in me than just another wretched lag. The thought was an uncomfortable one, and I was unsure where it had come from.

"I'm sure I'm not the only woman to have found herself sleeping in the street," I said.

He held my gaze. "I'm sure you're not. But as unfortunate as that is, I don't make a point of accommodating prisoners. I merely saw you as I passed by the church. You were clearly in need of shelter, and it seemed rather uncharitable not to offer it."

"I see." I hated being on the receiving end of his charity. Hated what I had been reduced to.

"If you are unhappy with this arrangement," he said, "you're free to leave anytime you wish."

I turned back to my bowl. I regretted raising the issue.

Blackwell took another mouthful of soup. "It's good," he said, after a moment of silence.

I managed a faint smile. Good, no, but I appreciated his kindness.

There was something about the civility of this; this act of sitting at a supper table, however crooked and rough-hewn, however foreign and ropey the meat. I couldn't remember the last time I had done something as refined as share a meal across the supper table.

Blackwell sipped the soup carefully from the edge of his spoon and I heard a laugh escape me.

"What's so amusing?"

"It's absurd," I said.

"What is?"

"This. Every bit of it. You, so careful with your manners; sipping your soup like you're at a gentleman's dinner party. And all the while we're sitting here in this mud hut with the roof falling down, eating heaven only knows what animal." I heard my voice get louder, bolstered by the awful liquor in my blood. "What point is there bothering with table manners when we're up to our knees in dirt like wild things? And," I said, dimly aware that I was making a scene, "you've never even thought to tell me your name. Am I worth so little I don't even warrant an introduction?"

He paused, his spoon hovering in mid-air. "I'm sorry," he said. "My name's Blackwell. Adam Blackwell."

I stuck a spoonful of soup in my mouth, embarrassed by my outburst. I couldn't remember ever speaking so openly, especially not in front of a man.

Finally, I dared to look up at him. And for a second it was as though the protective shell he hid behind had fallen away. I saw a flicker of a smile on his lips, a hint of warmth in his eyes. It caught me by surprise and I looked away hurriedly.

My eyes drifted to the book he had left on the edge of the table. "*The Vicar of Wakefield* was one of my father's favourites," I garbled, trying to take the conversation back to less hysterical grounds.

"You read?" he asked. There was a hint of surprise in his voice.

I nodded.

"If you wish," he said, "you may take it once I've finished. I know books are few and far between in this place."

His kindness emboldened me. "Why are you here?"

"Duty. Why else?"

"Well." I put down my spoon. "In London they used to say this place was an officer's dream. Land grants from the governor. Free labour. The freedom to choose a woman like we're fruit to be picked from a tree."

Blackwell raised his eyebrows.

"Isn't that why we were sent here?" I asked. "To keep all the lonely men company? To populate this place?"

He looked at me squarely. "You were sent here because you committed a crime."

I turned back at my soup. Found a chunk of gristle inside it. I scooped it out of the bowl and sat it on the table.

"This place could be better for you than England," Blackwell said.

I frowned. What did he know of my life in England? Who was he to make such judgments? I supposed he looked at me as the same as all the others. A street rat crawled from the Whitechapel slums. It was a fair assumption, I supposed.

I'd heard all the stories, bleated out by those poor sorry girls I'd been crammed onto the *Norfolk* with.

A loaf of bread to feed my boys.
A cloak to keep out the snow.
Tales of pity.

But Blackwell knew I was a reader. And how many of those poor sorry girls from the slums had their letters? Perhaps my attempts to disguise my polished upbringing had been more successful than I'd believed.

Let him believe I too was tale of pity. Bread pocketed from the market. A stolen cloak wrapped around my shoulders.

That was a far simpler story.

CHAPTER SIX

"Here," said Lottie as I made my way down the stairs into the jail yard behind the factory. She held out a small, misshapen pillow.

"What's this?" I sat beside her and Hannah on the patchy grass, a cannikin of lukewarm tea in my hand. The sun had vanished behind a cloud just in time for our afternoon break.

"Took it from old Bert's bed when he weren't looking," said Lottie. "Thought you could use it. Might make you a little more comfortable."

I shook my head, feeling a stab of guilt. After two weeks beneath Blackwell's roof, I'd still not found the courage to tell Lottie I was no longer sleeping on the street. "I couldn't."

She whacked me on the arm with it, making tea slop down the front of my dress. "Would you just take it, you madwoman? Bert won't even notice it's gone."

Maggie looked down at us from where she stood leaning against the wall of the jail. "Take it, Nell. She's right; old Bert's as blind as a bat. Everyone knows it."

"It's true," said Hannah, sipping her tea. "I saw him in the tavern last week asking some scrawny lobster for a dance." She winked at me. "The lad was quite pretty and all, but Bert would've got a right shock when he got him home."

Maggie laughed. "Look on the bright side, Lottie. Least he's too old and decrepit to get a child on you. When was the last time he managed to get it up?"

Lottie snorted. "Don't stop him from trying."

Maggie lifted her cannikin in a mock toast. "Good of you to take him off our hands, girl. You're to be applauded."

Lottie gave her a thin smile. "Ought to say the same to you. Must be hard keeping Patrick Owen under control with those wandering eyes of his."

"I will take the pillow," I said suddenly, desperate to steer the conversation away from their friction over Owen. "You're right, I'll be much more comfortable."

Lottie turned away from Maggie and tossed the pillow into my lap.

"Thank you," I said.

She flashed me a smile. "Of course. It's like I said, we look out for each other here."

I didn't reply. I wondered if that still held true where Patrick Owen was concerned.

With our break over, I went back upstairs to the carding machine, sitting on Lottie's pillow to keep it from the filthy floor. One day soon, I would tell her the truth. Return the pillow to her and admit I made Lieutenant Blackwell's supper each night. She would be angry, no doubt, at both my lies and my foolishness. Would likely speak to me in the same brusque tone she reserved for Maggie. I hated the prospect of that coldness. *We look out for each other* – and with each day I saw just how important that sisterhood was. With too much ease, the horrors of the factory were becoming commonplace – the settler taking a woman up against the factory wall, the girl sent back to the spinning wheels to birth her overseer's child. Talk of what the men did to their lodgers in the night. How were we to survive this place without another to lean on?

Footsteps thudded up the stairs, two male convicts appearing in the warehouse, guarded by a marine. One of the men was a familiar face; most mornings when I returned to the factory he'd be gallivanting around the place with a kiss for any woman who'd let him near. He grinned at the young girl sitting closest to the door. Picked up one of the sacks of cloth that sat in the corner waiting to be taken to the government stores. He murmured to her in words I couldn't hear over the thudding of the looms. But the thump of the soldier's rifle I did hear, as it struck the man on the back of the skull. He pitched forward, dropping the sack and spitting out a line of cursing.

"Keep your mouth shut and do your job," the soldier barked. I turned my eyes away hurriedly. Found myself turning the handle of the carding machine faster, in time with my racing heart.

Footsteps again, as the marine and the convicts disappeared. My tea sat heavily in my stomach. I could hear the thud of the rifle blow echoing in my ears. I'd never known of a place in which the balance of power was so one-sided.

The thought made me turn the wheel faster, as though by throwing my energy into the carding machine, I might let some of it loose from my body. I fed the fleece into the whirring drums, eyes glazing over.

I thought of Blackwell. I'd not seen the same brutality inside him, but perhaps it was naïve to assume it wasn't there. I had made an active decision not to fear him. An active decision to trust him. But I knew there was every chance it might turn out to be a foolish choice. The men in red coats literally held our lives in their hands. Perhaps it was wiser to fear the hand that wielded the power. Grow too close and he could burn me alive.

I felt a sudden burst of pain in my fingertips. Heard myself cry out. And then a hand on my arm, yanking me backwards before my fingers were drawn into the teeth of the carding drum.

I toppled from my stool, landing heavily on the floor beside Maggie. I gasped for breath, gripping my stinging fingers with my other hand. Maggie put a hand to my shoulder.

"Careful, girl," she said, her face close to mine. "Careful. Got to keep your mind on the job."

I tried to reply, but my mouth just hung open. I opened my palm to see a rivulet of blood trickling down my fingers. Pain was pulsing through my hand, but I knew it could have been infinitely worse. I nodded at Maggie, unable to form words.

She got to her feet, picking up Lottie's pillow from where it had fallen beside me. She brushed the muck from the bottom and sat it back on my stool. Then she reached down and offered me a hand.

"Thank you," I murmured. And as I climbed shakily to my feet, my throbbing hand wrapped around hers, I couldn't help but stare at the chain of bruises reaching up her arm.

"Are you all right, Eleanor?" Blackwell asked as he came into the hut that night. I was rattling around the place, in an attempt to make supper, unable to keep from trembling. All I could think about was what would have happened had Maggie not yanked me back from the carding machine. I reached for the frying pan and sent it crashing onto the floor.

I picked it up hurriedly and slapped a slab of meat into it. "I'm fine."

Blackwell hung up his jacket. "Has something happened?"

I shook my head, unwilling to speak of it. Thinking of my near accident made me feel as fragile as a bird. And fragility was something I could not afford to show in this place.

"Nothing happened." I took the frying pan to the hearth and sat it over the embers. I knelt on the floor and stared into it, watching the edges of the meat darken. The smell of the cooking flesh made my stomach turn.

I heard Blackwell at the washbin and kept my eyes fixed to the pan. For not the first time since I'd come to his hut, I was struck by the utter impropriety of our situation; of having a man who was not my husband so close upon me, washing, dressing, sleeping, breathing. In the fortnight we'd been sharing the hut, we'd fallen into an uneasy, wordless arrangement in which I'd dress beneath my blankets, and disappear into the garden while he washed and clothed himself each morning. In which he'd turn his back while I lifted my stockings and laced my stays.

On more than one occasion, the forced intimacy of the thing had felt too much. I'd thought to leave, to give him back the space he had so generously carved out for me. But each time, I arrived at the same conclusion. Without that scrap of space, I had not a single place to go.

I pressed the wooden spatula into the meat, watching as the juices ran clear. I carried the pan to the table and slid its contents onto Blackwell's plate. He looked down at the single slab of meat.

"You're not eating?"

I set the pan on the floor beside the door to cool. My bruised fingers throbbed in time with my heart.

"I'm not hungry." I took the bread from the shelf and sat it on the table for Blackwell. He stared up at me, a faint frown creasing the bridge of his nose. And that look, what was that? Something so close to concern that a part of me wanted to speak, to tell him of the foolish accident that had left me so rattled. But when I heard the words in my head, they sounded so petty, so inconsequential. Certainly nothing that would matter to a marine lieutenant. Just a thing that would reveal the delicacy I was trying so hard to outgrow. I nudged the bread towards him. "Here. It's still quite fresh."

Blackwell held my gaze for a long second, then slid around on his stool and reached for the rum bottle on the shelf. He filled a tin cup and placed it on the edge of the table.

"Drink it. It's quite dreadful, but it does settle the nerves somewhat."

I took the liquor and tossed it back, gasping as it seared my throat. I closed my eyes, feeling the drink slide through me, warming my insides and yes, somehow, faintly easing the nerves that were rattling through my body. A dangerous thing, I knew well, to find a little peace at liquor stills of the Rum Corps.

When Blackwell was asleep, I pulled on my boots and slipped out of the hut. My mind and body were exhausted, but my thoughts were racing. I knew sleep was still hours away.

The air was cold and clean; a silver cloud of breath appearing in front of me as I strode away from the hut. Laughter from the main street hung in the air, and I turned towards the church to avoid the throng of men and women outside the tavern. I followed the curve of the river as it snaked through the trees, needing the stillness, the calming sigh of the water.

In the pale moonlight, I recognised Maggie's figure leaning against the railings of the bridge. She looked up as I approached.

"Don't often see you out at night," she said. She brought a clay pipe to her lips and blew a line of smoke upwards.

I stepped onto the bridge and stood beside her at the railing. In the darkness the water was hidden, but I could hear it churning beneath us.

"Couldn't sleep," I told her.

Maggie held the pipe out to me. I shook my head.

She nodded in the direction I had come. "That Blackwell's hut?"

I wrapped my arms around myself. Said nothing.

Maggie gave me a short smile. "Don't worry. I won't tell Lottie old Bert's pillow is snuggled up next to her favourite officer."

I let out my breath. "I feel dreadful. I shouldn't have taken it."

"It's just a pillow."

"It's not just a pillow. It's the principle of the thing. I've not told her the truth."

Maggie lifted the pipe. "You think too much. That's why you got yourself in trouble today."

I lowered my eyes. I knew she was right. "I'd appreciate it if you didn't tell anyone about… my sleeping arrangements," I managed.

She chuckled. "If I were curled up beside an officer in the night, I'd be letting everyone know."

I shifted uncomfortably. "I'm not *curled up* beside him."

Maggie shrugged. "Ain't nothing to be ashamed of."

"How can you say that?" Necessity or not, sleeping beside a man in the night made me feel as though I'd abandoned every scrap of my morality.

"It's smart," said Maggie. "Getting in with an officer. You do him a few favours and maybe he'll do the same for you. Make your time here a little easier."

"He's not asked for any favours. He says taking me in was an act of charity."

Maggie gave a short laugh. "It's coming. You just watch. This ain't a place of charity. There's no room for that here. Even men like Blackwell, they're just trying to find a way to survive in this wilderness."

I shook my head. "That's not true. This place might be about survival for us, but it's not for the men who carry the rifles."

She shrugged. "Maybe you'd be surprised." An echo of breaking glass sounded from the street, followed by wild laughter. Maggie looked back towards the tavern. "Fucking animals."

"Is Owen in the tavern?" I asked.

She nodded. "The man's a right bastard when he's in his cups. I managed to get out of there when he was looking the other way. I'll pay for it later though, I'm sure."

I thought of the mottled bruising on Maggie's arms. Felt rather certain Patrick Owen was a bastard whether he was in his cups or not.

"Would you marry him?" I asked. "For a ticket of leave, like Sally Quinn got?"

"What other hope do I have? They ain't letting me out of this place til I'm dead."

My lips parted. "You're here for life?"

Maggie blew out a line of smoke. "Made one or two bad decisions in my time."

I gave her a small smile. "I know the feeling."

"Headed up a thieving ring back in London," she said. "Thought Lottie would have told you. The other girls ain't shy to remind me I'm the only lifer in the factory."

My fingers curled around the worn wooden rail of the bridge. Maggie was not the only lifer in the factory, but I couldn't bring myself to tell her. Couldn't admit to the shame of it. Speaking of it aloud was too brutal.

Instead, I asked, "How long have you been here?"

"Coming up on ten years. I were cleaning a man's house at first, til the old bastard turned over the perch."

I stared downwards, watching ripples emerge from the darkness. Who would I be after a decade in this place? Would I be desperate enough to chase a man like Patrick Owen? Seek some semblance of a future in the bed of any man who could offer it? This, I told myself, as my stomach turned over with dread, was why I could only bear to consider the moment I had before me. I felt a sudden, desperate need to return to Blackwell's hut.

CHAPTER SEVEN

Parramatta was still covered in golden dawn light as I made my way towards the factory. My boots sank into the mud as I walked. Cold wind whipped my hair against my cheeks and made my skirts dance around the top of my boots. Autumn was slowly becoming winter, though the trees were stubbornly green.

I stopped walking suddenly, my eyes drawn to the scrub on the side of the road. What had made me look? And as I realised what I was seeing, my breath caught in my throat.

I'd seen death before, of course. Seen my father, uncles, aunts laid out lifeless on the mourning table. But it was the unexpectedness of this that caused heat to wash over me. The presence of a body where a body should not have been. A white hand curled beneath the undergrowth; a thin wrist, a twisted arm, a motionless figure in a blue and white striped dress.

I stumbled backwards, my legs weakening. I felt as

though the world was tilting around me. I lurched into the main street, whirling around in search of someone to tell. Felt a hand on my elbow.

"What's happened, Nell?" asked Hannah. "What's wrong?"

"A body," I managed. "A woman." I had trouble forming the words.

"Where?"

I led her back to the white hand in the bushes. Bolstered by Hannah's company, I dared to look a little closer. The woman lay on her side among the undergrowth, her feet bare and her skirts tangled around her legs. I couldn't see her face, just the bundle of dark hair at her neck.

Hannah edged forward and touched the woman's shoulder. The body rolled over. I pressed a hand over my mouth to stifle my cry of shock. Maggie Abbott's blank eyes stared up into the trees. Her neck was dappled with red marks and bruising, her skin deathly pale against the darkness of her hair.

I swallowed a violent wall of sickness.

I realised we were not alone. People were gathering, clustered on the side of the road, trying for a look.

I felt a hand around my wrist. Lottie appeared beside me and stood with her shoulder pressed against mine, not releasing her grip on my forearm.

I stared at the bruises on Maggie's neck. "She was murdered," I said, more to myself than anyone else. My words seemed to ripple through the crowd.

She was murdered.

Lottie pulled me into her arms and squeezed tightly. And at last, here were the redcoats, elbowing their way towards the body. Blackwell was among them, his eyes skimming over me without showing a hint of recognition.

"Who found the body?" asked one of the soldiers.

"I did."

"This was how you found it?"

Her, I tried to say, but the word caught in my throat. I tried to swallow. "Yes," I managed. "I mean, no. She was on her side. We turned her to see who it was." I wrapped my arms around myself. "She was murdered," I said again.

Blackwell glanced at me then back at Maggie's body. "Escort the women to the factory," he told the soldiers. "And take the body to the hospital."

And then we were back in the factory, spinning yarn as though nothing at all had happened. I sat dazedly on my stool and stared into the spokes of the motionless spinning wheel. The chalky smell of the fire thickened the air, making it hard to breathe. I felt as though I might fall at any moment. Lottie reached out and squeezed my hand. I squeezed back, grateful for her nearness.

Despite the wall of nervous chatter that filled the factory, I was acutely aware of Maggie's absence. The place felt empty without her. Quieter somehow, despite the constant thud and groan of the looms and carding drums. Each time I closed my eyes, I saw her blank face staring into mine.

The superintendent clipped me over the shoulder, barking about my laziness. I drew in my breath, trying to stop the tremor in my hands. I felt moments away from another accident. And today Maggie wasn't here to save me.

I turned to Lottie. "She was lodging with Patrick Owen," I said, though I knew she didn't need reminding.

For a moment, she didn't speak. "That doesn't mean anything." Her voice was thin.

I glared at her. Why was she defending him?

But in the back of my mind, I knew. She was defending him because there was a part of her that desperately hoped Maggie had not died with Owen's hands around her neck. That her body had not been so carelessly tossed into the scrub by one of the men we drank at the river with. There was a part of me that was hoping the same thing. But what was the alternative? I had seen the bruising on her neck. Had seen the bruising on her forearms the day she had saved me from crushing my hand in the carding machine. Still, I told myself, this was a wild land. Perhaps it was the doing of the savages, or some nameless creature that lived out there in the bush.

Maggie was dead, yes, but the horror of it was more manageable if she had not died at the hands of someone within the settlement.

Lottie turned away from me, pedalling rapidly in a sign our conversation was over.

I thought of Maggie's body. Hoped she was being treated with a little respect. I knew the hospital was without a mortuary; had heard tales of bodies being discarded in the passageways. Was she being examined? Or did the Rum Corps see no point?

We were precious, yes, us women at the spinning wheels. But so achingly replaceable. One of us buried would be replaced by another the moment the next ship came in.

A sense of unease hung thick in the air as we pedalled and spun. Restless murmuring rippled through the room. A baby began to shriek, the sound making the muscles in my neck tense.

Heads turned as heavy footsteps thudded up the stairs. Blackwell and one of the enlisted men appeared in the doorway of the warehouse. They made their way towards the superintendent.

One of the women at the spinning wheels leapt to her feet and strode towards the soldiers. "What you going to do about this then? Are you going to catch the bastard what done this to Maggie?"

"There'll be an investigation in due course," Blackwell said shortly.

"An investigation?" Hannah cried. "What need do you have for an investigation? Everyone knows it were Patrick Owen that killed her!" She stood abruptly, knocking over her stool. "Whatever you may think of us, we ain't bloody fools."

The younger soldier strode towards her. "Sit down and shut your mouth." He reached for Hannah's arm, but she pulled away violently. He grabbed her arms and forced her downwards, pinning her to the ground. Hannah screeched and kicked against him. And at once, the women were on their feet, crowding around her, trying to tear the soldier away. Another baby joined in the wailing. Children scrambled towards their mothers. I stood as well. Somehow, staying in my seat and obeying orders felt like a slight on Maggie. A slight on Hannah.

Blackwell dashed towards the fight.

I saw Lottie's eyes fall to him. Saw the hatred, the anger. And I saw her grab her stool by the legs and swing.

I had no thought of what I was doing. I was only aware of my body pitching instinctively towards Lottie, shoving her away from the lieutenant. And then of shock jolting through me as the full force of the wooden stool struck me instead.

It took a moment for the pain to hit, but when it did, it seared through my temple and brought me to my knees. Blood ran into my eye.

"Jesus, Nell," Lottie cried, crouching beside me and gripping my shoulder. "What in hell are you doing?" She shrieked as she was yanked to her feet by the superintendent.

I felt a hand around the top of my arm, helping me stand. Blackwell's imposing figure loomed over me.

"Get your hands off her, you corrupt bastard!" Lottie kicked against the superintendent. "Do you hear me?"

Blackwell handed me over to the other soldier. "Take her out to the yard. And find something to stop the bleeding."

I stumbled dizzily down the stairs, the soldier's hand clamped to my elbow. I swiped at the blood with the hem of my apron. It kept spilling from the gash in my forehead, soaking through the fabric and staining the skin on my wrist. The shouting from the factory grew steadily softer. The soldier led me out to the jail yard and planted me on the narrow wooden bench beside the door. Beads of blood slid from my chin, turning black in the striped flannel of my skirts. The soldier produced a handkerchief from his pocket and pressed it hard against the cut above my eye. Pain drummed steadily behind my forehead.

Blackwell appeared suddenly in the doorway, his footsteps crunching across the stone path. I was surprised to see him.

"Leave us," he told the soldier. "I need to speak with her about the incident." He took the bloodied handkerchief and knelt in front of me. He pressed it back against my forehead, then looked down at the crimson mess of my skirts. "Head wounds always bleed heavily," he said. "But it isn't deep. It looks worse than it is."

I gripped the edges of the bench, my teeth clenched against the ache of it.

Though his eyes were level with mine, Blackwell somehow managed not to look at me. Did he know, I wondered, that it was Lottie who had done this? Had he seen me step in front of her flying stool? Or had it all happened so quickly he had no thought of it?

I was glad he didn't ask for an explanation. I would not have been able to give it.

He lifted my hand and brought it to the handkerchief, gesturing for me to hold it in place. Then he disappeared into the jail for a moment, returning with a small bowl of water and a clean cloth.

He knelt opposite me again, dragging the cloth through the thin grey puddle at the bottom of the basin. Dabbed gently at the jewels of dried blood I could feel forming at my cheekbones.

"Maggie was murdered," I said. It wasn't fresh information to him, of course. I just needed him to know that I knew.

Blackwell's hand tightened around the cloth. Water drizzled onto the path and disappeared into the earth. "Yes. I'm sorry."

Sorry for what, I wondered?

I said, "It was Patrick Owen."

Blackwell didn't reply. Just slid the damp cloth over the side of my neck.

I waited for his questions, his interrogation. Wasn't that why he had marched down from the factory after me? I had been the one to find the body.

But there were no questions. Just the rhythmic plinking as the water dripped from the cloth back into the basin. A crow glided across the jail yard and perched on top of the stair rail.

"Has it stopped bleeding?" I asked.

"Almost."

I got unsteadily to my feet, turning to face my reflection in the narrow window behind us. Lottie's attack had left a congealing red stripe above my eyebrow, but the cut was not as enormous as I had imagined it might be. The side of my eye was already cloudy with bruising.

I squinted at my reflection. It was the first time I'd dared to examine myself since I'd arrived in Parramatta. My hair hung in lank, coppery snarls, damp and darkened around my face. My cheeks were hollow, pink from the sun. But it was my eyes that caused my loud intake of breath. They were brighter and fiercer than I could ever remember; the flat grey planes of them alight with flecks of blue. There was my anger, my fear, my frustration. There was *four shillings*, and *I have shelter* and *who found the body?*

New South Wales had left a blaze inside me.

"I ought to go back upstairs," I said, "before the superintendent has me in the cells with Lottie and Hannah."

"You're to come with me to the courthouse," said Blackwell. "The magistrate wishes to speak to the person who found the body."

"So you were telling the truth. When you said there would be an investigation."

He looked me in the eye for the first time. "Why would you doubt that?"

I didn't answer.

We walked out of the jail towards the courthouse without speaking. I felt a faint flicker of nerves. The last time I'd been before a magistrate, I'd been transported upon the seas.

A few yards from the front door, Blackwell stopped walking. He looked down at me, eyes fixed to the cut streaking my forehead. "Eleanor," he said, his voice low, "you're not to put yourself in danger for me again. I don't require protecting."

He strode up the steps to the front door before I had a chance to respond.

CHAPTER EIGHT

I followed Blackwell into the courthouse, and down a long stone corridor with doors on either side. Our footsteps echoed in the stillness. He stopped at the door at the end of the passage and knocked loudly.

"Enter."

Blackwell opened the door to a small meeting room. A table took up most of the space, wooden chairs on both sides. White light filtered in from a window high on the wall. Inside, I could see the round-shouldered figure of Reverend Marsden, dressed in his customary black, along with two soldiers.

"Eleanor Marling, Reverend," said Blackwell. "She's the one who found the body."

The reverend walked slowly towards the door, rubbing a chin that disappeared into the mottled red folds of his neck. He looked me up and down, taking in the gash on my forehead, the blooms of blood on my Navy Board skirts. "You're a government woman." It was not a question. But I said:

"Yes, Father."

The bridge of his nose creased, then Marsden turned back to Blackwell. "It's not necessary for me to speak to her, Lieutenant. Please see her back to the factory."

Lottie and Hannah were put in solitary confinement for three days. A part of me was glad for the reprieve. I had no desire to try and explain my actions to Lottie. And I felt more than a hint of anger towards her over her attack. I knew Blackwell a target of the rebels, for reasons I didn't fully understand. And I knew Lottie was loyal to the Irish croppies. But surely that didn't warrant the whole stool-swinging debacle.

When she reappeared in the factory at the end of the week, she was uncharacteristically quiet. Shadows of exhaustion underlined her eyes, her hands discoloured with grime and the stale smell of the cells clinging to her skin.

For a long time, we sat beside each other without speaking. She glanced at the cut and bruising on the side of my face. I wondered if an apology would be forthcoming. But when she finally spoke, what she said was:

"Are you really sleeping on the street, Nell?"

I didn't look at her. "No," I said finally. I was surprised it had taken her so long to realise. I focused my gaze on my spinning.

Out of the corner of my eye, I could see her wheel was

motionless.

"Tell me I'm wrong," she said. "Tell me you're not lodging with him."

I knew there was no need to reply. I had been expecting an outburst, but her silence was much more brutal.

"No," she said finally. "You've got to get out of there. Do you understand me?" She looked at me with an intensity in her eyes I had never seen before. "The street is safer. Risking the savages is safer."

Anger tightened my chest.

"Is this about what Maggie said?" she asked. "About having sway with a powerful man?"

I laughed coldly. "Power?" I repeated. "You think this about power? I was desperate, Lottie. I was sleeping outside the church. A person has to think of survival before they can think of power."

She shook her head. "Any man in this place would have taken you in. And yet you went with Blackwell."

"You're mistaken about him," I said, my voice coming out thin. I wasn't even sure she had heard me over the rattle of the looms. Her long silence suggested she hadn't. But then finally, she said:

"You trust him then? Is that why you… did what you did?"

I gritted my teeth. Why I did what I did? Had she not even the courage to say it aloud?

Why you stopped me from attacking him…

"Nell?" she pushed. "Do you trust him?"

I did trust him, I realised. And perhaps that made me a fool. But curling up on his floor made me feel fleetingly safe. That was not something I was willing to give up.

"He's giving me food and a fire in exchange for sweeping his floors," I said. "Tell me there's another man in the colony who would do that."

Lottie laughed coldly. "Sweeping floors. Is that really what you think he wants you for?"

I didn't answer. I wanted so desperately to believe in Blackwell's goodness. *Needed* to believe in it. I would not have Lottie and her anti-English sentiments ruin it for me.

She was wrong. She had to be. I had been sleeping on Blackwell's floor for more than three months, and not once had he even so much as brushed against me in the night.

"You're lucky I got in your way," I said sharply. "You could well have been facing the hangman if you'd struck an officer instead of a factory lass."

"Aye, well, it were grand of you to sacrifice yourself for me."

"Your attack was unwarranted," I said, not looking at her. I'd planned not to raise the issue. I knew we had all been rattled after Maggie's death. None of us had been thinking straight. But her comments had sparked something inside me.

Lottie snorted. "Just promise me one thing," she said bitterly. "When he gets a child on you, you name him as the father. Let the colony see who he is. Don't go pinning it on Marsden like the other women do."

We turned back to the spinning wheels. I found myself pedalling faster, letting the wool fly through my fingers. The wheel whirred and hummed.

"It's because of Castle Hill," I said. "That's why you despise him so."

Something passed over Lottie's eyes. "What do you know of Castle Hill?" She sounded angry I had spoken of it.

"Nothing," I admitted. "What happened? What did Blackwell do?"

"Why should I tell you? I warned you away from him once and I now I find out you're sleeping beside him in the night. I'm sure whatever I tell you you'll manage to see it with the eyes of an Englishwoman. You'll find a way to make him the hero."

"That's not true," I snapped. "I just want to know the truth."

Lottie snorted. "You want to know? Ask Lieutenant Blackwell."

Maggie was buried the next day while we were at the spinning wheels. I knew it was a deliberate attempt by Marsden and the Rum Corps to keep the factory lasses away.

An investigation into the murder had begun. Our information was hazy – mostly comprised of gossip from the men at the river – but in the factory that morning there was word Patrick Owen had been taken to the magistrate for questioning. Committed to prison to await trial.

I felt a faint flicker of optimism. Three months of Marsden's weekly sermons had shown me his hatred of the Irish. And if that hatred was what it took to send Owen to the hangman, then so be it. There was no doubt in my mind he had been the one to kill Maggie.

When work at the factory finished that night, we went to her grave; a meagre pile of earth at the back of the churchyard, with a crooked wooden cross shoved at the head. There was not even any mention of her name.

I tried not to imagine what her burial had been like. With all the women away at the factory there would have been few – if any – people to mourn her. I couldn't bear the thought of her being lowered into the earth with no one but the grave diggers to attend her.

Lottie and I stood at each other's side, not speaking, settled into an unspoken truce. One of the other women murmured a prayer.

As we were making our way out of the churchyard, several of the men approached. I wondered distantly why they had come. Were they here to pay their respects to Maggie? Far more likely, they'd come to persuade us to the river and talk some fertile young girls into becoming their wives.

In the half-light I could make out the tall figure of Dan Brady and several of the other rebels. They looked incomplete without Patrick Owen among them. Sheep without a leader. How many of those loyal croppies knew the man they followed was a killer? Did they, like Lottie, feel the need to push aside the truth?

Brady laid a stone beside Maggie's cross. "Patrick Owen sends his regards."

Anger bubbled inside me. "How dare you speak of him here."

Brady took a step towards me, eyes flashing. "You mean to send him to the hangman, Nellie?"

I turned away.

He grabbed my arm, yanking me back to face him. "Hey. We all heard how you got carted off to Marsden. What d'you say to him? Were you the one who led him to Owen?"

"I didn't say a thing," I hissed. "Marsden wouldn't even let me speak."

"And what about Blackwell? You open your mouth to him?" He snorted. "Word is you been opening your mouth to him a lot."

My cheeks blazed. "I didn't say a word to anyone," I snapped.

I could feel Lottie's eyes burning into the back of me.

"This true, Nell?" she asked. "You were taken to speak with the magistrate?"

"Yes," I said bitterly. "And it's also true that he wouldn't even let me speak. I had nothing to do with them going after Owen."

"Leave her alone, Dan," said Lottie. "She says she didn't speak to Marsden, then she didn't speak to Marsden. Patrick'll be back with us before you know it."

"You think Owen innocent?" I asked her.

She looked at me squarely. "What proof is there he's guilty?"

"Maggie was lodging with him," I said, aware it was an argument I was beginning to overuse. "And her arms were bruised. Just like her neck was."

And Dan Brady was up in my face, his nose inches from mine. "Watch yourself, Nellie," he said. "You hear me? No one wants to hear you mouthing off about what you think happened."

Lottie shoved him backwards. "I told you to leave her be."

I looked back at Brady, determined not to let him see how much he had rattled me. "What does it matter what I think?"

"You're right," he said. "It don't matter." He turned back to the other men. And then they were off down the main street, striding towards the jail.

I hurried back to Blackwell's hut, desperate for an escape. Through the cloth window, I could hear voices, footsteps, shouting in the street. Angry men, yelling in Irish.

With Blackwell on duty, the hut felt too quiet. I sat at the table, cutting up vegetables for soup while the clamour in the street grew louder. The chalky smell of a bonfire drifted beneath the door. I did my best to block out the noise. I needed that hut to feel safe. I realised I was craving Blackwell's company.

My stomach was groaning by the time he returned. I guessed it close to midnight. I spooned the soup into bowls and sat them on the table.

He looked surprised to see me awake. But not angry.

"I attended Maggie Abbott's burial," he told me as he took off his coat and hung it on the nail beside the door.

"You did?" I felt a sudden swell of gratitude. "Tell me about it."

He sat at the table and stirred his soup. "It was simple. Respectful. Reverend Marsden prayed over the coffin."

"Who else was there?" I dared to ask.

"Several of the officers. Parker and his wife from the tavern. A few others."

I was glad of it. "Thank you for attending."

He nodded. Somewhere in the distance, I heard glass shatter. Blackwell's eyes darted towards the door.

"Are you to sit on the jury in Owen's trial?" I asked.

"Yes."

"And do you think him guilty?" I felt it my duty to Maggie and the other factory lasses to prise out as much information as I could. I knew there were few other women in the colony who had the luxury of sitting opposite a solider and holding a civilised conversation.

Blackwell gave my boldness a ghost of a smile. "I can't discuss that with you, Eleanor. You know that."

"There were bruises on her arms," I said. "She—"

"Yes." Blackwell's tone darkened a little. "You told me that before. And as I told you, there's no proof Patrick Owen gave them to her." I could hear the impatience in his voice. Knew I was pushing the issue.

I was saved by a knock at the door. Blackwell pulled it open and noise flooded in from the street. Two young soldiers stood outside the hut.

"I'm sorry to disturb you, sir," said one. "Captain Daley has asked for you at the barracks."

Blackwell nodded. "Tell him I'm on my way." He closed the door on them, then grabbed his jacket from the nail. He slid on his gorget and buttoned his coat to his neck. He glanced at his pocket watch.

"Don't venture outside tonight," he told me.

"The rebels are angry," I said. "Because Owen has been arrested."

He didn't answer. But I didn't need the confirmation. I'd seen the anger in the eyes of Dan Brady and the other croppies. Knew they were fighting for justice for their leader. And I knew that in their eyes, Patrick Owen could do no wrong.

The hut felt cold and empty after Blackwell had left. I threw another log on the fire and scraped the last of our supper into the trough, setting the unwashed bowls on the edge of the table. I'd wait until morning to fetch water from the river.

I blew out the lamp and curled up on my sleeping pallet. The cut on my head was drumming.

I thought of the crude cross at the head of Maggie's grave. Thought of her sashaying about the riverbank on Patrick Owen's arm. Lottie was right of course; I had no proof it was Owen. But there was a certainty within me that he had wrung Maggie's throat. And I ached for him to be punished.

The person I had been in London would never have let herself get drawn into such matters. Would never have prodded a soldier for answers or churned through evidence in my mind. I would have stepped back, hidden my eyes, told myself the world was as it should be. After all, the person I was in London had no reason to fight. I had everything I needed. I knew, of course, of the inequality in the world, but saw it as an unavoidable part of life. Back in London, the injustices of the world had largely fallen in my favour.

My father, in his own starched and stilted way, had loved me. I'd never doubted that. My mother had died in her childbed, and my father's way through the loss was to lavish me with care and attention. I grew up with an endless parade of nurses and governesses, music teachers and tutors. A good head for arithmetic and a convincing French accent, I suppose Father assumed, would go some way to making up for my gaudy appearance.

I knew I was no great beauty, but I was confident in my intelligence. Father made sure I knew it a good substitute. He brought in master after master to train me in subjects far beyond the scope of most young women of my class. And each night, as we sat opposite each other at the supper table, he would quiz me on the things I had learned that day.

How might I ask for my supper in Italian, Eleanor? Or; *Tell me about Herschel's new planet…*

As a child, my life had been laid out for me; dutiful daughter and conscientious student, then I was to become a wife and mother. I'd never imagined I could be taken in any other direction. For all my studies of the skies and foreign phrases, my world was narrow. Though I could point to any city on a map, I had no thought of how life might be in any place but London. When, as a nine-year-old child, I heard of our ships landing in Botany Bay, the place seemed as distant as a dream. Never in the stretches of my imagination could I have perceived ever walking these shores. Especially not as a prisoner.

Jonathan Marling was an accounting client of my father's; an ambitious young man who shared ownership of a jeweller's on Theobolds Road. He'd come to our door one day with a valise full of papers, and while I waited for my father to return home, I kept him entertained with mindless small talk and a pot of Indian tea. At the sight of us laughing together in the parlour, my father's face lit up, and he set about arranging our betrothal with far too much enthusiasm.

A week later, Jonathan was back at the door to ask for my hand, no doubt buoyed by the sizeable dowry Father had dropped at his feet.

I'd held out no hope of marrying for love, of course, but accepting Jonathan's proposal left a hollowness inside me. I found reason after reason to delay my wedding; the need to be married in spring, our priest's runny nose, the unavailability of sky-blue satin for my bridal gown. I had nothing against my husband-to-be. I was just not ready to become a wife.

When Father fell ill with smallpox, I was still finding excuses not to marry.

But Jonathan was there beside me while my father's body was lowered into the earth. And he was there to accompany me home from the service, to manage Father's affairs on my behalf, to hold me when the grief broke inside me.

With Father gone, I felt the emptiness stretching out around me. As his only child, he had left me a good inheritance, but the thought of being alone in the world was terrifying. I felt utterly incapable of managing my own life. And so three weeks after I had walked out of St James's behind my father's coffin, I was walking back down the aisle as Jonathan's wife.

I became the lady of a whitewashed townhouse in Clerkenwell, with a fortepiano in the parlour and a small garden in front.

My father would be proud of me, I told myself, as I managed our small staff and walked on Jonathan's arm to a parade of garden parties and banquets. Would have been proud of the well-respected young lady I had become.

But I knew he would not have pushed so hard for our marriage if he'd known I'd be a widow by the age of twenty-six. And he certainly would not have done so if he'd known that marrying Jonathan Marling would lead me onto a prison ship.

I lay wide awake for what felt like hours, listening as the yelling in the street continued. I could see the flare of the bonfire through the cloth window. Did the rebels plan to break Owen out of prison? Or was this chaos their way of announcing to the Rum Corps that they would not be kept down?

I got out of bed and lit the lamp, knowing there was little point trying to sleep. I went to the shelf and looked over the pile of books. Blackwell's collection was an eclectic one; a Bible interspersed with the novels of Goldsmith and Fielding, and an enormous brick on construction techniques that looked unbearably dull. I opened the novel at the top of the pile but it did little to hold my attention.

My gaze drifted to Blackwell's empty sleeping pallet, to the wooden storage chest beside it. I felt a sudden, desperate need to look inside. To learn just a little about this man I lay beside in the night. This man I had chosen to trust.

I picked up the lamp, my bare feet sighing against the dirt floor. I tiptoed towards the chest in which Blackwell kept a small piece of himself.

Guilt tugged inside me, but my curiosity won out.

I opened the lid and held up the lamp. The chest was filled with clothing; neatly folded shirts, trousers, a scarf and gloves. Beneath them, several more books and a large metal crucifix.

Tucked down the side, fallen between the books, was large oval locket. I clicked it open, holding it up to the lamp. A young woman peered back at me, pale hair falling in ringlets around a heart-shaped face. She had a delicate beauty, with large doe eyes and a smile at the edge of her lips. I remembered posing for a similar portrait in the year before my father's death.

Blackwell's wife, I wondered? I'd never been bold

enough to take the conversation in that direction. I clicked the locket closed, and tucked it back beneath the clothes.

I felt a hollowness inside me, though I couldn't fathom why. Guilt, perhaps? Or the inexplicable envy that his thoughts might have been on that curly-haired beauty while he was sitting at the supper table with me?

I regretted going through his things. I closed the lid and went back to my sleeping pallet, bringing my arms up over my ears to block out the chaos in the street.

CHAPTER NINE

"The Enemy hath so completely possessed himself of the minds of all ranks and orders here; that it is a matter of doubt with me, that His power will be ever seen in this place."

Letter from Rev. Samuel Marsden to Mary Stokes
October 1795

On Sunday morning, as I laced my boots for church, I said, "You're a man of God." My thoughts were with the Bible on the shelf. The crucifix within the chest. With a murmured prayer before each meal.

Blackwell buttoned his jacket. "Does that surprise you?"

I sat back on the chair, watching a tiny lizard dart under the door. "Sometimes it feels as though God has been forgotten here. At least within the factory walls."

He ran a comb through his hair and peered into his shaving mirror. "My father was the vicar of our parish," he told me finally. "So yes. I suppose I am a man of God."

I felt a faint warmth in my chest. It was the first time he had offered me a scrap of information about who he was.

I stood up and smoothed my skirts. "You go first," I told him. "I'll follow." I was always careful to distance myself from him when the colony was watching. I knew being seen with me would only bring him shame. There was talk of course; whispered at the spinning wheels and hollered over rum at the river. Talk of the factory lass who'd found a bed beneath the roof of an officer. I refused to speak on the subject; refused to give any weight to the rumours. I was afraid that if the gossip came too close, Blackwell might see the error of his ways and send me back to the street.

I pulled the door closed and made my way to the church. And into formation us government men and women went; lining up like children before we were herded into the front pews. Redcoats stood at either end, rifles at the ready. Sunlight blazed through the windows, making dust motes dance above our heads.

Reverend Marsden strode to the pulpit. Though the morning was cold, his cheeks were pink with exertion. His thick fingers curled over the edge of the pulpit as he looked out over the congregation.

I wondered if Maggie would make it into his sermon. A prayer for the departed. An acknowledgement that a crime had been committed. An acknowledgement that Maggie Abbott, a rough-spoken factory lass, had existed.

If anyone was going to speak out against Patrick Owen, I knew it would be the reverend. If there was anything Marsden despised more than the factory lasses, it was the croppies.

Maggie did make it into the sermon that day.

A loose woman, the reverend called her. *A harlot*. His steely gaze moved along the front row where the factory lasses were sitting. He looked into our eyes as he spoke of the perils of carnal immorality. Of the way a woman's active sexuality threatened the very order of society. Upset the precious balance of masculine and feminine.

I stared back at him, forcing myself to hold his gaze. The person I was in London would have nodded along with Marsden. Yes, a sinner; a loose woman who deserved all that came to her. But the day I had stepped out of the factory with nowhere to sleep, I had come to see that there was not always a choice.

"The immorality of this colony is a thing you should all be ashamed of," he said. "The extent of which will become clearer in the coming days and weeks."

Murmurs rippled through the congregation.

I turned to Hannah, who was sitting beside me. "What do you suppose he means by that?"

She snorted. "Don't waste your time dwelling on it. When you ever heard anything but drivel come out his mouth?"

"Behave yourselves," a well-spoken man called down to the convicts.

"You behave yourself," a young woman snapped back. I hid a smile.

"1 Corinthians 14," the man boomed down at us, like he was trying to be the very voice of God himself, "it is shameful for a woman to speak in church."

I returned to the hut before Blackwell, and gathered up

my dirty clothes. I took the washboard down to the river and crouched on the edge in the pale winter sun. My boots sank into the muddy bank as I dipped my apron beneath the surface. For a moment, I just held it between my fingers, watching it float ghost-like through the bronze haze of the water.

I scrubbed my clothes along the washboard until my fingers were numb, hanging each piece from a tree; marking the forest with my fleeting scrap of civilisation. The washing helped take my mind off things. Helped take my mind off Maggie Abbott's blank eyes staring out from within the scrub. Helped me stop wondering what Marsden had meant by revealing the extent of the colony's immorality.

I bundled my wet clothes into my arms and went back to the hut, draping my shift and petticoats over the table, wet stockings spread out across a chair. I felt as though I was possessing the place, making it my own. Strewn about Blackwell's hut like this, my clothes felt almost as inconsonant as they had hung up among the wilderness.

His footsteps behind me made me start. I spun around to find him holding out the book he had been reading a few nights earlier. I'd not even heard him come in.

"I've finished if you'd care to read it," he said.

I murmured my thanks. There was something alluring about escaping into a fictitious world for a time. A precious thing here.

He glanced at the ghostly shapes of my washing. "It's the Lord's Day. You ought to be resting." He nodded to the book. "Read it. I think you will enjoy it."

I took the book and went back to the river. Followed it downstream a few yards to where the mangroves gave way to a battalion of broad trees. There was a chill in the wind, but the sun was struggling through the clouds. I needed to be out in the daylight, not in the endless shadows of the hut.

I opened the book and stared at the first page. The words swam in front of my eyes. My mind refused to be drawn into the story. I had already been transported into another realm that I would have believed fictitious had I not been living it.

I became aware that Blackwell had joined me by the river. He had changed out of his uniform into dark trousers and a faded riding coat. There was a clay pipe in his hand. I'd not seen him smoke often. He looked upwards.

"These trees are very beautiful," he said. "Redgums."

I nodded.

"I come here sometimes," he told me. "For a little space."

"I'm sorry." I moved to stand. "I'll leave. I—"

He held up a hand to stop me. "I didn't mean for you to leave. I simply meant to say this place helps relax me."

"Why do you need help relaxing?" I knew it a foolish question. Maggie's murder. The Irish rebels. Owen's upcoming trial.

"You put me on edge," he said finally.

I looked up at him in surprise. "Why?"

"Well," he said after a moment, "there's the matter of my storage chest, to begin with."

I felt my cheeks colour with shame. How did he know I had gone through the chest? Had I not put things back neatly enough?

"I'm sorry," I said, meeting his eyes. "That was unacceptable."

His face was unreadable. He gestured with the pipe to

the grass-flecked earth beside me. "May I?"

I nodded.

For several moments we sat in silence, Blackwell's long legs stretched out towards the river, mine folded neatly beneath me. Water burbled in the stillness.

After a moment, he gestured back to the redgums. "I used a little of this wood in the roof of the hut."

"You built it yourself?"

"Mostly," he said. "I learned a little construction when I was at school. I've always found it most rewarding. A way of leaving your mark on a place." He chuckled lightly. "Although I can't imagine that hut lasting too many generations. Each time the sky opens I fear the rain will carry it away."

I ran my fingers over the faded leather cover of the book in my lap.

"You're not enjoying it?" he asked.

I lowered my eyes. "In his sermon today, Reverend Marsden spoke of revealing the colony's immorality. Do you know what he meant by it?"

"A muster," Blackwell said shortly. "Nothing more. The governor likes to keep track of who is holding land, how many colonial-born children have arrived. Which prisoners are on and off stores…"

"What does any of that have to do with immorality?"

He puffed a line of smoke towards the clouds. The pipe didn't suit him. He looked like a young man trying to whittle away the years. "Reverend Marsden is also to register the females in the colony. The service will take place next Sunday."

"Register us?" I repeated. "And? We are catalogued by

our place of birth? Our ages? Our children?"

"Yes," said Blackwell. "Among other things." He jammed the pipe back between his teeth.

"What other things?" I looked at him through narrowed eyes. "How does the reverend catalogue us, Lieutenant Blackwell?"

"You are to be catalogued by your marital status," he said finally. "Wife or concubine."

He spoke the words carefully, gently, but I felt the sting of them. I was not a wife. So it left no doubt as to what I was in Reverend Marsden's eyes.

As to what I was in the colony's eyes.

Once I had been a wife. But my husband had died and his spilled blood had led me to New South Wales. Now I spent each night lying on the floor beside a member of His Majesty's Army.

Concubine.

"What do you think of this?" I asked, my voice hardening.

He shrugged. "It is what it is."

"That is not an answer."

"I'll not fight with you, Eleanor," Blackwell said calmly. "I'll not be a dumping ground for your anger."

"I don't want to fight. I just want to know what you think of this muster."

He lowered his pipe. "Reverend Marsden is doing what he thinks is best for the colony. And the women within it." His words sounded rehearsed.

"Is that what you truly believe?" I asked. "Or is that just what you think you ought to say to me?"

He looked taken aback by my boldness. "The reverend

has been pushing for a women's barracks to be built. He believes the factory lasses' plight will be eased with a safe place to sleep each night. And he hopes the muster will support his cause."

"That may be so," I said, "but that's not what I asked. Do you think for yourself, Lieutenant? Or do you follow Reverend Marsden blindly?"

Blackwell's voice rose slightly. "What exactly do you mean by that?"

I gave a small shrug. My words had come spilling out half formed. But I was glad I had finally gotten a rise out of him. Glad I had finally seen a little emotion. I sat up on my knees so my eyes were level with his. "Do you believe us all immoral harlots, Lieutenant? Us factory women who curl up on your floors? You're a man of God. And the Bible says we must only do such a thing in the presence of our husbands. Is that what you're thinking each night I sleep beside you?"

Blackwell's neck reddened. And I saw then that my opinion mattered to him. What a strange thing, I thought distantly, that the views of a convict woman might hold such weight to a military officer. Perhaps I was not so insignificant. Perhaps none of us were.

"Reverend Marsden is not everything I believe in," Blackwell said shortly. He emptied his pipe into the river and disappeared inside the hut. I hugged my knees to my chest and watched the silver streaks of ash float away on the tide.

CHAPTER TEN

They blamed Maggie's murder on the blacks. Who could pretend to be surprised?

The verdict of Owen's trial had filtered through the factory that day. His version of events, which we had for days believed nothing but a garbled lie, had become the truth; Maggie had left his hut after supper the night of her death, with too much liquor under her skin. Wandered into the bush to be set upon by natives.

And perhaps that was all the Rum Corps believed she deserved.

"You don't know it a lie, Nell," said Lottie.

We were out in the prison yard, eating the slivers of bread we'd brought for mealtime. Clouds hung low, threatening rain.

"Her feet were bare when I found her," I said sharply. "Why would she have gone wandering into the bush without her boots?"

"She were a drinker," said Lottie. "You know that. She

probably weren't thinking clearly."

"And what about the bruises on her arms?" I asked. "She didn't do that to herself." I wrapped my hand around my teacup, craving its warmth. I never felt Maggie's absence more acutely than when I was out in the jail yard with Lottie and Hannah. Without her brassy interjections, our conversations felt painfully incomplete.

"The bruises," said Lottie with a sigh. "I told you before, they don't prove anything."

"I know you and Maggie weren't the best of friends," I said. "But—"

"That doesn't mean I'm happy about what happened to her," Lottie said pointedly. "It sickens me as much as it does you. But Patrick has been found innocent."

I whacked the arm of Hannah, who was sitting on the bench beside me. "Would you make her see sense?"

Hannah jabbed the remains of her bread in Lottie's direction. "Ain't no making this one see sense."

I pulled my eyes away from Lottie's glare. I could feel our friendship beginning to strain under the weight of our disagreement. For the sake of our relationship, I knew I ought to keep my mouth shut. I had already lost one friend that month. I couldn't bear to lose another. But nor could I not just sit back in acceptance while Patrick Owen walked free.

"I suppose it doesn't matter who killed her, does it," I said bitterly. "Because Maggie Abbott was nothing but a concubine."

"You still on about that damn muster?" Lottie asked. "It's just Marsden's blathering."

"It's not just Marsden's blathering. Lieutenant Blackwell says the register is to be sent back to England. Imagine what they'll think of us there."

Hannah gave a short laugh. "Sorry to say it, Nell, but whatever it is, I'm sure they're already thinking it."

Two days earlier, the women in the colony had been corralled outside the church before the service. We had presented ourselves to Reverend Marsden's secretary, and become nothing more than entries scrawled on a page. Name, age, marital status.

Widow, I'd said. But I knew when that register made its way back to England I would be listed upon it as *concubine*. I tried to tell myself it didn't matter. What difference did it make what men ten thousand miles away thought of us out here? But it mattered more than I wanted to admit. There was every chance the muster would be read by men who had known my father, known my husband. Men I had walked among at soirees and Christmas parties. The shame of being transported had been crushing enough. And now beside my label of *convict*, I would also be marked as a concubine.

I looked between Hannah and Lottie. "Doesn't this bother you?"

"Are you truly surprised by it?" asked Lottie, her mouth still half full of bread. "People like us, we're nothing. When are you going to realise that?"

Her words stung.

As a girl, I'd been led to believe I was a prize. Something to be awarded to the gentleman with the biggest income or the best family connections. I was preened and polished like a jewel, my dowry added to, my skills and etiquette polished until they shone.

But as we were herded back upstairs by a pimply soldier who looked half my age, I realised Lottie was right. We were nothing. Our names, our stories, our pasts; none of that was important. We were just marks on Marsden's register.

Concubine one.

Concubine two.

Three, four, five.

We could disappear, die at the hands of another, and who was there to care? We were just hands to weave the cloth. Wombs to carry the next generation. And there would always be more of us where we had come from.

"The blacks?" I demanded when I got back to the hut that night. Blackwell was dressed in full uniform, sitting on a chair and polishing his boots. I couldn't fathom why. They'd be caked in mud again the second he stepped outside. "You truly believe she was killed by the blacks?"

Blackwell didn't rise to my anger. It made me even more furious. I slammed my hand hard against the table, forcing him to look up. "Blame the blacks. Because it's easy. Isn't that right?"

"There was not enough evidence to charge Patrick Owen," Blackwell said, pressing the lid onto the pot of polish and setting it back on the shelf.

"Maggie was lodging with him."

"That's not evidence."

I paced back and forth, hot with anger. Anger at Owen's freedom, at Marsden's labelling of us. At Blackwell's calmness and his stupid need to polish his boots.

"Do you think him guilty?" I demanded.

Blackwell sighed as he stood up.

I planted my hands on my hips and glared as I waited for an answer. Somewhere inside, I suppose I knew this wasn't his fault. At least, not entirely. But seeing him there in his lobster coat, all I could think of was the officers on the jury who had let Owen walk free. The skewed authority, the injustices. Everything that was wrong with this place. Besides, I had to take my anger out on him, because who else would listen?

"Of course," I said. "You've no opinion on the matter."

"I have an opinion," he said sharply. "I'm just not obliged to share it with you." He glanced down at his pocket watch, then grabbed his scarf from the back of the chair and wound it around his neck. "You would do well to remember your place, Eleanor."

My cheeks flushed with a mixture of anger and embarrassment.

"Where are you going?" I asked, following him to the door. I didn't want him to leave. I wanted him to stay here so I could unload my protests on him.

"I've a council meeting." He stopped at the door and looked back at me. "Can you sew?"

I blinked, caught off guard by the abrupt change of subject. "Sew?" I repeated. "Yes, of course."

"Good." He nodded towards the pile of shirts on the end of his sleeping pallet. "I've several pieces that need mending. I'll pay you a half crown apiece. I know it falls outside our arrangement."

I clenched my hand around the edge of the door in frustration. Damn Blackwell and his decency. I wanted to be angry with him. *Needed* to be.

"I thought the lobsters only traded in liquor," I said sharply.

"You ought to have some money of your own," he said,

pushing past my comment. "And I'd hate to think you were resorting to... other means to earn yourself a little coin."

I felt my face colour violently. "No," I managed. "Of course I'm not."

Blackwell nodded. He looked away, as though embarrassed he had raised the subject. "Good," he said shortly.

I felt the loss of him as the door thumped shut. It was not just about needing to air my grievances, I realised. There was a part of me that wanted to be near him.

I hovered in the doorway for a moment, hot and disoriented by the realisation. Then I took the sewing tin from the shelf and carefully threaded a needle.

I heard voices outside the hut. Muffled, drunken laughter. I recognised Owen's drawl. I grabbed the lamp and stepped outside.

Owen and Brady were standing close to the door of the hut. There was something small and dark in Brady's hand. They were tying it to the post of the awnings with a length of rope. I squinted. Were they paws? And eyes?

"What in hell is that?" I demanded.

Owen looked unfazed at the sight of me. "A little gift for the lieutenant." He stepped back to admire his work. "Don't you go taking it down now, Nellie."

I realised they had hung the battered corpse of some poor creature from the edge of Blackwell's roof.

"This the best you can do with your freedom, Owen?" I hissed. But he and Brady were already walking away.

I went inside for a knife and sawed at the rope. The carcass fell to the earth with a dull thud. I picked the poor creature up by the legs and flung it into the bush.

CHAPTER ELEVEN

"[If Catholicism] were tolerated they would assemble together from every quarter, not so much from a desire of celebrating mass, as to recite the miseries and injustice of their banishment, the hardships they suffer, and to enflame one another's minds with some wild scheme of revenge."

Rev. Samuel Marsden
A Few Observations on the Toleration of the Catholic Religion in New South Wales
1806

"Wake up, Eleanor." Blackwell's voice was soft, and close to my ear. We had barely spoken since I'd confronted him about Owen's exoneration. I took his gentleness as a sign I was forgiven.

It was a Sunday. The bright morning light told me I had overslept. If Blackwell hadn't woken me I would have been late for church.

He was already at the door. "Meet me outside the hut after the service."

I pulled the blanket around my shoulders to cover myself. "Why? What do you need me to do?"

But he had slipped out the door before my question was fully formed.

When the service was over, I made my way back to the hut. Blackwell was already there waiting for me. He had changed out of his uniform into dark trousers and long black boots, his shirtsleeves rolled up to his elbows. I wondered distantly if he meant it as a gesture; wanted me to see him as something other than a lobster who'd let Maggie's killer walk free. The neck cloth tied loosely at his throat made him look boyish and young. A small hessian sack was bunched into his hand.

He started to walk. "Come with me."

I had to skip to keep up with his long-legged strides. "Where are we going?"

"To find a little space."

My lips curled up slightly at his hazy response. I didn't press him. I was coming to recognise that the way to prise answers from Adam Blackwell was to not ask questions at all.

He led me down Macquarie Street and into a thick tangle of trees. Soon, any hint of the settlement had disappeared. I followed close, disoriented by the absence of a path. I could see the undergrowth had been trampled in places. By the savages, I wondered? My heart began to beat a little quicker.

I heard a murmured voice carried on the wind. At the sound of our footsteps, the words fell silent.

"This way." Blackwell gestured with his head for us to walk in the opposite direction.

I looked back over my shoulder. "Who was that?" I asked edgily. "All the way out here?"

"Father Dixon, I assume," said Blackwell. "Holding his Catholic mass."

"Out here?"

"Well," he said, "the Irish want his services. What choice does he have but to hold them in secret?"

"You're not going to stop them?"

Blackwell looked ahead, shading his eyes from the sun. "I've more important things to do today."

"Lottie says Father Dixon was allowed to hold mass before the Irish uprising," I said as we walked. I wanted to grasp the workings of this colony, however brutal things were. I felt as though understanding this place was the best way to survive it.

I knew my education was worth little here. What did it matter in this place that I could dance a minuet, or play a Bach fugue? They were meaningless skills when life was stripped down to its necessities. In this place, it was a different type of knowledge that would save me; an understanding of who held the power and who was about to fall.

"Dixon failed to talk the Irish down from attacking at Castle Hill," Blackwell told me. "The mass was taken away as punishment." He pushed aside an overhanging branch, holding it back for me to pass.

"Were you fighting in Ireland?" I asked. "During the first rebellion?"

He nodded.

"They say the fighting was particularly brutal."

He watched the ground as he walked. "Yes," he said finally. "But it's the life a man signs up for when he chooses to fight for the Crown." The undergrowth crackled loudly beneath his boots.

"Must be a strange thing," I said, "finding yourself fighting against the Irish again in this place."

"Not so strange. I feel I've spent my whole life fighting against the same men. And fighting with the same men, for that matter." He gave a short smile. "For a place so far from home, this colony certainly has its share of familiar faces."

I smiled wryly at that. I'd not seen any faces from my old circles trudging the riverbank of Parramatta.

Blackwell pointed suddenly to a small purple flower poking out of the undergrowth. "Here. Look." He knelt down, gesturing to me to join him. "The chocolate plant," he said. "They've just started flowering."

I smiled crookedly. "Chocolate plant?"

He nodded. "Smell it."

I bent forward, inhaling the scent of the flower. A rich chocolate and vanilla aroma that brought a smile to my face.

Blackwell dug into the earth and yanked out the root of the flower. "We roast these," he said. "Eat them with a little salt and butter. The taste is quite something." He put the tuber into the bag. "There ought to be plenty of them out here."

I smiled. "How did you learn to do this?"

"I watched the natives do it once."

My shoulders stiffened. For a fleeting moment, I had forgotten we were in a world of savages and sharp-toothed creatures.

Blackwell got to his feet and dusted the earth from his knees. "Come on. There's more over here."

In spite of my unease, I followed him through the

undergrowth. Sprigs of purple leapt from within the carpet of green. I knelt down and began to tug the tubers from the earth. Dampness soaked through my skirts.

I inhaled deeply, drawing the clean, mint-scented air into my lungs. The bush rose up around me on all sides, the grey-green trees carpeting hills that rolled up towards mountains. A repetitive fragment of birdsong sounded above my head, its melody rising and falling. I sat back on my heels for a moment, trying to pick out the notes.

I felt suddenly, inexplicably calm. There was something about this vastness, this rugged beauty; the ability of this wild land to feel at once so empty and so alive. I had not imagined I would feel calm in such a place.

I allowed myself to get drawn into our search, hunting out the purple flowers from within the tangle of brown and green. I focused on the feel of my fingers buried in the damp earth; a foreign, raw sensation, but one I deeply enjoyed. My head felt pleasantly empty.

When Blackwell said, "That's enough," I found myself oddly disappointed. He swung the full bag over his shoulder. "Unless you want to carry some more back in your pockets."

I smiled, wiping muddy hands against my skirts. We began to walk back in the direction of the settlement.

The undergrowth rustled, and I heard the unmistakable crackle of twigs. Blackwell held up a hand, gesturing to me to stop walking.

My heart began to race. I felt myself edge closer to him.

Another hiss and snap of twigs. The sighing of branches. And the natives stepped out in front of us.

I heard my sharp inhalation. There was a part of me that had believed them a myth. A story told within the depths of the convict ships, like the two-headed monsters hiding in the bush.

But these were not the wild warriors of the stories I had heard. Three men stood either side of the group, two women in the middle, and children among them, ranging in age from perhaps twelve or thirteen to a baby pressed against its mother's hip. Each wore swathes of animal skin, reaching from their shoulders down to their bare feet.

The children stared up at us with wide, dark eyes. Clouds of black hair hung past their shoulders, their skin the colour of darkest coffee. My gaze lingered on the spear in one of the natives' hand; two heads taller than the man himself.

Blackwell stood close, reaching around me and pressing a hand to my shoulder to steady me. My chest tightened. Fear? Or the unexpected feel of his hand against my body? He put the sack at his feet and held up his free hand in a gesture of peace. Nodded to the natives in greeting. I could hear my heart thudding in my ears.

The tall man's hand shifted on his spear and I heard myself gasp. But then he gave us the faintest of nods. He murmured to the others in words I didn't understand, then they turned as one, disappearing back into the bush.

I felt my muscles sink in relief. The back of my shift was damp with sweat.

Blackwell's hand slid from my shoulder. "There's no need to be afraid," he said. "They'll not attack unless they're provoked."

"That's not what I've heard."

"The natives won't come any further east than Prospect," he said. "We've likely strayed into their land." He watched his feet as we stepped over a fallen tree. "It's the white men you ought to fear. Not the natives."

I didn't answer. What did he mean by such a comment? Was he speaking of himself? Or was he warning me away from Patrick Owen and the other Irish rebels?

He shoved aside a thicket of grass. "This way," he said, "I want to show you something."

The ground began to rise steeply, and I grappled at tangled tree branches to haul myself up the incline. And suddenly the trees cleared, the land opening out before us. I let out my breath at the sight. I could see out to a jagged mountain range, silhouetted in the late afternoon sun. It was achingly beautiful; the peaks dotted with snow beneath the harsh black of the rock. Golden winter light spilled over the hills, a stark contrast to the heavy gloom that pressed down upon England.

I sat on the hillside, hugging my knees to my chest. Let a sense of calm wash over me. I saw then that it had been a deliberate act; his bringing me here. He had known the mountains would be a tonic for my anger over Owen, over Marsden's register. He had known how much I needed it. I felt a sudden swell of gratitude.

I looked over my shoulder. He was standing several yards behind me, one hand shading his eyes from the sun. And for the first time, it was curiosity I felt about my new home, rather than terror. I thought again of the natives; of the mothers, the children, the tall man's nod of greeting.

I caught Blackwell looking at me.

"How long have you been out here?" I asked.

"Almost four years."

I imagined four years in this place must feel like a lifetime. The harshness of this land made time distort. My four months in New South Wales felt more like a decade.

"Do you miss home?" I asked.

"Sometimes."

I peered sideways at him, determined to eke out more than one-word answers. And then he sat beside me on the damp grass. I took it as a sign he was open to my questioning. I folded my legs beneath me, suddenly conscious of the shortness of my Navy Board issue skirts.

"Who is she?" I asked. "The lady in the portrait?"

Blackwell's dark hair streamed back in the wind. "My wife. Sophia."

"Where is she?"

I was expecting *dead*. Perhaps I was even hoping for *dead*. But, after a brief moment of silence he said, "London."

I heard a sound come from my throat. "Tell me about her."

He raised his eyebrows. "What do you wish to know?"

In truth, I wished to know nothing. The question had just fallen out in the surprise of finding her still living. I could tell from her portrait the kind of lady his wife was; polite, well-spoken, obedient. The kind of lady I was supposed to have been.

Blackwell had been four years away from his wife; four years, plus the length of the voyage. Had time apart made him long for her? Or had he pushed her to the back of his thoughts?

"Do you love her?" I asked boldly.

He didn't flinch. "Yes. She's my wife."

"A marriage does not necessarily equal love."

"No. But it did in our case." He shook his head. "It does." An afterthought.

"Children?" I asked.

"No."

And what was she doing now, I wondered, that lady in the portrait? Beautiful, curly-haired Sophia. Was she faithful to her husband, pining, praying, awaiting his return? Or had she long found someone to take his place?

"And you?" he asked. "Have you a husband?"

"No," I said. "He died." The words felt strange on my lips. It was the first time I had ever spoken of Jonathan's death, outside of the interrogation at least. I was surprised at the lack of emotion in my voice.

Blackwell said, "I'm sorry."

I nodded. Perhaps this was why I had never spoken of Jonathan. I didn't want the pity. Or the questions.

"You're not like the other women here," he said. "You did not commit a crime of desperation."

I gave a wry smile at that. His guess was not entirely accurate. My crime had been one of great desperation, just not desperation fuelled by an empty belly and starving children.

"Is this your way of asking how I came to be here, Lieutenant?"

"No." He got to his feet, slinging the sack over his shoulder again. "That's not for me to know."

CHAPTER TWELVE

The light had drained from the day by the time we returned to the settlement. Though I was warm from walking, the icy wind had made my cheeks and fingertips numb. I wished for the gloves I had lost on the voyage.

As we approached the main street, I held myself back, leaving space between myself and Blackwell. He looked over his shoulder at me, brow wrinkled in confusion. I wasn't sure if my gesture was for him or me. I did not want him to be seen in the company of a lag in mud-streaked skirts. And I did not want to fuel stories of me as his concubine.

As I approached the hut, I felt a stab of dread. The door was hanging open, the cloth on the window dangling by one corner.

Blackwell dropped the sack and strode towards the hut. The tubers spilled onto the road. I grabbed the sack and followed.

I let out my breath as I stepped through the door. The table had been knocked onto its side, the books flung from the shelves. Shards of glass jars were strewn over the floor between the remains of potted meat, and the wooden chest had been overturned. The place smelled of piss and spilled liquor. I hovered beside the grate.

"Why did they do this?" I dared to ask.

He ran a hand through his hair. "Because I'm a murdering bastard." His voice was low and dark. Was it sarcasm? Or self-disgust? I couldn't tell.

"A little gift from the croppies, Lieutenant," said a voice behind me. I whirled around to see Patrick Owen in the doorway. His arms were folded across his chest, and the grin on his face made me want to strike him.

Blackwell strode towards him and Owen backed out into the street. I put down the sack and followed.

Owen shoved against Blackwell's chest, making him stumble backwards. No retaliation. Blackwell had several inches of height on the Irishman, his shoulders broader, arms thicker. But he made no attempt to fight, or to reach for his weapon and threaten Owen into leaving. It made me nervous. I knew Owen was the kind of man who'd carry a pistol in his pocket. The lieutenant was in close range. If there was a shot, he'd not survive it.

I raced out into High Street, searching for the soldiers on patrol. I found them pacing the alleys close to Marsden's land. When they saw me charging towards them, their hands went instinctively to their rifles. But when I told them what was happening – *Patrick Owen* and *Lieutenant Blackwell* – they were off down the street without giving me another glance.

"Come on now, Blackwell," Owen was drawling when I raced back to the hut, "you can do better than that."

"I'm not going to fight you, Owen," he said. "Get the

hell out of here."

Owen swung a wild fist. The blow landed on the side of Blackwell's jaw, knocking him backwards into the wall of the hut. I heard a cry of shock escape me. The two soldiers darted forward, each grabbing one of Owen's arms and yanking him away from the lieutenant.

"You all right, sir?" asked one.

Blackwell rubbed his jaw. "Fine. Just get rid of him."

One of the marines shoved Owen hard in the back, making him stumble into the street. "Get out of here, you mad bog-jumper."

Owen chuckled. He dug his hands into his pockets and began to walk in the direction of the tavern.

"What?" I demanded. "He's just to walk away after—"

"Eleanor," Blackwell snapped, silencing me.

One of the marines glanced at me, then at the lieutenant. "Shall I get rid of the lag too, sir?"

"No. That won't be necessary."

I stood with my arms wrapped around my body, watching as Owen disappeared around the corner.

And I realised it then. Realised why the blacks had been blamed for the death of Maggie Abbot, when so many fingers pointed to Patrick Owen. I turned to look at Blackwell. He was staring after Owen too, a hand pressed to the side of his jaw.

"Owen is untouchable," I said. "He can do as he likes and he'll never be punished. I'm right, aren't I?"

Blackwell didn't answer.

"Why?" I pushed.

But he had retreated to silence. I could tell it was up to me to put the pieces together. I bent down to pick up one of the tubers that had rolled into the road.

"Fetch some water from the river," Blackwell said tersely. "There's a lot of cleaning to do."

The next day was a visiting day; a day when the men crowded the factory floor and watched as we paraded ourselves as potential wives. A settler just arrived from Sydney Town had been given his marriage certificate.

"A wife is required for this man," the superintendent said, sounding as though he'd never been so bored in his whole damn life. "Those willing to be married, please step forward."

For a moment, I thought of it. Choose me. Take me away from this place. Make me *wife*. My label of *concubine* sat heavy on my shoulders.

But I had seen how this circus worked. And I knew there would be questions.

Have you ever been married before? Yes? What happened to your husband?

I didn't want my whole shameful story spilled out on the factory floor.

I stayed motionless, staring at my feet. Women from the *Norfolk* stepped forward, along with several others. The settler seeking a wife was young and handsome. A far better catch than most of the pock-faced scrubs who came traipsing through this place.

He chose a young girl from the *Norfolk*; a scrappy blonde

thing who'd cried all the way to Gibraltar. Petite and birdlike, she made me feel like an ogre.

She gave the settler a tiny, shy smile, looking up at him with enormous blue eyes. I imagined her in her trial, weeping before the magistrate while telling a pitiful tale of a stolen cloak to keep out the snow.

"You ever been married before?" the settler asked her.

"No sir."

And I thought of Jonathan Marling with a bullet in his chest, sure I'd be at the factory forever.

We drank at the river in celebration of the tearful girl from the *Norfolk*. Within an hour of the settler's visit to the factory, she'd been hauled off to the church to sign her marriage papers. Now she was on her way to her new husband's farm with a ticket of leave in her pocket.

Lottie sat beside me on the log, and we passed the dregs of a rum bottle back and forth between us.

"I thought you would have put yourself forward," I told her. "Or did he not take your fancy?"

Lottie didn't return my smile. "You know it's not about that," she said. "Marriage is a necessity. It's the only chance I got of getting out of here. Getting out of old Bert's bed."

"So why did you not put yourself forward?"

Lottie hiccupped on the rum. "I've got to marry an Irishman, don't I. My poor da would be rolling in his grave if he knew his only daughter had married a *sasanaigh*."

I hugged my knees. The men had fashioned a cricket bat out of a fallen tree branch and were whacking a cloth ball across the riverbank.

"Do you truly want a lifetime shackled to some mindless

croppy?" I asked. "It's not your only way out. They say good behaviour will get us a ticket of leave."

We all talked about the ticket of leave like it was the key to the greatest treasure in the land. A mythical treasure, for while we all knew someone who'd managed to get a ticket, there weren't one of us who had ever laid eyes on such a thing.

They said the magistrate handed out tickets whenever it suited him. There was no rhyme or reason to it, as far as any of us could tell. Stories were told of gentlemen convicts who'd stepped off the prison ship and had a ticket pressed into their hands. Others swore they could bribe their way to freedom. I knew several women who had climbed off the *Norfolk* with their liberty. I'd tried not to think of what they'd had to do to earn it.

"Is it true then?" I'd asked Blackwell one night. "We can bribe the magistrate for our freedom?"

True or not, I knew it was nothing but wishful thinking on my part. For the magistrate of Parramatta was the Reverend Samuel Marsden, and there was no way his fine, upstanding soul was getting bribed by a lowly concubine.

"A ticket of leave is a reward for good behaviour, not bribery," Blackwell had said, his face as impassive and even as ever.

Lottie snorted. "When did a factory lass ever get her ticket of leave without marrying for it first? And besides, what good is a ticket if you got no man to support you?" Her eyes were on Patrick Owen as he strutted over from the cricket match. The back of my neck prickled with anger.

Untouchable Patrick Owen. His eyes caught mine for a second and he gave me a ghost of a smile.

I stood abruptly. I couldn't just sit there across from him, sharing a drink like everything was all right. Lottie grabbed my arm and pulled me back down to the log.

"You've got to stop this," she said. "He's innocent."

I snorted. "You can't truly believe that."

"Yes," she said after a moment. "I do. The Rum Corps hates the Irish. If they could have put Owen on the scaffold, they would have. So aye, I believe he didn't do it."

I wrapped my arms around myself. She had things the wrong way around, I was sure. Owen's innocence – or lack of it – had little to do with anything.

The Rum Corps hated the Irish, yes, but they knew Owen was revered among the rebels. Send him to the scaffold, and who knew what chaos would be unleashed? The night of his arrest, the settlement had been in disarray.

The authorities were playing a dangerous game; letting a criminal loose among us to keep the croppies down. I knew with grim certainty that Owen had killed Maggie. Maybe such a thing simply didn't matter to the men who ran this place. What need was there for justice where the factory lasses were concerned? Perhaps it was far more crucial that a second Irish uprising was quelled.

Lottie planted the empty bottle in the dirt and stood, grabbing my arm and pulling me up beside her. "Come on. The drink's finished. We need to get more."

She looped her arm through mine as we walked towards the tavern.

"I wish you'd just give him a chance, Nell. That's all I'm asking. He's a good man. He's got a real passion in him. He's just doing what he thinks is best for his people."

I decided not to tell her about Owen's attack on

Blackwell the night before. Nothing I said would make her change her mind, especially not where the lieutenant was involved. I knew it would only lead to conflict between us. And I didn't want that. Having a friend in this place was far too precious.

But my hatred for Owen was roiling inside me, pushing against my chest. That morning, the side of Blackwell's face had been purple with bruising after their altercation in the street. And one of the shelves Owen had kicked at had fallen in the night.

As we approached the tavern, I felt my stomach knot. I'd not set foot inside since the night I'd stolen the potatoes. Some foolish part of me was afraid I'd be recognised.

Lottie shoved open the door and we stepped inside through a curtain of pipe smoke. Men were clustered around the counter in mud-streaked shirts, cannikins of drink in grimy hands. I kept my eyes down as I followed Lottie to the bar. I recognised the woman serving as one of the convicts from the factory. Lottie reached into her pocket and handed over enough coin for the new rum bottle.

"Stay and keep us company, ginger," said one of the men at the bar, sliding a hand around my waist. I shoved him away, his friends' laughter ringing in my ears.

On the walk back to the river, Lottie was harping on about Owen and his cohorts again. My head was beginning to ache.

"Some of the croppies," she began, "they were sent here after the rebellion in Ireland without their convict records. They were only sentenced to seven years. But it's coming on eight now, and there's no word of them being freed." She turned to look at me, her hazel eyes shining. "Tell me you wouldn't be angry if you that were you."

I frowned. "I understand that, Lottie. But this is about Owen killing Maggie and leaving her body on the side of the road."

Her eyes hardened. "You don't understand," she said. "How could you? How could you have any idea? How could you have any idea what it's like to struggle and fight and not know where your next meal is coming from?"

I sat back on the log and began to trace a stick through the dirt. I'd not spoken a word to Lottie about my privileged upbringing – I'd not spoken a word about it to anyone. But I was beginning to see it was not a thing I could easily hide.

"You think I don't know, Nell?" Lottie pushed. "You think I can't hear it in the way you speak? And the way you bleat on about Marsden's register as though once you were actually worth something?"

I didn't reply. I felt chastened; an intruder in someone else's world.

"Why a toff like you was caught thieving I'll never know," said Lottie. Her tone suggested she was not interested in my answer.

I'd not been transported for thieving, as I'd told Lottie I had. I'd not needed coin, or food to fill my empty belly. But I'd craved security, nonetheless. Needed someone to show me how to live my own life. And so, when my husband had held out his hand and told me to follow him down the wrong path, I had done it without question.

I took the bottle from Lottie and gulped down a mouthful, coughing as the rum seared my throat.

Look at us!, I wanted to scream. Here we were side by side in matching slops, matching blisters on our fingers, the same rum bottle passed back and forth between our hands.

But I knew all the blisters in the world would not make me understand what it was like to grow up with nothing. I had no thought of what it was to struggle and fight because I'd never had to do it before.

Lottie stood suddenly, and made her way towards Owen and the other men. I rested my aching head against my arms, letting the drunken conversations wash over me.

I found myself longing for London; for the glittering, diamond and ruby world I had once known.

There was nothing for me to return to in England, of course. My husband and father were dead, and I would never be welcomed back into my old circles after leaving this place on a prison ship. But I ached nonetheless for the cluttered grey skyline, the constant rattle of hooves and wheels, for the twists and turns of the river. Ached for a world I would never see again. Most of all, I wished for my own ignorance, for my ability to turn a blind eye. I wished for the naïve fool I had been when I had married Jonathan Marling.

I gulped down the rum, seeking drunkenness, seeking foolishness. I wanted my thoughts to still; wanted them to stop churning over Owen's exoneration and Maggie's blank eyes. But for better or for worse, I didn't know how to live in ignorance anymore.

My thoughts did not still. Instead, they crystallised. I wanted to speak to Reverend Marsden. Wanted that conversation I had been denied when he'd sent me on my way after seeing me at the courthouse in my bloodstained convict slops. At the back of my mind, I knew nothing I said would make a difference – Owen was free, Maggie was dead, and the female register was on its way across the seas. But just for a moment, I wanted to be seen. To be heard. To be more than an insignificant concubine. I would tell the reverend of the bruises on Maggie's arms. Tell him of the way she spent her nights by the river to escape Owen's fists. Pander to Marsden's hatred of the croppies and make him see that Patrick Owen deserved to be hanged.

Rum churning through my blood, I stood dizzily and strode towards the vast expanse of Marsden's land on the north-eastern edge of the settlement. I pressed my shoulders back and lifted my chin. I was a well-spoken woman from Clerkenwell who deserved to be taken seriously. Tonight I would make sure Reverend Marsden saw that.

As I approached the gates, a soldier came out of the blackness. "Where do you think you're going?"

I lifted my chin. "I wish to speak with Reverend Marsden," I said, trying my best to sound like an educated lady and not a lag filled up with rum. I wished I were wearing my worsted gown.

"Reverend Marsden don't have nothing to do with your kind," he said on a chuckle.

His dismissiveness made anger burn inside me. More than that, I hated that one look at me had told him I was a government woman. It was far too dark to see the tell-tale blue stripes on my skirts. What was it about me that told him I was not just the wife of a settler? Perhaps it was that bitterness in my words, or the fire in my eyes. Perhaps Hannah had been right when she'd claimed I couldn't blend into a place if I tried.

"It's very important," I said, continuing my march towards the house. It had never felt more pressing that I be permitted that conversation.

He grabbed my arm, fingers digging in hard. "Did you not hear me? The reverend don't have nothing to do with the factory whores."

Sudden anger tore through me. Before I knew what I was doing, I was swinging my arm, striking his nose and making blood spurt down the front of his coat. I stared open-mouthed, unable to believe I'd done such a thing. In a second he was on top of me, pinning me to the ground and wrenching my arms behind my back. Pain lanced through my shoulders. I felt hot drops of his blood against my ear. A shout into the night and two more soldiers came running. They yanked me to my feet, delivering me to the factory and the waiting hands of the superintendent.

CHAPTER THIRTEEN

"I would rather die than go out of my own country to be devoured by savages."

Convict Sarah Mills
Refusing transportation in favour of the death sentence
1789

They threw me into the cells on the bottom floor of the jail. Five days of solitary confinement. I'd not been given so much as a chance to explain myself, though I knew, even if I had, I'd have found no excuse for what I'd done. What did the Rum Corps care that I'd been mortally offended?

The cell was near lightless. Nothing to sleep on but the cold stone floor. I could only guess at the time of day by the clatter of footsteps up and down the staircase leading to the spinning room. Shivering in a corner, I drifted in and out of sleep, and soon lost any sense of whether the footsteps on the stairs made it morning, night, or somewhere in between. Once a day, a hunk of stale bread and a cannikin of water appeared inside the door, bringing with it a precious and fleeting gasp of light.

My anger at Marsden and Owen shifted into anger at myself. I was troubled by what I'd done. I'd been a criminal for some time, of course, but my crime had been carefully calculated. I had never acted so violently, so rashly in my life. I scared myself. My attack on the soldier had been rum fuelled, yes, but it had been a reaction to the injustices I saw in the world around me. I began to wonder what else I was capable of.

My dreams were vivid, filled with lags and blood and Jonathan. Time began to lose meaning, and I felt as though the whole rest of my life would be consumed by this dark cell.

I lost myself in my thoughts. My world was no longer Parramatta, populated by Owen, by Blackwell, by Hannah, by Lottie. Instead, I was back in a townhouse in Clerkenwell, with roses in the front garden and a fortepiano in the parlour.

I'd known from the first days of our marriage that Jonathan had secrets. There were many nights that he'd return home late, his explanations vague and insubstantial. I assumed he had taken a mistress, and like a dutiful wife, I did not ask questions. On the rare occasions we saw each other, he was affectionate and kind, full of questions about the books I was reading, the pieces of music I was learning, the ladies I had taken tea with.

It had never occurred to me that Jonathan might be bad with money. His jewellery business was flourishing; churning out fine pieces for ladies of our class and beyond. I had everything I needed; staff in the household, fine clothing in my wardrobe. Food and wine on the table and a bookshelf that reached the ceiling.

I had no idea that, with each day of our marriage, my dowry and inheritance were being frittered away in a string of bad business investments, and the occasional sorry night at the gambling halls.

A week after New Year, Jonathan took me to Hanover Square to hear a Handel cantata. A generous thing, I'd thought, for him to indulge my love for music, when I knew such a thing would bore him to tears.

As the carriage rattled its way back to Clerkenwell, he slid across the bench so his shoulder pressed against mine.

"Did you enjoy the evening?" he asked.

I smiled. "Very much. The music was magical."

"I'm glad." He took my hand and pressed it between both of his. "Nell," he said, "there's something I ought to tell you."

I was expecting to hear of the mistress. Couldn't believe he was planning to admit to it with my hand sandwiched between his. But Jonathan spoke in a tentative half voice, outlining the coining enterprise he and his business partner had been operating since the early days of our marriage.

The cellar of the jeweller's filled with silver, with copper, with scales, weights and crucibles. Moulds and tankards and bottle after bottle of aqua-fortis. For each gold necklace that had been finely crafted over the years, there was a pouch of counterfeit shillings and sixpences, put out to pay off gambling debts, or exchanged at the bank for legal white notes.

I forced a laugh. "I see." I waited for him to break into a smile. Waited for the confirmation that this was some wildly unamusing joke.

It didn't come.

"Is this what you do?" I asked. "When you're out late at night?"

Jonathan picked at a non-existent piece of lint on his greatcoat. "Mostly, yes."

I didn't know whether to be horrified, or relieved he had not spent our entire marriage in bed with other women.

I looked out across the coach, with its embroidered benches and gossamer curtains. Looked down at my silk gown, at the gold ring on my finger. How much of this had been paid for with counterfeit coin?

Jonathan's eyes were on me, waiting for my reaction. My insides were churning and my skin was hot. But I knew better than to unleash my anger on my husband. Paid for illegally or not, I knew how easily that coach, that gown, that ring could be taken away from me.

"And was this your idea?" I asked, careful to keep my voice level.

"No." As the glow of a streetlamp shafted through the window, I saw Jonathan had the good grace to look ashamed. "It was Wilder who proposed it in the beginning."

I shifted uncomfortably on the bench seat. Even the mention of Henry Wilder was enough to make my every muscle tense. I had met Jonathan's business partner several times in the past. An enormous man with a bald head and tiny, darting eyes, he would take my hand in his sweaty palms and press a kiss against it that made my stomach turn over. I had no difficulty imagining him in some shady cellar with a pile of counterfeit coins in front of him. Jonathan, however, was a different story.

I looked him up at down, taking in the neat contours of his face that were so familiar to me. In the half-light of the carriage, he felt suddenly like a stranger.

"Wilder asked you to be involved?"

"Yes." Jonathan picked at the stitching on the edge of the bench seat. "As he made clear, we have both the skills and the means to run such an enterprise. It seemed rather a logical progression for our business."

I let out my breath in disbelief. "A logical progression?"

Jonathan squeezed my fingers. "Don't get angry, Nell. It doesn't suit you."

I pulled my hand out from under his. "Why?" I asked.

He turned to look out at the passing street. Streetlights glittered through the glass, painting jewelled patterns on the carriage windows.

There were money issues, my husband told me then. Debts to be settled. Bills to be paid. He gave me a strained smile. "Perhaps you ought to have foreseen such things when you married a mere jeweller."

"Don't be so foolish," I said. "You're as fine a man as any." But I could hear the thinness to my words. For my kind and decent husband had just revealed himself to be entrenched in criminality.

"Wilder knew I owed money," he told me. "Said he could help me make what I needed. And plenty more."

I wished for my old ignorance. Wished to be sitting in Hanover Square with closed eyes, letting the lush arpeggios of the cantata wash over me.

"Why are you telling me this now?" I asked.

Jonathan reached for me again, covering my wrist with his long, thin fingers. "Because we need you to be involved."

An expansion of their business. Thanks to contacts Wilder had curated, he and Jonathan had a seemingly endless array of apprentices, servants and cashiers across London, all responsible for handling their superiors' money. Each would pay a fee for the counterfeit pieces, and exchange them for the genuine coins in their masters' coffers. Send the forgeries out with the business and keep the authentic coins for themselves. There was great wealth to be made, Jonathan assured me. Wealth that would ensure we lived a life of concert halls and diamonds until the day we died.

But with he and Wilder working long hours at the jeweller's, they needed a third person to run the coins to each business and manage the payments.

This, I realised then, was the reason for the evening at Hanover Square. The reason my tone-deaf husband had sat through two hours of wailing sopranos. It was not just to please me. It was to make me agreeable.

"You've plenty of time on your hands, don't you, Nell." It was not a question. "It's not as though you've children to take care of."

His tone of voice said it all. During the five years of our marriage, Jonathan had watched his friends' wives produce child after child, while I had failed to give my husband an heir. Though he had never once said as much, I knew myself a failure as a wife. With each month, each year that passed, I became more and more certain he would find another woman who could give him the son he craved. Each night he returned home to me, I found myself almost surprised. I had no thought of what I would do if Jonathan left me. Running counterfeit coins across the city felt like the least I could do for the man who had saved me from facing the world alone.

And so when he looked me in the eye and said, "You'll do this for me, won't you, my darling?", I found myself agreeing.

For more than a year, I skulked across the city with coins in my reticule, liaising with the apprentices, the servants, the cashiers. Each of the clients had been groomed by Henry Wilder himself; men he knew would keep their mouths shut and their eyes down in exchange for a little wealth.

Though I knew, of course, that I was breaking the law, I pushed the reality of it to the back of my mind. I told myself I was doing no more than helping my husband, as a dutiful wife should. Making up for my failures, proving I was of use.

I'd had no thought the thief-takers were following until I got back to our townhouse. They accosted me at the front door and demanded to know why I was carrying a bag of coins, and the ledger recording the businesses I had received them from.

Jonathan had made sure I had a story prepared – *my husband has requested I assist with the banking* – but I told it in such a pathetic, trembling voice that even the densest of men would have known me lying. And with my husband away at the jeweller's, I could only stand and watch as the thief-takers tore the house apart, finding the counterfeit coins I was yet to bank hidden at the bottom of my husband's desk drawer. I had no thought of which of our clients had turned us in. But I knew it didn't matter.

With striking efficiency, I was escorted to the thief-takers' wagon, while our staff watched wide-eyed and murmured between themselves. My terror eclipsed any hint of shame I felt at the staff seeing me this way.

In front the magistrate, I admitted to it all. I told him how Jonathan had sat beside me in the carriage and outlined his plans. Admitted I had called at each of the businesses on the ledger that day, and had been doing so for the past fourteen months. Somewhere, at the back of my mind, I knew I was likely condemning both Jonathan and myself, but I had been raised believing my job was to appease the men around me, and I told the magistrate exactly what he wanted to hear. I was hoping for leniency, for mercy. Hoping blindly to return to that townhouse in Clerkenwell with little more than a slap on the wrist.

"Are you aware the crime of coining is considered high treason, Mrs Marling?"

I wasn't aware. Jonathan had played down the crime I was committing. I was nothing but a courier, he'd assured me, my hands clean of the silver dust and chemicals that saw the coins churned out into the world. And he had led me to believe we would not be caught. I had accepted it because I needed to.

"Are you aware of the punishment you will likely face for such a crime?"

In a hollow, expressionless voice, he told me how I would be drawn to Old Bailey Road to face the Newgate hangman.

I heard a laugh escape me. That same disbelieving, bordering-on-hysterical laugh I had given when Jonathan had first told me about his coining enterprise. I heard the sound of it hang in the still air of the interrogation room. My body went cold, then hot, and I saw the world swim.

"And my husband?" I managed.

But Jonathan was never to make it to the hangman. The

day of my arrest, he took a bullet to the chest in the front garden of our townhouse. The constable delivered the news to me in such a blank, matter-of-fact tone that his words barely registered. I was far too shocked to feel anything; not grief, or anger, or regret. All I could make sense of was that I would not be returning to Clerkenwell, or Hanover Square. There would be no more townhouse, and no more fortepiano. No more roses in the garden where my husband's body had fallen.

My other realisation was that I knew who had killed him. There was no doubt in my mind that Henry Wilder had come after him to prevent Jonathan from speaking his name. Prevent him from revealing him as the architect of the enterprise.

But I stayed silent. I'd been taught never to speak out. Never to make waves. I told the magistrate I knew nothing of who the shooter might be. And with closed eyes and death hanging over me, I turned my back and let my husband's killer walk free.

Once, back in the blissful days of my ignorance, Jonathan and I had passed a prison hulk rotting on the banks of the Thames. We were returning by boat from two days at the seaside, and the sight of the sorry vessel beached in the mud at the low tide had yanked me back to reality. Men in ragged clothes moved about on deck and I could hear shouts and groans coming from within the lightless shell of the ship.

I found myself watching, unable to tear my eyes from these men who had been reduced to little more than animals. Stripped of dignity, of privacy, of freedom, a future.

"They'd be better off dead," Jonathan said, a hand to my

shoulder ushering me away. I nodded along, forever in agreement.

And perhaps there were convicts on that hulk who wished they had faced the hangman. But when I was sent to New South Wales for the term of my natural life, I found myself sobbing with relief.

I kept to myself as the *Norfolk* slid down the Thames and into the English Channel. At least as best as I could with elbows in my face and women on every side of me. I couldn't fathom that this was my life now. Somehow, engaging with the chatter, the gambling, the out-of-tune singing made my new life far too real.

I'd managed the seasickness well enough in the early days of the voyage, when the *Norfolk* traced the coast of Europe and slid smoothly into the Bay of Gibraltar. But in the open ocean, the ship was seized, and down in those airless, lightless quarters, we lost all sense of up and down.

Water poured in through the hatches and the sea was thunder against the hull. Most of us were too sick to stand, to speak, to do anything except huddle in our own mess, and the pool of seawater gathering at our feet. I shivered and retched, and clung to the edge of a bunk until my fingers were raw. I tried to close my eyes, but that only made things worse. I had no idea of how many days and nights had passed. All I knew was that, there in the bowels of the ship with months at sea ahead of us, I wanted to die.

With my eyes half closed, I was dimly aware of a woman weaving her way through the bunks and groaning bodies. Hannah Clapton. I couldn't fathom how she was on her feet.

And then she was standing over me, offering me a gentle

smile.

She held out a small hunk of bread. "Here, love. You ought to eat something."

I shook my head.

"You'll feel better for it. Trust me."

I took the bread. Forced down a mouthful. It wasn't like I could feel any worse.

"That's it," she said with a small smile. "It'll help. Take a little more."

She watched me like an anxious mother as I took another minuscule bite.

"Why are you not sick?" I asked. My throat was burning, and my mouth felt horribly dry.

Hannah shrugged. "Spent half my childhood on my pa's fishing boat. Seems I still got my sea legs after all these years." She tilted her head to look at me, chuckling to herself. "And I here I were thinking you couldn't speak."

I leaned my head wearily against the edge of the bunk. "What are you talking about?"

"You've not said a word to any of us since we boarded," she said. "Me and some of the others were wondering about whether you was soft in the head."

I would have been insulted had I not been too sick to care. I felt shame wash over me then. Shame that came not from hunching in a corner of a convict ship with half my insides on my skirts. But from looking down upon these women crammed below decks with me.

Hannah was right; I'd hardly spoken a word since London. I'd told myself I was above them; all those dirt-encrusted women I shared a shit bucket with. I had been raised to look down on people of their kind. But with each day, my old life grew more distant, and I began to see things as they really were. What place did I have to look down on these women? What separated us other than the fact that they had stolen to feed their families, while I had carted counterfeit coins around the city? That didn't make me better than them. It made me a fool.

When the door of the cell finally creaked open, I started at the sound. I cowered in the corner, squinting into the shaft of light from the soldier's lamp.

"What day is it?" I asked, my voice husky from disuse. "Am I to be released?"

The soldier chuckled. "Unless you fancy another night in here."

With a hand pressed to the wall for balance, I made my way out of the cell and into the street. I stood outside the jail for a moment, inhaling deep lungfuls of the clean, fragrant air. I stretched my arms above my head, and rolled my shoulders, my whole body aching.

It was night, but after the blackness of the cell, the lamp above the jail door made it feel as bright as morning. I walked across the bridge towards High Street. A peal of laughter rose from a group of men outside the tavern. And in that moment, Henry Wilder and Jonathan were gone. I was relieved to have escaped the dark, and the past it had pulled me into.

I walked slowly back towards the hut. It wouldn't have surprised me if Blackwell wanted me to leave. After all, I'd struck one of his fellow soldiers.

I could see the lamp flickering through the window. It made me realise how much I did not want him to send me away.

I stood outside the door for a moment, debating whether to knock. I decided against it. That little mud hut was the closest thing I had to a home. I wanted it to feel that way.

Blackwell was stooping by the fire, stirring the embers to life. A pot hung on the hook above the grate. He looked at me for a long second, his eyes giving nothing away.

Suddenly, I was acutely aware of the grime on my skin and the blood on my hands. Aware of the stench of the cells that had followed me back to the hut. Without speaking, I went to my little pile of clothing in the corner. Took my clean dress and shift, and hurried outside, making my way to the river. I could hear the water sighing in the dark.

I took off my boots and stepped into the river. The iciness of it stole my breath, making me gasp aloud. But there was something exhilarating about the feel of the water against my skin.

With the river lit only by the moon, I stripped myself naked and stepped deeper into the river. The tide was high, and I could feel the swell trying to tug me towards the sea. I kept my feet firmly planted in the mud as I scrubbed at my skin. Above my head, an owl let out its husky, jagged cry. I lifted my face to the sky, inhaling the clean air. I plunged my head beneath the surface and the sounds of the world around me fell away, leaving only a deep, sighing silence. I felt the water move around my face, the cold making my blood pump hard. I emerged breathless and shivering, but blessedly clean.

I stepped out of the water and pulled on my clean clothes. I squeezed the water from my hair and let it hang wet down my back.

When I returned to the hut, Blackwell had placed a bowl of soup on the table. He nodded towards it. "Sit down. You must be hungry."

I paused. "What about you?"

"I've eaten already. I wasn't sure if you were to be released today. But there's enough left for another bowl."

I perched on the edge of the chair, looking up at him. "Will you sit with me?" I asked. "I'd appreciate the company."

Blackwell sat. Pretended not to watch while I spooned the soup into my mouth. It was thin and flavourless, but its warmth was achingly welcome after five days of bread and water. After only a few mouthfuls, my stomach felt full and slightly unsettled.

"You're lucky you didn't hang," said Blackwell. "It's a serious crime to strike an officer."

I nodded, eyes down. I knew that well, of course. Knew who held the power in this place.

I wanted to speak; to put into words that desperate need to be seen I'd felt the night I'd gone to Marsden's property. To be more than just a discarded convict, sent to New South Wales to be forgotten. And I wanted to speak of the wild anger that had torn through me when the soldier had looked me up and down and called me *whore*.

When I looked up at Blackwell, his eyes were on me, intense and dark in the candlelight. I felt seen. Unforgotten. And in that moment it was enough to be sitting at the table with another human being, feeling warm soup sliding down my throat.

"You're right," Blackwell said after a moment. "About Patrick Owen being untouchable."

I stopped eating suddenly, the spoon halfway to my mouth.

He said no more, as though he knew he had crossed a line. Told me something he shouldn't have. "I think there's a little bread," he said, sliding back on his chair to search the shelf. "Would you like some?"

I pushed past his question. It was too late to pretend he hadn't spoken. "And what's to be done about it?" I asked.

Blackwell sighed. He met my eyes with a dark, pointed look. Yes, I understood. This conversation was never to go further than this table.

"Nothing," he said tautly. "It's the way things have to be. Or else more people will die."

CHAPTER FOURTEEN

"Many of the Irish Convicts are well acquainted with the art of war, and all the secret intrigues that can work on the minds of the ignorant and unwary."

Rev. Samuel Marsden
A Few Observations on the Toleration of the Catholic Religion in New South Wales
1806

And so it was; the way things had to be. Around the other women, I steered my conversations away from the rebels, from Castle Hill, from Blackwell. Away from anything that might disrupt the sense of solidarity I felt at the spinning wheels. I needed my friendship with Lottie. I would not let Owen take that from us. But at Blackwell's supper table, I asked questions.

"Why is he untouchable?"

Sometimes the lieutenant kept his thoughts to himself. Other times, he seemed to want to speak.

"The government fears another uprising is imminent," he told me one night, tossing a log onto the fire. "They fear that if the rebels see their leader strung up it will incite them to violence."

I felt a flicker of self-satisfaction that things were as I had imagined. That I was beginning to develop an understanding of the world around me.

"And what of Maggie?" I asked, at the table with a cannikin of tea in my hand. "Does she not deserve for her killer to be punished?"

I was careful to keep my voice even, controlled. Though he had stood on Owen's jury, Blackwell was being open with me now. Allow myself to let my anger loose and I would destroy this precious chance at knowledge.

"Yes. She does." He jabbed the poker into the fire and made a log break noisily in the grate.

I thought of Jonathan and Henry Wilder. For all his faults, my husband deserved justice just like Maggie did. Deserved for his killer to face to the gallows. And yet I had kept silent out of fear. Let Henry Wilder walk free. I knew my guilt over doing so had fuelled my desire to see Owen punished.

"But it's like I said," Blackwell continued, taking the teacup I had nudged across the table, "if Owen is hanged and the rebels retaliate, far more people will die."

It was the closest I'd come to hearing him acknowledge Owen's guilt. I wasn't sure if it felt like a victory or a defeat.

But I was acutely aware that he was sharing far more with me than he ought to. I knew as a factory lass I had no place knowing these things. But sometimes, with the fire burning and cups in our hands, Blackwell and I felt oddly like equals. Strange that we might seem to be standing on such even ground when we were at different ends of the scale of power. It was not just the information about Owen, but the small pieces of himself he would toss out into conversation.

I always dreamt of seeing this place.
My mother died when I was twelve.
I much prefer coffee to tea.

I feared the moment would come when he would realise he had let me too close. Allowed me to step onto ground on which a factory lass was forbidden to stand.

"And what of you?" I asked. "Owen is untouchable. Are you not afraid he'll come after you again? With a pistol this time?"

Blackwell turned the cup around in his hands. "His immunity goes only so far."

"So his immunity doesn't stretch to killing an officer. But it does stretch to killing a factory lass."

Blackwell took a sip of tea, meeting my eyes. A wordless response. But the words did not need to be said.

"If Owen dares come after me, the other officers will have him on the scaffold," he told me. But I could hear the uncertainty in his voice.

After church that Sunday, I set out for the market. I lifted my face to the sky, letting the spring sun warm my cheeks.

The rain had stopped for the first time in days, a dazzling blue emerging from within the clouds. The surrounding bush smelled clean and damp.

I filled my basket with meat and vegetables from the farmers' stalls set up in the backs of wagons. As I passed the clothes stand, I stopped, my eyes falling on a swathe of violet fabric on the racks of gowns and cloaks.

That colour, I knew it well. I pushed aside the cloaks to reveal my worsted gown. There was the neat pleating at the waist, the single brass button, the delicate scoop of the neckline. Whoever had stolen it from the ship must have sold it for a few pennies.

I ran my finger over the skirts. They were as soft as I remembered, despite their months at sea and subsequent kidnapping by some nameless woman on the ship.

The stall owner caught me looking. "Yours for a crown," she said. I felt for the coins in my pocket. I knew it was foolish to spend what little I had on something I would never even wear. I could hardly strut into the factory in a pleated gown. But I needed it back. It was my last piece of a life I thought had gone forever.

I handed the coins over before I could change my mind.

I was glad to find the hut empty. The fire was still crackling mutedly from the bread I had baked that morning, and the air was thick and humid. With the fire still lit, I knew Blackwell couldn't have gone far.

I pulled off my dress and stepped into the gown, fastening the hooks and closing the single button below my throat. I felt the weight of the skirts around my ankles.

I took Blackwell's small shaving mirror and peered into

it. My hair had come loose from its plait and hung over my shoulders. With my free hand I bundled it into a knot on my neck, searching out the gentleman's wife I had once been.

I could not find her. The eyes that looked back at me were hardened. The eyes of a woman who did not belong in a worsted gown.

I put down the mirror. I didn't want to see my reflection. I didn't want that reminder of who I'd once been, of all I'd squandered with my terrible choices. Nor did I want Blackwell to return and see me in the dress. Perhaps for a fleeting moment, a part of me had wanted him to see that I had once been more than just a factory lass. But that lady in the worsted gown was nothing to be proud of. What pride was there to be felt when I'd let that life unravel so dramatically?

I undid the hooks and let the gown slide from my shoulders. I stood for a moment with it in a pool around my feet, before stepping out of it and tossing it into the fire. It caught with a burst of orange light, and I sat back on my heels to watch. I felt the blaze warm my cheeks.

The door creaked open and I leapt to my feet, suddenly aware I was standing there in searing daylight in nothing but my underskirts.

My eyes caught Blackwell's for a second and I grabbed my striped dress, holding it to my body. He disappeared again before I could speak.

I dressed hurriedly and stepped out into the street, feeling the need to apologise. It had been wrong for me to strut around the hut indecently in the middle of the afternoon. I couldn't bear for Blackwell to think I had been parading myself for his benefit.

I called after him, but he didn't respond; just kept striding out towards the edge of the settlement.

I followed. I wanted to explain myself. But I also wanted to know where he was going.

We climbed into the hills, along a narrow track beaten into the scrub. I stayed some distance behind, not wanting him to know I was following, but close enough to keep track of him as he wove through the trees.

We walked for over an hour, perhaps closer to two. Sun streaked through the trees, insects dancing in the needles of light.

I could see a clearing up ahead. I hung back, hiding myself among the trees.

I peered out between the gnarled white trunks. Rows of graves, each marked with a crude cross, like Maggie Abbott's.

Blackwell walked slowly among them, eyes fixed to the crosses. I stood motionless, barely daring to breathe.

My heart lurched. Why had he come here? Who lay beneath his earth?

I darted into the undergrowth so he wouldn't see me. Held my breath as he walked past, back onto the narrow path.

Once his footsteps had disappeared, I stepped out into the makeshift cemetery. A heaviness hung over the place. A coldness, despite the warmth of the air. There were shallow engravings on the wooden crosses and I bent closer to read them. No names appeared in the inscriptions, but there were snatches of Gaelic, carved in a rough hand. And then English words that made my breath catch.

Castle Hill 1804

Had the battle taken place among these trees? I had learned from some of the men at the river that the site of the main conflict lay further to the north, where the Rum Corps had surrounded the rebels and brought them to their knees. But I also knew there had been men killed in the uprising from Toongabbie to Sydney Town; days of underhand warfare following the main attempted rebellion. I imagined the redcoats storming through these trees, imagined rifle fire shattering the stillness.

How many of these men had been sent to their graves by Blackwell's bullet? Was it guilt that had brought him here?

Surely it was no easy thing to be a soldier; to shoot to kill on another's bidding. Could a man still be haunted if he were acting in the name of duty?

I stood suddenly, unable to bear the oppressive atmosphere of the cemetery. I turned back the way I'd come, seeking out the narrow path that snaked back towards civilisation.

When I returned to Parramatta, I detoured to the river so Blackwell wouldn't ask about my absence.

"Oh," I said, in the world's worst attempt at feigning ignorance, "you're back. Collecting the chocolate flowers?" I set the bucket of water on the ground beside the hearth.

He returned my smile, but it didn't reach his eyes. "Something like that."

I had hoped, of course, I might nudge him into speaking of the burial ground. But I could tell today he was to be tight-lipped.

"I'm sorry about earlier," I said. "I didn't mean for you to see me that way. I dirtied my dress and I…"

Blackwell shook his head dismissively. "It's no matter." He slid the Bible from the shelf and sat at the table, opening the book in front of him. His message was clear: conversation over.

The weight pressing down on him was almost a physical thing. A part of me longed to ask him outright about the cemetery. I couldn't bear the thought of him locking all that regret away to be passed over.

"I saw you come from the north," I said clumsily. "What's out there?"

Blackwell eyed me. I could tell, even without him saying a word, that he knew I had followed him.

Beneath the table, I saw something slide through the shadows. I shrieked, and bounded onto the empty chair. "Snake!" I yelled, pointing wildly.

Blackwell stood, his chair toppling. He reached down to pick it up.

"Be careful!" I cried. "Did you not hear me? A *snake*!"

His lips curled into a smile. "I heard you, yes."

My eyes widened as he bent to straighten the chair. I watched the creature slither out from beneath the table. I couldn't pull my eyes from it. There was something horribly entrancing about the way it glided across the floor. I glared at Blackwell. "Do something!"

"Stop yelling, Eleanor," he said, with a calmness I found unfathomable. He took his rifle from where it rested beside the shelf.

"You're going to shoot it?" I demanded.

He laughed. Brought the butt of the rifle down on the snake, mashing its head into the floor. He picked up its limp body and carried it outside. I found myself peering frantically around the hut, searching for other intruders.

I was still teetering on the chair when Blackwell returned.

"You can come down now," he said, offering me his hand. I climbed down carefully, before beginning a thorough search of my sleeping pallet. I heard him chuckle.

"It's not funny," I said. "What if it had gotten into the blankets?"

"I didn't imagine you to be afraid of snakes," he said, sitting at the table and opening the Bible again.

"What kind of madman would not be afraid of snakes? Did not you see the way it moves? It's completely unnatural."

Blackwell laughed again, eyes on the book as he turned the page. I straightened my blanket and tried to catch my breath. My heart was still beating fast. But I was glad I had made him smile.

In the morning, I awoke to find the brass button from my worsted gown on the floor beside my head. Had Blackwell found it in the fireplace? I stared at it for a long time; that fire-tarnished piece of my old life I couldn't burn away. His message was clear; I had my past and he had his. They weren't for each other to know.

I took the button from beside my bed. Stepped out of the hut in the early morning and buried it beside the river.

CHAPTER FIFTEEN

On Christmas Day there was no spinning.

After Marsden's service, we were given the day to ourselves. While the scent of roasting lamb floated from settlers' houses, we gathered at the river with slabs of mutton and pork, and enough rum to drown a whale.

The men set a bonfire roaring on the riverbank and soon had the meat roasting over the embers.

The sun blazed through the trees, painting long shadows across the earth. Insects swarmed the surface of the water as we languished in the sultry heat that lay over the land.

Two of the factory lasses hacked up the meat and shared it among us; on plates, in wooden bowls, or into bare hands. The men stretched out shirtless on the edge of the water, women with their feet dipped into the swell. The convicts and emancipists took turns telling stories as they passed the liquor bottles between them.

"Helped myself to a side of pork like this from my master's kitchen," said one of the lags who worked Marsden's land. "Woulda got away with it too if it weren't for the dog. Bloody thing were only six inches high, but it had a bark like pistol fire. Held me up by the back gate."

An enormous roar of laughter.

"You've got a tale or two for us, don't you, Nell?" asked Lottie, nudging my shoulder with hers. "You can tell us a little about how the toffs live." There was a playful smile on her face.

I whacked at the giant ant crawling up my ankle. "Nothing as interesting as being held up by a dog."

Lottie passed me the rum bottle. She'd seemed to have made peace with who I was – or rather, who I had been. I was glad of it.

I ate until my stomach was straining against my bodice; a long-ago, forgotten sensation. I sat with my back up against the great white trunk of a gum tree, a pleasant liquor haze pressing down on me. I could feel the embers of the bonfire warming my cheek.

"Well," said Hannah, wiping greasy hands on her skirt, "this is a damn sight better than last year, ain't it."

I smiled. Our last Christmas had been spent in the depths of the *Norfolk*. We'd not even been sure of the date until we'd been pulled out onto deck for the church service.

As the afternoon stretched into evening, the gathering grew. Settlers emerged from their meat-scented houses and men I recognised as soldiers sat among us in shirtsleeves. Dark clouds rolled across a blazing sky, the air thick and humid, and scented with rain.

Someone arrived with a fiddle, and Owen, who'd been drinking since before noon, struck up a jagged beat on an empty crate. The music drowned out the birdsong and the constant burble of the river. Songs in Gaelic burst up around us, and everyone was dancing. I felt a smile on my lips. It had been far too long since I'd heard music. Lottie grabbed my hand and yanked me to my feet.

"I don't know the steps," I said on a laugh.

"It's easy," said Lottie, whirling around and pulling us into a circle of other dancers. "Like this. The Fairy Reel... Watch, Nell... *Watch!*... No, like this, other way!"

I gave up, whirling around in the circle and making up my own steps. I shrieked with laughter as we galloped around the uneven riverbank. I danced until I was breathless and a line of sweat ran down my back. Some blessed soul hurled Owen's drum crate onto the bonfire.

As the sun slipped away, the fire drew everyone towards it, making cheeks sweat and hair curl. It was no weather for a fire, of course, but this was all we knew. Fire was the centre of the Christmas celebration, no matter if snow was falling or the land was cracked and dry.

I thought of childhood Christmases spent behind ice-speckled windows, candles lighting our dinner table. Father and I working our way through roast meat and pudding, or gingerbread by the fire. For a moment, I missed him deeply.

I looked out towards the water. Patrick Owen had an arm slung around Lottie's shoulder, as they sat close together on the ground beside the river. I watched her laugh at something I was sure wasn't funny. I tried to catch her eye across the flames. I hated seeing them together. Lottie turned her back, avoiding my eyes.

I slipped away from the gathering. Stumbled down the road towards Blackwell's hut. The shrieking cicadas began to take over, pushing the raucous sounds of the party to the background.

I peeked through the gap in the door. I could see the lieutenant at the table, a quill in hand.

Writing to his wife, perhaps? Good wishes for Christmas, dear Sophia, that she would receive some time next September. There was something about him sitting there alone on Christmas night, hunched over his ink pot while the rest of us drank and danced. Something that made my chest ache.

I pushed open the door, making it squeal noisily against the floor. He looked up from his letter in surprise.

I sidled up to the table with what, in my drunken state, I assumed was an alluring strut. I peered down at the letter, not even pretending to be discreet.

'Dear Father,' it read.

"What are you doing?" I asked stupidly.

"Writing to my father." His sleeves were rolled up against the heat, his shirt open at the neck. I could see the sparse curls of hair at the top of his chest.

I leant over his shoulder to look at the letter.

'Governor Bligh has earned himself no favour with his order to destroy the liquor stills. The colony is still so short of currency – can he truly be against trading liquor for a sack of grain? It galls me that a naval officer might stride into this place and interfere with military order.'

I said, "There's a party going on."

"Yes," said Blackwell, his quill hovering above the page, "I can smell it on you." Ink dripped from the edge of the nib and splattered onto his letter. Insects flickered around the lamp.

"You ought to come," I told him. "It ain't right to be alone at Christmas." Sometimes the drink made me enunciate like a queen. Other times, I spoke as though I'd been hauled out of Whitechapel with a bottle of gin in my hand. "The other soldiers are there," I said. "Ensign Cooper and that one with the nose hair."

A smile played on the edge of Blackwell's lips. He tilted his head, considering me. He leant back in his chair, his arm brushing against my hip. "Go back to the party, Eleanor," he said after a moment. He dipped his quill back in the ink and continued writing, without looking at me again.

Dejectedly, I strode back towards the river.

"Where d'you go?" Lottie drawled when I returned. I was glad she had dislodged herself from Owen's claws.

"Just a walk is all." I slid my hand around her arm. "Let's have another drink."

"Fine idea," she said, looking around for someone with a bottle for us to steal.

I needed it. Needed to forget my childhood Christmases and the sight of Owen with his arm around Lottie. Needed to drown the emptiness that had come when Blackwell had sent me away.

Dan Brady was strumming a fiddle like a lute. He spoke to Lottie in Irish, though his eyes were fixed on me. Lottie looped her arm through mine. "You leave her alone now, Dan," she said in overenunciated English. "She's all right. Aren't you, Nell?"

Brady's eyes cut into me.

"Watch yourself, Johnny," Hannah hollered to some farmhand who was wading shirtless into the river. "Them eels will get you and pull you all the way to China."

I looked past her at the towering figure of Blackwell striding towards the river. I felt a smile on my lips. He went to the cluster of soldiers on one side of the fire. If he was going to stay with his own kind all night, so be it. I was just glad he was out of the hut. Glad he'd finished that dizzyingly dull letter.

Lottie followed my gaze. She looked back at me with fire in her eyes. I ignored her. What place did she have being angry at my seeking out Blackwell when she was swanning around the place on Patrick Owen's arm?

I sauntered over to the soldiers with a bottle in my hand. I recognised one of the men who had sent Owen on his way the day he had attacked Blackwell. Even out of their uniforms, the Rum Corps exuded authority. One of the officers, an older man with a thick grey moustache, looked me up and down. Disapproval on his face, but something else beneath. I had already watched several of the enlisted men disappear into the bushes with factory lags attached to them.

Blackwell was on his feet before the man with the moustache could get his pipe out of his mouth.

"I learned the Fairy Reel," I announced. "I'm going to teach you."

A faint smile passed over his face. "No you're not."

I held out the rum bottle. "This will change your mind."

Blackwell laughed. His face lightened, giving him a sudden and unexpected beauty. If he was irritated at my storming his side of the party he didn't show it. He took a gulp of rum, his nose crinkling in distaste.

"That's awful," he said.

"Bought it for a sack of grain," I told him. "Though Governor Bligh didn't like it."

He gave a short chuckle. "I see you managed an eyeful of my letter."

"Well," I said, "we must make a stand against those who dare interfere with military order."

He failed to hold back a smile.

I took the bottle, my fingers grazing his. "The Fairy Reel?" I asked. I was acting inappropriately; a part of me was well aware. I was also well aware that I'd never been so drunk in my entire life. It was a blissful, liberating feeling.

"No," he laughed. "Still no Fairy Reel." He nodded to where Hannah and Lottie were chatting by the edge of the water, heads bent towards each other, their brows creased in deep concentration. "Looks as though they're solving all the colony's ills. Perhaps you ought to join them."

I nodded, knowing even in my drunken state it was his polite way of telling me to disappear.

Blackwell returned to the marines, and I went and sat with Lottie and Hannah. As I'd guessed, the only thing they were solving was who'd drunk more of the liquor. The party was going to pot quickly. Bodies were dozing around the fire, upturned bottles scattered across the riverbank. Hannah disappeared into the trees with some mud-coated scrub, and Lottie made her way to the remnants of the bonfire, hands all over Patrick Owen. Sounds of pleasure drifted out from between the trees.

The first time I had heard such a thing on the *Norfolk*, I had been horrified. I'd been taught that my wifely duties were never to be spoken of, an act that took place behind locked doors. I had always been silent in the bedroom out of fear the staff might hear. I couldn't bear the thought of anyone knowing what we were doing.

But I had come to understand it was different here. For the women, such a thing was not a duty, but an act of survival.

And it didn't matter who witnessed it.

Sitting alone on the log, I felt a tug of loneliness. And in spite of everything I knew was decent and right, I found myself wishing I were one of those women sitting beside the river with a man's arms around her. I longed to forget myself, to forget where we were, and what my life entailed now. Until the morning at least.

A distant roll of thunder and the air seemed to grow thicker.

I felt the log shift beside me as someone took the place left empty by Hannah. The man's words were garbled. But his hand on my knee left no doubt as to his intentions.

I let that hand move up my thigh. Let him bend over and kiss my neck. Let myself sink into the warmth of another's touch. I could let it go no further, of course, but in that fleeting moment, I relished the company.

"Fetch me a drink," I said.

And he got to his feet unsteadily, giving me a smile. I felt a tangled mix of disgust and desire. And a tug of guilt at having let him think I was offering more than I was. I watched him saunter over to the bottles that sat ridiculously close to the bonfire.

"Don't." A voice close to my ear. "He's not a good man."

I opened my mouth to speak, my words dying in my throat when I turned my head and saw Blackwell's eyes inches from mine.

I watched him for a moment, trying to make sense of what I was feeling. Anger at his intrusion? Or flattery? The liquor was tangling my thoughts.

"Why do you care who I spend my time with?" I asked.

"I just don't want to see you get yourself in trouble."

"Why are you looking out for me?"

He frowned slightly. "Why do you need to ask that?"

Because I was lulling myself into the belief I might be worth caring for. That the safety of a convict woman might matter to a lieutenant in the Rum Corps. And I knew they were dangerous beliefs.

Lottie turned back from the bonfire and her eyes met Blackwell's. Then she glared at me. I looked away.

Thunder rumbled again, closer this time. Raindrops the size of marbles began to pelt the dry earth, sending wisps of steam spiralling up from the fire. With the arrival of the rain, the oppressive heat vanished, and I drew down a long breath, lifting my face to the sky.

My suitor returned with a fresh bottle, confusion wrinkling his face when he saw me with Blackwell. I could tell he was trying to remember which woman he'd been after.

Blackwell stood suddenly, as though he had only just become aware of how close he was to me. "I'm going back to the hut," he said.

He began to walk. For a moment, I sat motionless, unsure if his words had been an invitation to join him. He glanced back over his shoulder and I got to my feet. Hurried after him.

He opened the door and lit the lamp. His letter and inkpot were still spread out across the table.

I sank to the ground, not quite making it to my sleeping pallet. The earthen floor felt soft beneath me. My skirts and boots were splattered with mud.

Blackwell sat beside me on the floor, his long legs stretched out in front of him and his knee knocking against mine.

"Your letter," I said. "It's very boring."

He chuckled. "Yes, I know. My father is not the most vibrant of men. I'm playing to my audience." I could smell the liquor on his breath.

I made some sort of response, halfway between an acknowledgement and a groan. I rolled onto my side, my back to him. I closed my eyes against the violent tilting of the world.

"You shouldn't spend your time with men like that," he said after a long silence.

I didn't answer at once. His comment felt intrusive. Who was he to demand such things? Who was he to care?

I opened my eyes a crack, watching the flame dance inside the lamp. "Sometimes this place just feels overwhelmingly lonely," I said finally.

"Yes," said Blackwell. "It does." And I felt his body curl around mine, his big hand gripping my wrist as water drizzled in from the roof and put the candle out.

CHAPTER SIXTEEN

"The poor girl who yields to a misplaced passion, no matter how her ruin has been effected ... is immediately fallen. She has passed the threshold over which there is no return."

Thomas Beggs
An Inquiry into the Extent and Causes of Juvenile Depravity
1849

On the twelfth night, the officers gathered at Government House for a celebratory dinner. I watched Blackwell peer into the shaving mirror and glide his razor along his cheeks.

He had been distant since Christmas night. I could tell he regretted the way he had acted. But which part of it, I wondered? His drunkenness? Or the fact he had let himself get close to me?

The morning after Christmas, I'd woken alone on the

floor beside the hearth. Blackwell had been back on his sleeping pallet on the other side of the hut. No doubt when the liquor had faded he had seen the gross impropriety of curling up beside me in the night. I had seen it too, of course. But it had not felt like impropriety at the time. It had felt far too natural. Far too easy. A thing both of us had needed.

After he left for Government House, I sat at the table staring into the spluttering candle. I was exhausted, having sat hunched over the carding machine all day, but I felt too alert to sleep.

I took Blackwell's shirt from the back of the chair, where I had hung it for mending. I had little doubt he was hacking at his hems on purpose. A reason to put coins in my hands and keep me from selling my body.

Threading a needle by candlelight, I stitched the torn hem carefully, the rough linen warm in my hands. The Parramatta cloth was thick and coarse. I wondered how many of Blackwell's shirts had been woven by my own hands. His musky scent infused the linen. Made me feel close to him. Closer than I, as a mere convict woman, ought to be.

These thoughts felt sinful in so many ways. There was Sophia, of course, and the ghost of Jonathan, not long enough in his grave for me to be thinking of another man.

It was improper, my governess had taught me, for a lady to feel desire. Only a loose woman, a harlot, a *concubine*, would let her heart quicken in the presence of a man.

There was regret in me that I had let Blackwell see my desire. I knew as a military man, he was expected to look down on a factory lass like me. To see me as the loose woman the female register painted me as. But I knew my attraction was not one-sided. On Christmas night, while rain pelted the roof, I had felt his body slide closer to mine. Felt the warmth of his hand against my bare forearm. That night, as I had laid my cards on the table, Blackwell had also laid his.

I finished the sewing, folding the mended shirt and placing it on the end of his sleeping pallet. I undressed and blew out the lamp, curling up on my blanket beside the unlit hearth. The air was thick and humid, frogs clicking loudly in the river.

Voices came towards the hut, along with a spear of light. I sighed inwardly, wondering what gift Owen and the other rebels had for the lieutenant this evening. I glanced across the hut to where the rifle was leaning against the wall. If I burst out the door and threatened the rebels with it, would they be afraid? I smiled wryly to myself. Do such a thing and I'd find myself celebrating the twelfth night back in solitary confinement.

I grabbed my shawl and threw it over my shoulders, yanking open the door to confront them. "Get the hell out of here," I hissed. Owen and Brady charged towards me. I stumbled back into the hut. Felt hands around the tops of my arms. I thrashed against them. "Get your damn hands off me!"

"You're coming with us," said Owen. "It's important."

My heart thundered, Maggie Abbott's blank stare flashing through my mind. I tried to scream, but Owen clamped a hand over my mouth before the sound could form.

"Keep your bloody mouth shut. We can't have that lobster of yours coming running."

They yanked me back towards the door. "My dress," I spluttered. "And my boots." If I was going to be found in the undergrowth like Maggie, I at least wanted to have a little decency about me.

After a moment, Owen nodded reluctantly. He and Brady released their grip. I yanked my dress on over my head. As I bent to lace my boots, I felt a pang of regret. If I were found with my dress and boots on, it would look as though I had left the hut on my own accord.

But it was too late. Owen's hand was back around the top of my arm and I was being marched out towards the river.

"What's this about?" I demanded. Fear lurched inside me. Was I to be the next body found in the scrub? Did the croppies still believe me responsible for turning Owen over to the authorities? Or had they some twisted idea that they could punish Blackwell by harming me?

When we reached the river, I found Lottie pacing back and forth across the bank, arms wrapped around herself. Wind was rippling the surface of the water.

"Lottie?" I demanded, shaking myself free of Owen and Brady's grip. "You knew about this?"

"I'm sorry, Nell," she said. "I told them to bring you here. There are things you ought to know. Things between you and Blackwell have gone too far."

"What do you mean 'things between me and Blackwell'?"

Lottie sighed. "Come on, Nell. I'm no fool. We all saw the two of you together on Christmas night. Breathing on each other's necks. You mean to tell me there's nothing between you?"

"I clean the lieutenant's house," I snapped. "Nothing more."

Lottie took my arm and led me towards the log. She sat, tugging me down beside her.

"Are you truly warning me away from Blackwell?" I

hissed. "When you're spending your time around Patrick Owen? He terrified me, charging into the hut like that! I thought I was going to end up like Maggie!" I knew Owen could hear me. I didn't care.

"I'm sorry," said Lottie. "I didn't mean for you to be afraid."

"And what exactly did you imagine I might feel?" I glared at her, then looked up at Owen and Brady. "What's this all about?"

Lottie looked up at the two men.

"You ever heard of Castle Hill?" asked Brady.

I felt the muscles in my neck tense. "Yes," I said tersely. "I know of the uprising." I couldn't help feeling a tiny flicker of self-satisfaction. The men had clearly been hoping to catch me unaware. I got to my feet, needing to face them. I was eye-to-eye with Owen, but Brady still towered over me.

"He told you then?" said Owen. "The things he did?"

My silence brought a smirk to his face.

"Thought not." He took a step closer, his breath hot and stale against my nose. I wrapped my arms around myself tightly.

"That lieutenant of yours is a murderer."

I kept my gaze steady. "He's a solider," I said. "Of course he's killed."

A cold laugh from Brady. Lottie looked up from the log, her eyes darting between me and the men. Above our heads, the trees rustled in the hot wind.

"We just wanted freedom," said Owen. "A ship to take us home. There weren't no one needed to die. But the lobsters marched up from Parramatta and surrounded us at Rouse Hill. Told us they were willing to parley. But when our leader come down the hill to speak with them, Major Johnson put a damn pistol to his head. Ordered his men to open fire."

"What were you expecting?" I hissed. "That the army would just stand by and allow prisoners to sail out of this place?"

I turned to leave, but Owen grabbed my arm, yanking me back.

"The lobsters were sent out into the bush," he told me, his nose close to mine. "To hunt down those of us who got away. Hunt us down like animals. All throughout the settlement. Just like they did in Ireland."

I stiffened, unable to look at him.

"Lieutenant Blackwell, he went downriver. Three of my cousins lived out near Squires' inn, all of them sent out together after the rebellion in Ireland. Two of them weren't even at Castle Hill. But Blackwell, he just saw croppies and pulled the trigger. Charged into their hut and shot the three of them without asking no questions."

His words hung in the stillness for a second. I held his gaze.

"I don't believe you," I said. "I know him. He wouldn't do such a thing."

"He's telling the truth," Lottie hissed, getting to her feet.

"Is he? And how do you know that? Were you there?" I turned back to Owen and Brady. "Were any of you there?"

"I was there," Owen spat. "I went out after the fight to check on my cousins. Bullets in their chests. Point-blank range." He leaned close to me. "My cousin's wife was hiding in the woods. She saw it all. I went out into the bush after I found the bodies. Saw Blackwell riding off. Too far away for me to shoot."

I started charging away. Lottie called my name. Her footsteps crunched behind me and she snatched my arm. I yanked away.

"Let go of me."

"Listen to them, Nell." Her voice was pleading.

"Listen to them?" I repeated. "Listen to these lies they're spouting? Do you actually believe this?"

"Yes," she said. "I do."

I shook my head in frustration. "You've been blinded by Owen. All of you, you think he's your way to freedom, but you're wrong. Following a man like him is going to destroy you."

"You've no idea what you're on about," Lottie hissed. "You're the one who's been blinded. You're so desperate to believe you got someone who cares about you that you're refusing to accept the things he's done."

I kept striding back to the hut.

"Nell," called Lottie. "I told Owen to come for you because you need to know this. I'm scared for you. Blackwell; he's dangerous."

I whirled around to face her. "All the while you're spending your time with the man who killed Maggie?"

Lottie didn't answer.

"Stay away from me," I hissed. "And tell those bastards to stay away from Blackwell."

I paced back and forth across the empty hut, anger bubbling inside me. With too much energy and no thought of what to do with it, I went back to the river to fill a bucket for cleaning. Water sloshing over the sides, I took it back to the hut and unloaded everything from the shelves, dumping it onto the table. There was the locket containing Sophia's portrait, tucked in between the books. I wondered when Blackwell had taken it from the chest.

I scrubbed violently at the dusty shelves, rage at Owen shooting through me. There was rage at Lottie too. For the first time since I'd sat beside her at the spinning wheels, we were not sisters. We were Irish rebel and *sasanaigh*. The reality of it stung.

I was still scrubbing when Blackwell shoved open the door. His hair was windblown and I could smell tobacco on him. He eyed me, and then the contents of the shelves I had upended across the table. Books and candles and soap and razors were piled high.

"You're still awake," he said sharply. "Why are you still awake?"

I raised my eyebrows, hand planted on my hip. "I'm cleaning the shelves."

"I didn't ask you to do that." He slid off his jacket and hung it on the nail beside the door. "I hoped you'd be asleep."

I tossed the cloth back in the bucket of muddy water. I didn't deserve this sharpness. I had not dragged him to the Christmas party. I had not poured the liquor down his throat, or forced him to fall asleep on the floor with his body pressed to mine.

"I'm here as your housekeeper," I snapped. "And you are to reprimand me for cleaning your house?" My words came out drenched with my best high society inflections. Blackwell looked taken aback.

For a moment I thought to tell him of the way I had been dragged from the hut by Owen and the other men. Something to shift his anger from me to the rebels. But no. I did not want him to know what tales were being told of him.

He took the rum bottle from the table and poured himself a cup. Sank heavily into a chair and brought his drink to his lips.

I hovered beside the bucket of water, twisting the cloth between my hands.

Blackwell filled a second cannikin and set it on the edge of the table. The chair creaked noisily as I sat beside him. In the centre of the table, the candle hissed and spluttered. I wrapped my hand around the cup, but didn't drink.

He lifted Sophia's portrait from the top of the pile. With one hand, he clicked it open, then closed it again quickly.

"Do you miss her?" I asked.

"Sometimes."

I ran my finger around the rim of the cup. "Just sometimes?"

He didn't speak at once. "It's as though she belongs to another life," he said finally. "Another world."

His eyes were down as he spoke. Was he ashamed of the distance he felt from his wife? Or was he feeling the inappropriateness of sharing all this with a mere convict woman? He sat the portrait back on the table and took a mouthful of rum.

"Forgive my coldness," he said after a moment. "It was not about you."

I nodded, though I did not believe him. I knew this had plenty to do with me.

"How were the celebrations?" I asked.

He scooped back the dark liquid of his hair, his shoulders relaxing visibly. "Captain Daley's wife singed her eyelashes playing Snapdragon."

I smiled. "I almost did the same as a child once. My father was horrified. He told me it was most inappropriate for a young lady to set herself on fire."

And so there it was; my admission that I was not a pitiable story of stolen eggs and squalid slums. I was a long-ago lady who'd fallen from a world of twelfth night balls. It felt right to tell him, after his brief moment of openness.

He peered at me, turning his cannikin around in his hands. I could tell there was much he wanted to ask. Could tell he desperately wanted to break that unwritten rule and ask me what had led me to my prison ship. Instead, he said:

"And how did you spend your Christmas once the Snapdragon was forbidden?"

I smiled. "Father had me play carols on the fortepiano."

It seemed impossible that such things had happened on the same earth as this. Blackwell was right; it was as though our old lives belonged to another world.

"You play the piano?" he asked.

I nodded faintly. "At least, I used to." I was quite certain I would never do such a thing again.

"Captain Macarthur's wife owns a fortepiano," he said. "Downriver."

"Really?" I heard the light in my voice. While I knew, of course, that a lag like me would never get her hands to it, it filled me with inexplicable joy that the instrument had made it to this outpost of the world. It made me feel less like I were living on the wildest edge of the planet.

"I had a lesson or two when I was a boy," said Blackwell. "My mother used to play. But I rather think I gave my tutor nightmares."

A laugh escaped me. It hung in the stillness of the hut.

Brought a crooked smile to Blackwell's face. I found it oddly easy to imagine him as a boy, bashing at the keys of his mother's piano.

A smile moved across his face. A smile of reminiscence? Or was he simply enjoying the present moment? I wished I could see inside his head, if just for a second.

He emptied his glass, chuckling to himself. "I must say, Eleanor, of all the strange things I've seen in this place, you are by far the most surprising."

I raised my eyebrows. "I'm not sure how I ought to take that."

"You ought to take it as it was intended. As a compliment. A sign I value your company."

Stillness hung between us, half pleasant, half terrifying. I wanted to scream to break the silence, wanted to hold it forever. Wanted to step towards him, wanted to run away.

Lottie had warned me away from him. But my trust in Lottie had splintered. She had been standing there at Patrick Owen's side, spouting tales so vicious they could only be lies.

I was no fool. Blackwell was a soldier. I knew there was blood on his hands. And I knew much of that blood had likely come from the rebel uprising at Castle Hill. But how could I believe the word of Patrick Owen, who had wrung Maggie's throat and left her lifeless in the undergrowth? How could I let Owen stain my image of this man who had been so good to me? Perhaps Lottie was right; I had been blinded. But I didn't want my sight returned.

I pushed Patrick Owen from my mind. I didn't want him in the hut with us.

Blackwell reached for my hand and held it in both of his. He turned it over in the lamplight as though it were the most fragile of specimens. The contact made my heart thunder. He looked at my hand closely, the faintest of frowns on his forehead, as though he had never seen a woman's fingers up so close before.

Had he ever seen his wife's body, I found myself wondering? Had he ever cast his eyes over the female form in its entirety? In my head, Sophia Blackwell was the kind of meek and submissive lover who hid beneath the covers and slid her shift to her hips. Sophia Blackwell, if she were here, would be labelled *wife*.

I wanted to challenge him. Wanted to break through that cursed shield he hid behind. I wanted to see how far I could push him, how much power I had. Here, in this lamplight, with lust in a man's eyes, was the only place a woman had the upper hand. Playing on his desires was the only way to make a man weak. I had to take control any way I could.

I rose to my feet, bringing Blackwell with me. Slowly, I unbuttoned my dress and stepped out of it, letting it fall to the floor with a sigh. I stood before him in my underskirts, my shoulders ghostly white in the candlelight. I could feel his eyes moving over every inch of me.

He took a step closer. Pressed his palm to the top of my arm. I heard myself inhale, sharp and loud. His hand felt rough against my skin. The hut rustled and creaked around us.

I tilted my head, offering him the bare white slope of my neck. Up his fingers went, over the protrusion of my collarbone, over my throat, pushing aside the flaming snarls of hair, tracing the constellation of freckles on my cheeks. His other hand went to my hip, feeling the shape of me.

Fingers slid along my collarbone, pausing at the top of

my stays. I heard his breath. Fast. Shallow. Or perhaps it was my own.

At the feel of him against me, it went past my need for power. Now it was about my need for him. I was burning beneath his touch.

His hand was motionless, his thumb resting on the laces of my stays, and two fingers held against the place my heart was beating. He breathed heavily, caught in hesitation.

"No one would ever know," I said, trying to wrestle this back to a thing of power. But my skin was hot and my heart was beating between my legs. Blackwell had the control now, and I cursed myself for it.

But even as I spoke, I knew it was not a matter of who in the colony would see. God would know; would see him break his marriage vows; would see him lie with a woman who was not his wife. He would become an adulterer. And I would become a concubine.

I stepped away, leaving Blackwell's hand hovering in the dark space between us. I felt cold and hollow. But I could not be what Reverend Marsden had accused us of being. I picked up my dress and held it tight against me. I felt ashamed of my boldness, of all I had tried to do.

"I'm sorry," he said, his voice little more than a whisper. I wondered why he was the one apologising.

Blackwell moved quietly across the hut. He blew out the candle, leaving me standing alone in the blackness.

PART TWO

CHAPTER SEVENTEEN

"Nell Marling," the superintendent barked. I looked up from the spinning wheel. "You're to go with Corporal Anderson." He nodded towards the sunburned young soldier dithering at the top of the stairs. "You're being assigned. Housekeeper to Mr Robert Leaver. You'll be escorted to his property shortly. He has a room ready for you."

I swallowed. "A room?"

The superintendent chuckled. "I trust that's to your liking."

I traipsed down the stairs behind the soldier, feeling stupidly unsteady.

Had Blackwell had a hand in this? I couldn't tell.

I looked back over my shoulder as I climbed down the staircase from the factory. A place that, for all its horrors, had become strangely comfortable in its familiarity. The life I had scratched together here – days at the spinning wheels, nights on Blackwell's floor – was something I knew I could cope with. But here I was facing the unknown again.

It was almost a relief to be leaving the stool beside Lottie. In the three days since Owen had manhandled me to the river, we had barely exchanged a word. Each night as I'd left the factory and walked back towards Blackwell's hut, I could feel her eyes on me. Once, I'd thought to call out to her, make some attempt at resurrecting our friendship. But it felt like the time for that had passed. It had disappeared the night Owen had dragged me from the hut and told me lies about Castle Hill.

Or perhaps it had disappeared on Christmas night when I had shown the colony the way my heart sped for Adam Blackwell.

My new overseer, Robert Leaver, was waiting outside the factory. The soldier escorting me squinted as he read from the crumpled paper in his hand.

"Eleanor Marling, sir. Twenty-eight, childless, healthy."

Leaver was a short man with a wide, sun-streaked forehead and pale tufts of hair that reminded me of tussock grass. Forty perhaps. Maybe younger. I knew this place had a way of ageing you. He looked me up and down.

"She'll do."

Leaver was building himself a farmhouse on the eastern end of the settlement, downriver from the military barracks. As he led me wordlessly down the front path, I saw a number of what I assumed were government men, constructing the walls of the house from large sandstone bricks. Beyond the skeletal outlines of the new rooms, two wide paddocks had been hacked out of the forest. Sheep and cows dotted the patchy brown grass.

Leaver deposited me in the main house with little more

than a nod, abandoning me to his tiny, blonde-haired wife. Mrs Leaver was much younger than her husband, with a soft, doll-like face and dimpled cheeks. I guessed her little more than twenty. She glided around the house with a curly-haired child pinned to her hip.

"It's good to have you, Eleanor," she said in a girlish voice. "We've just had our last government woman finish her sentence." She set off down the hallway, gesturing for me to follow. "Quite a shame, I have to say. She were a good worker and all. But never mind. I'm sure you'll fill her shoes just nicely." She launched into a rapid tour, waving a hand at each room as we passed. The parlour, the dining room, and this will be my husband's smoking room… "The place is only half finished, I'm afraid. But we've room enough for you to have a little space of your own." She led me down a small set of stairs off the kitchen, the child squirming out of her arms and barrelling down the hallway like a wild rabbit. Mrs Leaver pushed open a door and nodded at the tiny room. A narrow bed sat against one wall, with a wash basin and chair beside it. "This will be your lodgings. I trust it has everything you need."

I murmured my thanks. The last time I'd slept in a proper bed, I'd been lying beside Jonathan in Clerkenwell.

"You've belongings?" she asked.

I thought of my old stockings and spare dress, tucked into my cloth bag beside my sleeping pallet. I would go for them later that night, when Blackwell was on duty. "Yes," I managed. "I can fetch them this evening." It would be far easier, I knew, if I was just to grab my belongings and disappear from his life. Pretend not a thing had passed between us. After all, nothing could come of it. If I hadn't known that before, I certainly did now.

"Very well." Mrs Leaver lurched for the child as he made a grab for the candlestick on the nightstand. She swung him back onto her hip. "The windows are due to be cleaned today," she said. "I trust you can see to that now, please? The polishing rags are in the kitchen. The cook will help you find them."

Her request was polite and achingly reasonable, but I bristled as I went to the kitchen for the rags. Once I had been the young wife, directing the staff to clean the windows. And now here I was with the polishing cloth in my hand.

My own bitterness infuriated me. How had I managed to dig up a scrap of my old spoiled self when I'd just been hauled from the spinning wheels? I knew women considered themselves lucky when they were chosen to leave the factory. As housemaids and cooks, the hours were better, the food better, the lodgings better. But I'd not had the experience of the other women, had I? I'd not had to sell my body to eat. I'd not taken men behind the factory to pay for a roof over my head.

In the back of my mind, I knew what this grief was really about. That tonight when I slept, I would not hear Blackwell breathing beside me. I hated that I could not control my attraction to him – that in his own quiet, underhand way, he had exerted his power over me.

It was better this way, I told myself, as I wiped acres of dust from the Leavers' windowsills. Best that I tried to forget.

But that night, when I crawled into my bed, feeling the softness of a mattress beneath me for the first time in two years, I felt nothing but sadness pressing down upon my shoulders.

My days became filled with laundry and bed-making, dusting and polishing, and the constant thud of hammers as the Leavers' house grew up around us.

While Leaver employed a small army of convict farmhands, there were just three of us inside the house; a pink-faced cook who had come over as a free settler and young housemaid, Amy, who broke glasses with disturbing regularity.

One morning, Amy and I made our way into town with an endless list of errands. A thick heat haze drifted up from the land, and the track into town crunched beneath our feet. The tuneless hum of insects rose from the grass.

Amy walked with her eyes down, twisting the corner of her apron around her finger. In the month I'd been at the Leavers', I'd barely heard a word from her.

"You come over on the *Norfolk*, didn't you," she said as we walked. "You was friends with Hannah." Her voice was tiny and bell-like.

I felt a tug of guilt then; I'd not had any thought that we'd travelled to this place together, lost in my own thoughts as I'd been for much of the voyage. But yes, with the reminder, I remembered shy, soft-spoken Amy. She'd been one of the youngest convicts on our ship. I guessed her little more than thirteen.

I swatted the flies from my face. "Have you been working for Leaver all this time?"

She nodded. "He took me off the ship. The place weren't

no more than a few tents on his land when I first got here."

"And how do you find him? Has he treated you well?"

She shrugged, looking back at her feet. She barely reached my shoulder. "Could be worse. Could have been sent to the factory."

I smelled the butcher's stall long before we reached it. The acrid stench of flesh floated on the hot wind, making my stomach roll.

"You go for the fruit and vegetables," I offered, pressing the list into Amy's hand. "I'll fetch the meat."

And I stopped walking abruptly, caught off guard by the figure of Blackwell striding out of the government stores. Since I'd begun working for the Leavers, I'd barely seen more than glimpses of him; sometimes at Marsden's services, sometimes here at the market, or on his way to the courthouse. I'd been careful to hide myself. What point was there in speaking? We both knew what had passed between us on the twelfth night had been a mistake. I had crossed a line that should never have been crossed.

But today, he had seen me. I knew I could not turn away without appearing petty and childish. Amy glanced at me expectantly, but I said nothing, just watched frozen as Blackwell strode towards us. He offered something vaguely resembling a smile.

"Good morning, Eleanor."

I hated the formality in his voice. Hated that the wall around him I had spent eight months chipping away at had so quickly been rebuilt. I gave a short nod. "Lieutenant."

Amy's eyes were fixed to the ground. She chewed her lip, knotting her fingers together in front of her chest. Blackwell towered over her.

A strained silence hovered between us, punctuated by the clatter of leg irons coming from the chain gang across the street. A wagon full of vegetables rattled past.

Blackwell's stiltedness left me in no doubt he had been the one behind my going to the Leavers'. Was it a punishment, I wondered? My penance for luring him to break his marriage vows? For daring to bring shame to his door? Perhaps I deserved what came to me.

I value your company, he had told me that night, as I'd reached up to unbutton my dress. And I had been foolish enough to believe his words. Had been foolish enough to believe I mattered.

"How are you getting on with Leaver?" he asked finally.

My hand tensed around the handle of the basket. "Fine, thank you."

He nodded. "I've heard him a decent man."

I looked up at him then. "Have you?" My voice came out sharper than I intended.

Blackwell made a noise in his throat and I regretted my outburst. Because standing there by the market, caught between a chain gang and the shadow of the courthouse, I saw the two of us as what we really were. Government lag and military officer. I saw I had no place to question him, to speak back to him, to stand in the lamplight and slide my dress from my shoulders. If he wanted me gone from his hut, who was I to fight it? I swallowed.

"And you?" I asked stiffly. "Are you well?" My skin felt damp beneath my shift.

"I'm well, yes. Thank you."

I wanted to ask him more; whether he'd had any trouble with Owen and Brady. What book he was reading now. If he had any shirts that needed mending. But I knew it was no longer my place to do so. Perhaps it never had been.

He glanced down at my empty basket, then back at me. "I'll let you get on with your business." And then he was gone.

Amy dared to look up, staring after Blackwell as he disappeared around the corner. Threads of blonde hair blew across her eyes. "Do you know him?" she asked in an awed half-voice.

My jaw tightened. "Barely." I felt longing, felt anger. Felt like a worthless lag who'd been slapped down to where she belonged.

I put a hand to Amy's shoulder, ushering her towards the fruit stall. "Come on. Let's get the food. It's far too hot to be out here."

At the end of February, Leaver put in a good word with the magistrate and one of his farmhands was given his ticket of leave.

When we had finished serving dinner to the family, I joined the other workers out by the barn for a farewell drink to the lucky man. The night was hot and still, cicadas shrieking in the paddocks and the musky smell of animals thick in the air.

Amy sighed heavily as we sat beside each other on the brown grass. "Wish it were me leaving this place." She stretched her legs out in front of her and began rubbing at a stain on her skirt.

I nodded. I knew we were all thinking the same. All wished we were the one with the ticket of leave being pressed into our hand. I picked up a twig and dug it listlessly into the earth.

Was I being foolish to imagine I might get such a chance? I knew with my life sentence and a stay in solitary confinement, there was not much to pin my hopes on. I had little to do with Leaver beyond his gruff orders for more food, but his young wife had taken a liking to me. Perhaps with a few well-placed words in her husband's ear, such a thing would become possible.

I had to believe it so. I couldn't spend the rest of my life scraping out another woman's hearths. I knew I would never see England again, but I didn't want to die in chains.

But even with a ticket of leave, what prospects would I have? I knew if I were to have any chance at a decent life, I would have to put myself forward at the marriage market. I would have to speak of my past; of my first husband's death, and hope the wife hunters saw only the obedience that had led me to New South Wales.

I left the celebration early and crawled off to bed, hanging my dust-streaked skirts over the chair in the corner of the room. I'd grown used to my tiny, silent bedroom; to the feel of waking alone each morning. I closed my eyes, my body aching with exhaustion. I craved the escape of my dreams.

From the back of the property I could hear the distant laughter of the farmhands. The steady wail of the cicadas. I shifted on the mattress, the air hot and stifling. And as I waited for sleep to pull me down, I heard another sound.

Rhythmic footsteps, like an army in motion. Approaching, passing, fading away.

CHAPTER EIGHTEEN

"Our servant burst into the parlour pale and violent in agitation ... he told us that the croppies had risen ... we then learnt that Castle Hill was in flames. The fire was discernible from Parramatta. It was recommended that as many ladies as chose should go to Sydney, as constant intelligence was brought into the barracks of the near approach of the Irishmen."

Elizabeth Macarthur
1804

I was on my way to the apothecary for Mrs Leaver when the chain gang shuffled out into the street, arms laden with hammers and saws. With chaotic footsteps, and leg irons rattling, they edged towards a building site close to Government House. Two soldiers marched along beside them. I recognised one of them as Ensign Cooper, who had sent Owen away the day he had attacked Blackwell.

I stood watching for a moment, the empty basket held against my chest. New South Wales had left its mark on me – the scar above my eyebrow, the calluses on my hands, the restlessness in my heart – but at that moment I was grateful for the hand I had been dealt since I'd stepped off the *Norfolk*. And perhaps I was even grateful to be a woman. My ankles were not scarred from chains, and my back was not flayed when I stepped out of line. I did not spend my days breaking rocks and building the government's houses. But gratitude felt like a dangerous thing. A thing that could so easily be taken away.

One of the convicts glanced at me and I turned away, unable to bear the sorrow in his eyes.

"What did you say?" I heard Cooper roar, his voice coming from nowhere and making me start. He loomed over two men at the back of the chain gang. Jabbed one in the side with the nose of his rifle. "What d'you say, bog-trotter?"

The man looked up at him with blank, frightened eyes.

"He don't speak no English, sir," the man behind him ventured. Cooper slammed the butt of the rifle into his nose. The man crumpled, blood spurting down the front of his shirt.

Several of the convicts began to shout in protest, others kept their eyes down. People appeared from inside the shops and taverns, watching as the convict's blood vanished into the mud. I pressed my back against the wall of the apothecary.

Here came more soldiers, marching in step, their coats stark against the muted earth and green.

"They're plotters, sir," I heard Cooper say to the captain striding towards him. "Bloody Irish rebels." The captain bent down and unlocked the shackles of the beaten man, along with the prisoner who had defended him.

"Take them to the cells. Find out what they're planning."

I hurried back to the farmhouse with the tonics for Mrs Leaver.

Plotters.

Take them to the cells.

Did the soldiers truly believe the men were planning another uprising? Or was this just a show of strength? A warning to the wayward Irish?

I found Mrs Leaver sitting up in bed, blankets piled up over her knees. With her second child on the way, she was pale and weak with nausea.

I placed the tonics on the table beside her bed. "The apothecary said these will help. Shall I boil up the ginger? Make you some tea?"

"Yes," she said. "Thank you." She sat her book on the nightstand and looked up at me. "Are you all right, Eleanor? You look a little out of sorts. Has something happened I ought to know about?"

I shook my head, smoothing her blankets and collecting the empty tea tray from the floor. "Nothing you ought to bother yourself with."

And why, I wondered, was I so bothered by it myself? Why had the mistreatment of two Irish lags made me so unsettled? Was I afraid of a second rebellion? Afraid for Blackwell's safety? Yes, but I was coming to see it was more than that. In the abuse of those croppies, I saw every injustice in the colony; the women with no place to sleep, the rations of rotted meat, Maggie's murder and Owen's freedom.

Since I'd made the choice to be ignorant no longer, I felt as though I were absorbing everything; the fear, the anger, the grief of the people I shared this place with. Everywhere I looked, I saw a thing to spark my anger; a thing that made me rail against my complete and utter powerlessness. I knew one day soon I would no longer be able to keep that rage inside.

The cup rattled against its saucer as I carried the tray towards the door. I looked back at Mrs Leaver and forced a smile. "I'll fetch you that tea."

After supper that night, Amy knocked on the door of my room. I was sitting cross-legged on the bed, mending the hem of my striped gown.

"There's a woman here for you. Says she knows you from the factory. She's waiting for you out back."

I put down my sewing and grabbed my shawl, murmuring my thanks as I headed for the door.

I found Hannah waiting for me outside the farmhouse, a blanket wrapped around her shoulders to keep out the icy wind. I was glad to see her. It had been many weeks since I'd sat at the river and drunk with the factory lasses. There was too much coldness between Lottie and me. Too much hatred in me at Owen. Too much sadness and anger over Maggie.

In the flickering lamplight, I could see Hannah's smile was strained. "All right, Nell? How they treating you?"

Wind tunnelled across the paddocks and I tugged my shawl around me tighter. "Can't complain." I looked at her expectantly. I knew this more than a visit to see how I was faring. "Has something happened?"

Hannah knotted her gnarled fingers. "Patrick Owen came to the factory today. With his marriage certificate."

I closed my eyes. "Lottie."

Hannah nodded.

"No. She can't have. She can't." What in hell was she doing? Surely she couldn't think this was the only way.

"Were there others who were willing?" I asked.

"One or two," said Hannah. "Far less than normally put themselves forward. But Owen didn't even look at the others. He wanted Lottie. It were obvious from the start."

I wondered sickly whether the two of them had discussed this earlier. Had he spoken to her of his plans to marry one night while we were drinking at the river? Had she known he was about to strut into the factory with his marriage permit in his hand?

"They're saying he got himself land in Sydney Town," said Hannah. "He's planning on taking her down there."

I began to march down the side path and out into the street. "I've got to speak to her."

I went to the hut of old Bert, the ex-convict Lottie was lodging with. Did he know, I wondered, that his concubine had betrothed herself that afternoon?

The hut was tucked away at the end of Back Lane, in a darkness so thick I could barely see the edge of the street. I walked towards the faint light shafting beneath the door. Unlike Blackwell's mudbrick home, Bert's hut was made almost entirely of wood, and it leaned dramatically to one side. A thin line of smoke curled up from the chimney. When I knocked on the door, it was Lottie herself who answered.

She sighed resignedly. "Had a feeling you'd show up tonight."

Peering over her shoulder, I could see no sign of Bert, just a small firelit hovel with a crooked table and a single, narrow sleeping pallet.

"You can't marry Owen," I said bluntly.

"No word of congratulations, Nell?" Her words were thick with sarcasm.

"Why are you doing this?" I asked.

She folded her arms across her chest. "You know why I'm doing this. Because I got more than three years of my sentence left and I don't want to spend them weaving cloth and sleeping beside an old man."

I softened my voice. "Is lodging with Bert truly so bad you'd risk your life by marrying Owen?" I wanted our old friendship, our old closeness. But Lottie had her guard up.

She laughed coldly. "Lodging with him? Is that what you imagine this is? Just lodging with the man?"

The bitterness in her words chilled me.

"And do you imagine things with Owen will be any better?" I asked.

Lottie held my gaze for a moment, her eyes narrowing. "The thing is done," she said finally. "The papers have been signed. We're to be married on Thursday. Leaving for Sydney on Friday. It's too late for any of this."

I heard the soldiers marching again that night. Crunch

and thud from the direction of the barracks. This time I was wide awake; thoughts of Lottie and Owen keeping me from sleep.

I slipped out of bed and peeked through the curtain. My window looked out over the front of the farm, but I could see little in the darkness. I pulled on my dress and boots and slipped out of the house.

One of Leaver's farmhands was leaning against the stone fence at the front of the property, blowing a line of silver pipe smoke up into the dark. I stood beside him and watched in silence as a parade of redcoats strode out into the wilderness.

"Is there trouble?" I squinted into the night, trying to pick out Blackwell's figure.

The farmhand took his pipe out from between his teeth. "Just a drill, I'd say."

"A drill?"

"The Rum Corps likes to be prepared."

"Prepared for what?" I asked. "Another rebel uprising?"

He nodded.

I frowned. This had to be a new development. When I'd been staying with Blackwell, I'd never known him to leave in the middle of the night. I was a light sleeper. I was sure I would have heard.

"The government fears another rebellion?" I asked. I thought of the Irishman in the chain gang, his blood disappearing into the mud. "Has something happened?"

The farmhand shrugged. "They've been fearing another rebellion since Castle Hill."

I pulled my shawl tighter around me. I realised I was fearing another rebellion too. "Were you here in Parramatta?"

I asked. "During the uprising?"

He nodded.

"What was it like?"

He took a long draw on his pipe. "Phil Cunningham raised an army of croppies at Castle Hill. Went from farm to farm recruiting men, taking weapons. There were a mad panic here when we heard it were happening." He chuckled. "Reverend Marsden jumped in a boat and fled the place like a scared cat."

I felt a small smile in the corner of my lips.

"Croppies had no chance though," the farmhand said. "The redcoats marched out to meet them and the battle only lasted a few minutes. Could hear gunshots for days, mind you, what with the lobsters sent out to find all the rebels who got away."

I felt a sudden tightness in my throat. Owen's story about what had happened at his family's cottage echoed at the back of my mind.

I went out into the street, staring through the darkness the soldiers had disappeared into. I wrapped my arms around myself and shivered.

It felt as though this fragile colony was teetering. I had little doubt the army would quell another rebel uprising as quickly as they had the first. But I knew they would not do so without blood being shed. And I knew if the croppies rose up in battle, Blackwell would be a target. Would likely be the first to die.

I whirled around at the sound of footsteps. Found Dan Brady standing in the road behind me. Had he been watching the soldiers too?

I felt the sudden urge to hurry back to the farmhouse. But I didn't want to give him the satisfaction of knowing he unnerved me.

"I thought you'd be out there pounding down the jail doors," I said. "Trying to free those two croppies they locked up. Or are they not as important to you as Patrick Owen?"

Brady chuckled humourlessly. "If we rose up every time a croppy were mistreated there'd be none of us left."

"I know," I said. "It's not right. I was there when it happened. Any fool could see they were just speaking their own language."

Brady tilted his head, considering me. I could tell he was surprised by my agreement.

"And yet here you are," he said, "staring out into the night after your lieutenant."

I felt my cheeks burn. Was grateful for the darkness.

I didn't reply. Admitting to it made me feel like a fool.

Brady jabbed his pipe in the direction the soldiers had disappeared. "You think this is right, *sasanaigh?* The redcoats out training to take us all down? So Blackwell can take more innocent lives?"

I clenched my teeth, forcing my anger away. "Instead we're all just to sit back and let the croppies take over the colony? Do you truly think that's what's best for this place?"

Brady chuckled. "What does a factory lass know about what's best for this place?"

I said nothing. He was right, of course. What did I know?

"I know how it feels to be powerless," I told him. "Just like you do."

"That's right," said Brady. "You do." He took a step

closer, pointing a long finger at me. "But here's the difference between us, Nellie. Us croppies fight for what we want. The factory lasses just sit back and accept things the way they are."

CHAPTER NINETEEN

"A light punishment for rebellion will excite revenge, not terror ... Transport all prisoners in the gaols and give full power to the generals."

Advice from England to Undersecretary Cooke, Dublin
The Rebellion Papers
12th March 1797

The next day, the Irishmen from the chain gang were dragged from the cells for a flogging. Robert Leaver, the most patriotic of Englishmen, herded us all from the farmhouse to watch. A crowd had gathered, the murmur of voices thick in the air. Soldiers lined the edges of Jail Green, rifles held at the ready. Reverend Marsden paced in front of the triangle, thick arms folded across his chest.

The two prisoners were dressed in grimy shirtsleeves and breeches that reached just past their knees. They were led out to the green, a mess of bloodied faces and swollen eyes.

I thought of untouchable Patrick Owen, merely sent on

his way after striking an officer. Protected from punishment by his position as the rebels' leader.

Was this the government's way of striking back against the Irish? Flogging two lowly convicts for speaking their native language? Surely no one truly believed them capable of inciting another uprising. These were simply men they could punish without fearing backlash. Or was I just being naïve?

The first of the prisoners was shoved towards the triangle, shirt yanked from his body and his arms bound to the structure, high above his head.

I glanced around the crowd for Blackwell. There was no sign of him. No doubt he had marched off on last night's drill. I wondered stiffly what he would think of all this.

No. I knew what he would think of this, and the thought was an uncomfortable one. Blackwell was a lieutenant in the New South Wales Corps. He had fought in the Castle Hill uprising. Had fought in the rebellion in Ireland. Hardly a man who would sympathise with a couple of lowly croppies. I pushed the thought aside. What difference did it make? The only one of Blackwell's thoughts that mattered was his decision to send me away.

The first crack of the whip made my shoulders tighten. The prisoner cried out as it tore through his bare skin. Beside me, Amy murmured and turned away.

The flogger hurled the cat again. The prisoner tried to swallow his cry.

"This isn't right," I said, to no one in particular. "These men aren't plotters."

On the other side of me, Leaver's farmhand chuckled, taking the pipe out from between his teeth. "I hadn't picked you as a rebel sympathiser."

"I'm not a rebel sympathiser," I said. "Those men just didn't understand what was being asked of them. Any fool could see that."

"Aye." He took a long draw on his pipe. "It's politics. It weren't about their crimes. It were just about the government making a point."

I clenched my teeth. There hadn't seemed to be a point to make when Owen had his hands around Maggie's throat.

I felt horribly on edge. Each crack of the whip rattled through me, as though the cat were striking my own body. I felt my muscles tighten, my stomach turn over. My thoughts were storming; with Maggie, with Lottie, with Owen. With *wife* and *concubine* and these blood-streaked convicts.

The officer overseeing the flogging stepped close to one of the prisoners, their noses inches apart. "What are you planning?" he hissed.

The prisoner groaned out a line of Irish.

"Give him another hundred," said the soldier. A murmur rippled through the crowd.

Afraid as I was for Blackwell, I understood then why the Irish felt the need to rise up, to fight against the hand they'd been given. I thought of what Dan Brady had told me the night the Rum Corps had left on their drill.

The factory lasses just sit back and accept things…

There'd been anger among us the day of Maggie's murder. But how quickly we'd been put back into our place. How easy we were to tug back into line. While the croppies plotted and planned rebellions, we just lifted our skirts so we might have a place to sleep. Bared our skin in the lamplight so we might have a little sway. We were weak and voiceless.

"This isn't right," I said again.

I felt a firm fingers digging into the top of my arm. Turned to see Leaver inches behind me.

"Shut your mouth," he hissed, breath hot against my cheek. "Just who do you think you are?"

I clenched my teeth, closing my eyes as the whip fired again. I felt as though an enormous weight were pressing down on me.

Tonight those prisoners would sleep with flayed backs because they had dared speak their own language. Marsden's register was on its way around London, painting us as concubines. And now Owen, the man who had taken Maggie from us, was to take Lottie as well.

For the rest of the day, I went about my chores in a daze. I felt hot and disoriented. Unable to see clearly. I spoke to Amy and the cook in terse, one-word answers. And when the house grew dark, I went to the kitchen and pulled a knife from the drawer.

I felt oddly outside myself as I made my way across the farm and stepped into the street. My thoughts were hazy. Likely, there was a part of my brain preventing me from thinking too clearly in case I saw the foolishness of my behaviour.

I strode towards Owen's hut, my hand tight around the handle of the knife. I felt a surge of determination.

Once, I'd blindly followed my husband, believing I had no other choice. But I saw now that I had had a choice, and I'd made the wrong one. I'd made the choice to believe myself powerless; to let circumstances carry me away like the tide. And now, in this place, where I felt more powerless than ever, I'd made the decision to be powerless no more.

My hand tightened around the knife handle. I would die for this, of course; some distant part of me knew that. But it didn't matter. It was hard to value my own life when no one else did. I would face the hangman, but Owen would finally have his punishment. Maggie would have justice and Lottie would be safe. And men would learn they would not get away with murdering a factory lass.

The darkness was thick and cold; just a few stars straining through the cloud bank. I could feel the emptiness all around us. A day by barge to Sydney Town. Half a lifetime to the existence I had once known. The place felt inescapable.

I stood several feet from the door of Owen's hut, feeling the smooth bone handle of the knife between my fingers.

How would it be, I wondered? Was there someone in the hut with him? Someone who would witness his death? Was Lottie in there?

A part of me hoped so. She would see the things I was willing to do to save her. She would see that, even though we had grown distant, I still loved her like a sister.

How would I do it? A blade through the heart? Or perhaps the throat. The thought caused me to inhale sharply. When had I become a woman who could do such a thing? It was a natural progression, I supposed; obedient daughter to obedient wife, convict to murderess.

I felt capable. And I felt ready.

Here were the footsteps again. Distant, dreamlike. The soldiers returning. They would drag me to trial, put a rope around my neck. But not before Owen was dead.

"Eleanor. What are you doing?"

It took a moment for me to register that Blackwell's voice had not come from inside my head.

I turned to look at him. He stood a foot behind me, dressed in full uniform, his rifle slung across his back. I slipped the knife into my pocket, keeping my fingers wrapped around the handle.

Blackwell looked at the shack, then back at me. "This is Patrick Owen's hut."

I squeezed my eyes closed. "Go away."

"What are you doing?" he asked again.

I turned back towards Leaver's farm, unsure what else to do. Blackwell took my arm gently, preventing me from leaving. "What's happened?"

I felt tears threatening. No, this was all wrong. I was not supposed to fall apart. I was supposed to charge into Owen's home and deliver the justice he had so far escaped. But instead, Blackwell was leading me towards his hut, his hand around my wrist, and I was going without hesitation.

Inside the hut, everything was just as I remembered, except for the bare space on the floor where my sleeping pallet had been. I wanted to leave. But his hand was still firm around my wrist and I couldn't find the strength to pull away.

I shifted my fingers on the handle of the knife, to stop it falling from my pocket. Blackwell lifted my hand in his, bringing the blade out into the light.

He looked down at the knife, then back at me. "What were you doing at Owen's hut?"

"He's to marry Lottie," I said, not looking at him.

"And so you will kill him?"

"He deserves to die," I said. "He murdered Maggie."

Blackwell stood motionless for a long second. "You don't want to kill him," he said evenly.

"And how do you know that?"

He stepped closer, pushing gently against my shoulder, urging me to face him.

No, I didn't want to look at him. Didn't want him to see this darkest side of me. I felt tears spring up behind my eyes.

"Because once you kill another, it never leaves you." His voice was low. "The look in their eyes, it stays with you forever. It's a stain you will never be rid of."

I thought of Blackwell hunching beside the rebels' graves. Thought of the heaviness that had hung about him when he had returned to the hut that day. How many ghosts haunted Adam Blackwell, I wondered? Whose invisible eyes watched him at night?

But he was wrong. There was a part of me that did want to kill Owen. To hell with the consequences and the ghosts and the unerasable stain. I wanted to look into Owen's eyes and see fear. See the realisation that a woman held the power.

For those few precious moments I would be more than *concubine*. I would hold life and death in my hands.

"You don't have it in you," he said.

"Is that what you think?"

But I knew he was right. I had walked that path from obedient daughter to convict, but *murderess* was still beyond me.

Blackwell wrapped his fingers around mine, his hand dwarfing my own. "Please, Eleanor," he said, "put the knife down."

My fingers tensed around the handle. I couldn't release my grip on it. What I would do with it now, I didn't know, but it felt like all the power I had in the world. How could I let that go?

"Lottie's going to die," I coughed. "Just like Maggie.

She's going to die and no one will think twice on it. They'll blame her death on the blacks and Owen will walk, just as he always does."

Blackwell looked down at the knife. "So you will sacrifice yourself for her? Send yourself to the hangman?"

I felt my shoulders sink, as though the earth was tugging me down. I let him take the knife from my hand. He placed it on the ground between our feet. He slid the rifle from his shoulders and opened the chamber, setting the balls and cartridge on the table.

Inexplicably, the gesture made rage flare inside me. I thought of all the dominance, all the strength, men like him had over the rest of us, casually taking the shells from his weapon with a practised ease. And all I could see was him standing on the jury and letting Patrick Owen walk.

I swung at him suddenly, my blows pounding his chest, his shoulders, his arms. For several moments, he stood still, letting me take my anger out on him. But when I bent to pick up the knife, he grabbed my wrists, pulling me up to him and forcing me into stillness. His nose grazed mine.

"Wave that knife around and you'll hang for it," he hissed. "It doesn't matter if you kill Owen or not. You're a factory lass. Just carrying it will be enough to put you on the scaffold."

I shook my head. "I don't care."

His hands tightened around my wrists. "*I* care."

My tears spilled suddenly; tears of grief, of exhaustion, of frustration. And his arms were around me, holding me tightly.

I closed my eyes, feeling myself sink against him. I buried my head against his broad chest, so he couldn't see me cry.

He slid his hand over my hair, holding me close. I could

feel the warmth of his palm against my neck. Could feel his body rising and falling with breath. A little of the distress inside me began to still.

I wished for my old sleeping pallet beside the hearth. I wished for the sound of him breathing beside me in the night. Nothing more. Just that reassurance that someone was there to know, to care if this place swallowed me whole. I felt my fingers tighten around the edge of his coat. And with the gesture, he pulled away, his hand ghosting over the plait that hung down my back.

"I'm sorry, Eleanor," he said huskily, "you need to go back to the farm."

On Thursday, I made it a point not to step off Leaver's property for a minute. I couldn't bear to be out in a world in which Lottie was marrying Owen.

The next day I woke before dawn, lighting the fires and laying the table. Then I slipped out of the house and made my way to the river, desperate to catch Lottie before she sailed away on the morning barge.

I found her waiting on the riverbank beside Owen, a few other travellers clustered by the jetty. She stood with her arms wrapped around herself, staring across the murky plane of the water. Owen was pacing back and forth across the riverbank, hands dug into his pockets to keep out the cold.

He looked up, his face breaking into a grin. "Nice of you to come see us off, Nellie."

There was a positive to their leaving of course; no more dead animals hung from Blackwell's hut, no more rocks through his window. Perhaps in Sydney Town, Owen would learn to forget the anger he held towards the lieutenant. And perhaps with Owen gone, Blackwell could move out from beneath the shadow of Castle Hill.

But with Owen gone, Lottie would be gone too. And the thought of it made me ache.

I made my way towards her. I wanted to plead with her one final time, but I knew there was no point. The marriage permit had been signed, the ceremony complete. Instead, I just pulled her into my arms and held her tightly. I couldn't shake the fear that the next grave I would be standing at would be hers. Her arms slid around me, pulling me close.

And here came the barge, gliding up the river, ready to carry her away. Ready to carry her to a life as Patrick Owen's wife.

"Be safe," I managed, my voice coming out broken.

When I stepped back, Lottie's eyes were glistening. "And you, Nell," she said. "He's not who you think he is."

CHAPTER TWENTY

I opened my eyes to thick darkness, aware something had jolted me awake. It had been several months since Owen had left Parramatta, and I thought constantly of Lottie. Thought constantly of Blackwell and the redcoats out on their midnight drills.

To still my thoughts, I'd thrown myself into my work. As Mrs Leaver's confinement approached, I'd become something of a lady's maid to her, running to answer the ringing of her bell throughout the day and night. My devotion to her earned me the occasional smile from Leaver, who was clearly besotted with his young and pretty wife.

I sat up in bed, listening for Mrs Leaver's bell.

No. That was not what had woken me.

Murmurs were coming from Amy's room. Male grunts of exertion.

I climbed out of bed. Had one of the farmhands crept into her room? Had he been invited?

I stood outside her door, debating whether to intervene.

A muffled cry came, followed by another grunt; this time one of aggression. I darted instinctively into the room.

In the shafts of moonlight streaming through the gap in the curtains, I could see the square figure of Leaver on the bed, trousers around his knees and Amy struggling beneath him.

I snatched the candleholder; the only meagre weapon I could find.

"Get away from her," I hissed.

Leaver whirled around and stumbled from the bed, yanking up his trousers and buttoning them hurriedly.

Amy was watching open-mouthed, her blonde hair ruffled, eyes wide with fear. Her nightshift was tangled around her knees.

"Go," I told her.

She scrambled off the bed and disappeared out of the room.

Leaver came towards me, forcing me backwards. His face was darkened with shadow, his untucked shirt hanging around his knees. "Who the hell do you think you are?" he demanded, voice thin. Beneath his miserable attempt at forcefulness, I could hear the uncertainty, the embarrassment.

I held the candleholder out in front of me. "She's just a child."

"She's my lag. I can do with her what I like." He tucked in his shirt, looking at me with flashing eyes. "What will you do? Go to the Rum Corps? You think they'll give a shit?"

"The Rum Corps won't care," I said. "But I'm sure Mrs Leaver will."

I watched a look of horror pass over his round face. What a weakness it was, I thought distantly, for a man to care what his wife thought. He pointed a finger at me. I could see it trembling. "One word to my wife and I'll kill you."

I smiled thinly. My time in this place had shown me the difference between men who could kill and men who just talked. Robert Leaver was a man who just talked.

"You'll not kill me," I said.

He looked taken aback by my boldness. "What do you want?" he hissed.

I faltered. Let out a short laugh. "Are you trying to bargain with me?"

He clenched his jaw. "I said, what do you want?"

And I saw it then. I had power. For the first time since I had stepped onto these shores, I had the upper hand.

I thought of Lottie, wed to Patrick Owen, carted off to Sydney Town. And I said, "I want my ticket of leave."

I signed my name and the paperwork was handed to me.

'It is His Excellency the Governor's pleasure to dispense with the attendance at government work of Eleanor Marling...'

Below it was a detailed account of my appearance, my voyage on the *Norfolk*, and my trial at the Old Bailey. But it was the last line that had my attention:

'Permitted to employ herself in any lawful occupation within the district of Parramatta.'

No. I couldn't be imprisoned here in this settlement. Not while Lottie was in Sydney.

I stared down at the page. Demanding Leaver go to the

magistrate on my account had been selfish. I ought to have bargained with him for Amy's freedom. Not my own. I had done as I had out of a desperate need to help Lottie. But this would not help anyone.

I bought myself a room at the lodging house on Macquarie Street. At the market, I found two poplin dresses for sixpence each. They were threadbare and their prints faded, but with a little rehemming, they both blessedly reached my ankles. I stood in front of the mirror in my room at the lodging house and fastened the hooks to my neck. For the first time in almost two years, I was not dressed the same as every second woman in Parramatta. Nor was I the lady I had been when I had last stood in front of a mirror like this and fastened a lace collar at my throat. The relentless sun had darkened my skin and lightened my hair, almost two years of labour scarring my hands with callouses. But I knew the changes this place had wrought on the inside were far greater. Parramatta had stolen my ignorance, my ability to turn away. Twenty months in New South Wales and I was a woman who walked with a knife in her hand.

I looked down at my papers I had laid across the bed. Though I had little else, I had freedom of sorts. The enormity of that was not lost on me, despite the underhand way it had come about. I felt little guilt at having blackmailed Robert Leaver. Twenty months in New South Wales had also taught me there was little place here for decency.

I combed and pinned my hair, scrubbed my skin clean. And when dark had fallen thick across the street, I went to Lieutenant Blackwell.

I stood outside the hut and knocked, my heart pounding harder than it had the night he had first brought me here.

The door groaned as it opened.

He stooped in the doorway, looking at me without speaking. His eyes glided over the floral print of my skirts, my neatly pinned hair, the hint of lace at my neck. Beneath the callouses and the second-hand dress, I had conjured up a little of my old refinement. Chin lifted, shoulders back; a way I'd not carried myself in many months. Last time Blackwell and I had spoken, I'd been a chaotic mess with a knife in my hand. I needed him to see I was stronger than that. Capable. I needed to him to do as I asked.

I held out my paperwork. I knew one glance at the page would tell him I was here for life. But as he glanced over it, his face gave nothing away.

"You have your freedom," he said finally, passing the papers back to me. "That's wonderful."

I shook my head. "It's not wonderful. I can't leave Parramatta. And I need to get to Lottie in Sydney Town."

Finally, Blackwell took a step back, gesturing for me to step inside the hut.

"I'm sorry, Eleanor," he said, "this is the way things are. But do things right and perhaps one day it will become a pardon."

I couldn't wait for a pardon. Not while Lottie was lying beside Patrick Owen in the night.

I looked up at him. "You could persuade the magistrate on my behalf," I said. I knew there was little point dancing around the issue.

Blackwell scooped back his hair, exhaling. "This is highly inappropriate."

"Yes. I know." I looked him in the eye. And I kept my distance. Perhaps there were ways I could have persuaded him. Gentle fingers down his arm, lips on his neck.

Concubine.

I stayed fixed to the floor, my papers held out in front of me. "Please," I said. "Lottie is in danger."

"Danger you plan to walk right into."

He cared for me; yes, I saw that. And a part of me was grateful. But I didn't want to be cared for right then. I wanted – *needed* – that extra gasp of freedom.

"You were the one who arranged for me to work for Leaver," I said suddenly.

"Yes."

I swallowed, taken aback by his blunt admission. "Why?"

His eyes shifted. "You know why."

"I want to hear you say it."

"Because when I'm around you, I fear I will be unfaithful to my wife."

The words fell heavily into the silence. They did not bring me nearly as much satisfaction as I had expected.

"I thought it better for both of us," he said. "I know working in the factory is difficult."

Perhaps he was right. Perhaps it was better for both of us. But that didn't stop me from feeling as though I'd been discarded.

My hand tightened, crumpling my papers. "Patrick Owen should never have been allowed to walk free," I said. "We both know that."

I saw his jaw tense.

"I need to get Lottie away from him."

"How?"

"I don't know," I admitted. I only knew it was not something I could do from the depths of Parramatta.

"Please," I said. "You know how important this is to me."

Blackwell rubbed his stubbled chin, exhaling deeply. Finally, he reached for the papers. "Let me speak to the magistrate."

The following day, the factory burned. Flames roared up from the warehouses above the jail, a cloud of smoke drifting across the sun.

We all stood by the river, watching flames pour out the side of the building. The smoke stung my eyes and made my throat burn.

The women from the spinning wheels milled about in the street, staring up the fire. They chattered among themselves, some with children clamped to their hips. The men from the prison below the factory stood lined up in their shackles, guarded by a row of soldiers. Convicts and enlisted men formed a line from the river, passing buckets of water up the chain to be flung onto the blaze.

I sought out Hannah, who was standing among the women. I could feel their eyes on me, taking in my floral skirts, my straw bonnet. I felt myself shrink under their scrutiny. For so many months, I had longed to be more than a miserable factory lass. But now I felt painfully disconnected. Caught between two worlds.

"What's this about then?" asked Hannah, gesturing to my dress.

I shook my head dismissively. "Had a little spare coin is

all." I couldn't bring myself to tell her I'd wrangled a ticket of leave.

I stared up at the factory, imagining the spinning wheels ablaze. "What happened?"

"Started in the kitchen," she told me. "Some logs come out of the grate and landed on the girls' blankets."

Fitting, I thought, that that dreadful place might turn to ash. It deserved little more. But I feared what it would mean for the women and children who spent each night on its floor.

I edged away from Hannah and the other women, feeling an inexplicable tug of guilt. Guilt that I might escape this place. And guilt that fate had fallen in my favour and led me to Blackwell's door.

I felt his presence before I saw him. He stood at my side and pressed a piece of paper into my hand.

I unfolded it, heart pounding. My ticket of leave.

And there, at the bottom of the page, was the thing I had longed for:

'Permitted to employ herself in any lawful occupation within the district of Sydney.'

I looked up at him with gratitude in my eyes. I was going to find Lottie.

And then?

I couldn't bring myself to think that far ahead. I was terrified of what I might find.

"Thank you," I murmured. He was standing close; close enough for me to see the dark blue flecks in his eyes. At the back of the crowd we were hidden; Parramatta's eyes on the burning jail.

"Be careful," he said huskily. He bent his head and kissed the salty skin on the side of my neck.

Before I could reply, he was gone.

PART THREE

The courtroom is hot and cramped. I stand pressed between the other prisoners, their shoulders hard against mine. I can sense their racing hearts, can smell the sweat on their skin, feel as though I'm drowning in their fear.

Our trials are cursory, and we are given little chance to speak. The magistrate metes out punishments like a dull schoolroom recitation.

Assault of an overseer: to the coal mines in Newcastle.

Theft of government stores: remainder of sentence at Toongabbie.

And then I am brought forward; my name spoken, my charges read out.

I am given the chance to speak, but I know nothing I say will save me. I am a factory lass who has robbed a man of his life. I have taken that final step: murderess. *I am to be made an example of; a cautionary tale of a woman who took the wrong path. A warning to the other factory lasses to be quiet, be moral, be obedient. I grip the railing of the dock, praying my legs will hold me when the inevitable verdict comes.*

The magistrate's words are no surprise.

For the murder of Adam Blackwell, you are sentenced to hang by the neck until you are dead.

CHAPTER TWENTY-ONE

With my ticket of leave in my pocket, I climbed back onto the barge. The morning was hot and hazy, eels wrestling beneath the surface of the river. I watched over my shoulder as Parramatta and the charred shell of its factory vanished behind a wall of forest.

I felt focused as we wound along the river, my eyes fixed on the road of coppery water. I had no plans beyond finding Lottie, no thought of what shape my life would take now. But my days as a Parramatta lag were behind me. I had more freedom than I had ever imagined I would have again.

The sun was sinking when the barge bumped against its moorings in Sydney Cove. In my twenty months away in Parramatta, Sydney Town had grown. I saw hints of London in its neatly carved stone and the church spires that interrupted the vastness of the sky. Rows of jetties had sprung up out of the mudflats and the sprawl of huts and cottages had begun to take over the forest. And the people; more people than I'd seen since England. Sailors and soldiers, ladies and lags, filling the streets with chatter, with colour; overwhelming in their sheer number.

How was I to find Lottie among the expanse of this place?

Hastily built taverns teetered on the waterfront, men clustered outside them, roaring with laughter. I dared a glance through the window of one, and saw hordes of sailors at bare wooden tables, some stumbling drunkenly into one other. I kept walking. On the corner of the road weaving inland from the harbour, I found a smaller tavern without the men gathered out the front. A wooden sign squeaked above the door, announcing my arrival at the Whaler's Arms.

I stepped inside. The bar was small, with dark wooden panelling, barrels and bottles lined up neatly behind the counter. Round tables were dotted about the room.

"Close the door behind you, lass," called the man behind the bar. "Flies'll take over the place if you let them."

The door groaned loudly as I yanked it shut.

"I'm looking for a man named Patrick Owen," I told the barman. "Do you know him?"

The man was big and bearlike, with a dark beard that reached halfway down his chest. "Never heard of him."

"Irishman," I said. "Fair hair, handsome."

The barman chuckled. "Taken your fancy has he? Sorry lass, afraid I can't help you."

As I made my way towards the door, I heard a tangle of Gaelic. I stopped walking. The voices came from a group of older men, crowded around a table in the corner of the bar. I had little doubt that Owen had caused as much of a stir among the Irish in Sydney as he had in Parramatta. I made my way towards the table.

"Patrick Owen," I said. "Do you know him?"

One of the men blew a long line of smoke in my direction. "Who's asking?"

I hesitated. "I'm a friend of his wife."

And a gnarled brown finger was pointing in the direction of the street. "Owns a place out past the cemetery. Not too far from here."

By the time I stepped out of the inn, the last of the sunlight was draining away. The sea slapped rhythmically against the docks, interspersed with horse hooves and the crunch of cartwheels against stone.

I followed the directions the man had given. Owen's property was small and simple; a stone cottage at the front of few square paddocks. A lamp flickered at the front of the house, but it scooped out little of the darkness.

I made my way up the narrow path and knocked on the door, heart pounding. Was I scared of Owen, or scared of how Lottie might react when she saw me? Perhaps a little of both. Most of all, I was scared I would be too late.

A young woman in a mobcap opened the door. She looked me up and down. "Yes?"

I faltered. I hadn't expected Owen to have a housekeeper.

"I'm looking for Lottie." I swallowed. "For Mrs Owen."

The girl knotted her apron around her finger. "Mrs Owen ain't here no more."

My stomach clenched. "What happened to her?"

"I heard she went to the Rocks."

I frowned, not understanding. Still no wiser as to whether Lottie was alive or dead.

"The Rocks," she said again. "Down by the cove."

I let out a sigh of relief. "Why is she there?" I asked.

The girl chewed her lip, avoiding my gaze. Mothwings pattered into the glass of the lantern.

I gave up. It didn't matter why. "Down by the cove," I repeated.

She nodded. "But best you don't go there yourself, miss. It ain't a good place to be venturing at night."

The knot in my stomach tightened. "I've no choice."

CHAPTER TWENTY-TWO

"I observe that [when they are let out of the barracks on a Sunday, the convicts] run immediately to the part of the town called the Rocks, where every species of debauchery and villainy is practised."

Major Henry Druitt
Chief Engineer of New South Wales
27th October 1819

The Rocks was a noisy, narrow, London kind of chaos. Mudbrick and sandstone jostled each other for space, houses climbing up rock terraces and threatening to topple into the alleys below. Clothes lines were strung across the streets, hung with linen and stained shirts. Men and women gathered outside houses, laughing, drinking, blowing pipe smoke into the sky. Two children barrelled past me, knocking into my hip.

I thought of the slums of Whitechapel, a place I'd only

ever heard stories of. A humid haze hung over the place, and I could smell the stench of human waste, of unwashed bodies, of food gone sour in the sun. Beneath it all, the salty breath of the ocean.

I peered down one of the narrow alleys that snaked off the main thoroughfare. Two women were sitting side by side on the street, babies squirming in their arms. One of the children stared after me until I reached the end of the lane.

Down another alley, another, another. The streets felt circular and maze-like. Another turn and I was at the sea. I drew in a long breath, filling my lungs with the clean, salty air. I looked out over the dark plain of the ocean, listening to the water clop between the rocks. I could see the faint flicker of a lamp glowing on an island in the bay.

My feet were aching, my body weighted with exhaustion. I knew I ought to find myself a bed. But I couldn't bear to leave without finding Lottie. Not now I was so close.

I turned and walked back down the alley. And here were men coming towards me; all rolled up shirtsleeves and puffed out chests. Three of them. No, four.

I realised I'd made myself a target. A foolish target who had learned barely a scrap of street sense in her time in Parramatta.

I put my head down and walked faster, but I had lost all sense of my bearings.

"Don't leave us, darling," called one of the men, making the others roar with laughter. I suppressed the urge to run, sure it would make them chase me. But as one of the men reached for my arm, I grabbed my skirts in my fist and darted around the corner, deeper into the narrow warrens of the Rocks.

When I felt another hand at my wrist, I swung away wildly.

"Nell," said the familiar voice. "It is you."

I stopped running and gulped down my breath.

"Saw some lunatic charging by," Lottie said, before I could speak. "What in hell are you doing here?"

I threw my arms around her, overcome with relief. "I came looking for you. I…"

She looked at me with questions in her eyes – and yes, I knew there were many questions. A firm hand around my arm, she led me back down the alley I had run through. A narrow doorway led into what looked to be a dimly lit kitchen. The room was crammed with women in ragged clothing; some huddled on the floor, others herding children, a couple bustling around a cooking pot hung over the fire. The heat was stifling.

"Where are we?" I asked.

"A woman named Mary owns the house," said Lottie. "She made her fortune once her sentence were up. Helps out those of us with no place to go. Gives us a place to sleep."

Still holding my wrist, she led me to a corner of the room where a filthy grey blanket was spread out over the flagstones. A straw basket sat beside it. Inside was a sleeping baby.

My stomach knotted. I had many questions for Lottie too, of course.

"What happened?" I asked. "Why are you here?"

She shrugged. "Got sick of me, didn't he." She was trying for lightness, but the tremor in her voice betrayed her. As did the vicious streak of anger. "Threw me out."

She didn't look me in the eyes. Afraid, perhaps of *I told you so*.

On the other side of the room, a child began to wail.

I felt anger roiling inside me. This place was crammed full of women and children. Had they all been as carelessly discarded as Lottie?

I sat beside her on the blanket. The stench of hot bodies was making my stomach turn.

"Who are all these women?" I asked. "Where did they come from?" I was dimly aware that I sounded like a naïve young lady from Clerkenwell.

Lottie shrugged. "Some finished their sentences and couldn't find nowhere else. Or their husbands had enough of them. Decided they could do better."

I didn't answer. I couldn't find the words.

"So what then?" she asked. "You a runaway? Or that lieutenant of yours get you a pardon?"

I hugged my knees. "I've a ticket of leave," I said simply, not wanting to venture into details.

Lottie made a noise in her throat. I could tell she didn't want details either.

A throaty wail came from the basket beside her. She bent over to scoop up the baby.

"How old is he?" I asked. "She?"

"He's four months," she answered, her eyes meeting mine for the briefest of moments.

Four months. I realised then that Lottie had been with child long before she had left Parramatta. Long before she and Owen had married.

I swallowed. "Why didn't you tell me?"

I knew the answer of course. She and I had barely spoken in the months before she had left. And even if I had known, what would I have had to offer her but another diatribe of abuse towards Owen? What good would any of it done?

She unbuttoned her bodice with one hand and wrangled the baby onto her breast.

"Is he Owen's?" I asked.

She nodded, not looking at me.

"Did he force you?"

Lottie let out her breath. "What do you want, Nell? To prove you were right and I was wrong? To show me how well you've done for yourself? Is that why you've come?"

"Of course not," I said. "I was worried about you. I worried for you every day. I just want to help you."

She shook her head. "You ought to have stayed in Parramatta with your lobster. How d'you even get here? You have him swing things for you? Persuade him to get you a little more freedom?"

I clenched my teeth. Said nothing.

"You left him," Lottie said after a moment. "I didn't think you would."

I lowered my eyes. "There was nothing to leave." Heat flushed the back of my neck. I knew myself lying. But I couldn't let Lottie know how far things had gone between Blackwell and me.

I stood up. "I'll leave you then. If that's what you want."

Lottie rubbed her eyes with her free hand. "Where will you go?"

"I don't know," I admitted, heading for the door.

She sighed. "Come back, Nell. It's not safe to go wandering about out there with no place to go. You're better off here. Safety in numbers and all that." She spoke without looking at me. "I'll deal with you in the morning."

As the salty smell of broth seeped across the kitchen, the

women made their way towards the fire. A young girl at the cooking pot brought a stack of bowls from the shelf, and ladled a thin puddle of soup into each. One by one, the women filed their way towards the table in the centre of the room and took the soup bowls back to their own corners. A well-practised routine. I wondered how long some of them had been here.

"Make yourself useful," Lottie told me, wiping the baby's mouth with the hem of her dress. "Fetch us some supper."

I took two bowls from the table and carried them carefully back to Lottie. We huddled together in the corner, angled towards the wall so we might block out the world around us. Lottie bent over her bowl to scoop a spoonful into her mouth, the baby fidgeting in the crook of her arm.

I ate in silence, unsure what to say. Whatever was to come out of my mouth, I felt certain she wouldn't be interested in hearing it. She attempted another mouthful of broth, swatting the spoon out of the baby's grasp.

"Let me take him," I said, as I swallowed my last mouthful. She dumped the child in my lap and picked up her bowl to drink from it.

I peered down at the baby. Tiny pink fingers were darting in and out of his mouth. He felt small and fragile in my arms.

Patrick Owen's child. And Lottie's.

"What's his name?" I asked.

She gulped down a mouthful. "Willie. After my da."

He wriggled in my arms and began to whine.

"How long have you been here?" I asked, rubbing his back.

She didn't look at me. "Half a year maybe."

I said nothing. Half a year. I wondered if Patrick Owen

had ever laid eyes on his son.

"I know what you're thinking. But he did what I wanted. He got me out of the factory." She lifted her bowl to her lips to drain it, then sat it on the floor beside her, pulling Willie from my arms.

"It's good to see you," I said finally. Both an understatement and a lie. I was inexpressibly glad I had found her alive. But my heart ached to see where she had ended up.

"It's good to see you too," Lottie said, giving me a ghost of a smile.

I leant wearily back against the wall. There was so much more I wanted to ask, but I had learned a precious skill in my time around Blackwell. There was nothing so good as silence to encourage an answer.

"Things were good," she said. "At first. He was kind to me. Decent."

"Why did Owen come to Sydney?" I asked. "Why not stay upriver? He had it good in Parramatta."

"He served his time there," said Lottie. "Can you blame him for wanting a fresh start?"

"I suppose not." I hugged my knees, watching a women steer a bare-footed child away from the fire. "And the rebels?" I asked. "Is he involved with them here in Sydney?"

Lottie eyed me. "I suppose so. Dan Brady came down here not long after we did. And there was croppies at the farmhouse all the time. Talking among themselves. But I never heard what they were saying."

"Are they planning another rebellion?"

She sighed. "How would I know that? Look where I am." And she turned her eyes away, making it clear the conversation was over.

That night I slept curled up beside Lottie on the floor of the kitchen. The flagstones beneath my head were cold, despite the thick, wet heat pressing down on us. I kept my knees pulled to my chest to avoid kicking the women around me.

Before I had closed my eyes, Lottie had lifted the corner of Willie's blanket to reveal a pistol tucked into the basket.

"Here," she said. "In case anyone troubles you. Door don't lock so good. We have visitors in the night sometimes."

I stared down at the pistol, feeling an inexplicable tug of dread. "Where did you get that?"

"Stole it from Patrick."

"Does he know you have it?"

"Course not."

I closed my eyes and tried to breathe. Far from reassuring me, the sight of the pistol was unnerving. *Visitors in the night. Door don't lock so good...*

This was what I wanted, I reminded myself. This was what I had cajoled Blackwell to get. The freedom to come to Sydney Town and find Lottie, in whatever state she might be in. The freedom to get her out of it.

I wanted to believe there was hope for us. For me. For Lottie. For her son. I wanted to believe we could cobble together a decent life from the wreckage of our mistakes.

My sleep was broken and shallow, interrupted by footsteps and dreams and Willie's midnight shrieking. I was glad when the first hint of morning strained down the alley.

But I was nervous about the day ahead. And every other day after that. My only plan had been to find Lottie, and now my life stretched out hazy and uncertain. I needed to find work. Somewhere to live. But I had little idea how to go about doing either. Every day of my life, I had been told where to sleep. At least until my ticket of leave had been pressed into my hands.

"Come with me," I told Lottie, as I tried to smooth the creases from my skirts. After a night on the floor of the kitchen, they were in dire need of a wash.

"Come with you where? I've a child. I can't take him out into the world with nowhere to go."

"You can no more keep him in this place." My words came out sharper than I'd intended. I had offended her, I could tell. But surely she could see this was no place to raise a child.

"Get out of here, Nell," she said. "A ticket of leave lass can do far better."

I shook my head. "Not without you."

"If you stay, it's just another person I've got to look out for. Another person I got to worry over. I'm walking around with another man's child on my hip – no one's even going to look at me." Her eyes met mine, and her tone changed suddenly. "But you got a chance. You can make a go of things." She pressed a hand to my wrist and gave it a gentle squeeze. "Don't waste it."

I trudged out towards High Street. I wasn't abandoning Lottie, I told myself. Getting out of the Rocks and finding a way to earn some money was the best way to help her and her son. It was the best thing for all of us.

I had no thought of where I was to go from here. I was a free woman. Free for the first time in almost three years. It was a lost, shipwrecked feeling.

Here I was without a thing to anchor me. No Father. No Jonathan. No Blackwell. My entire life I had been shaped into what men wanted me to be. How was I to craft a life on my own? I felt horribly, sickeningly free. A concubine let loose in the streets of New South Wales.

A lodging house, I supposed was the logical first step. I had a few coins left in my pouch, courtesy of Blackwell's incessantly unhemmed shirts. Enough for a bed for a few nights at least.

I went back to the Whaler's Arms where I had asked after Owen.

"I need a room," I told the barman. I could hear the tremor of uncertainty in my voice and I cursed myself for it. After all I had been through, was it truly asking for a room that had my nerves rattling?

"Pound a night," he said.

I reached into my coin pouch and handed over enough to cover me until the end of the week.

For three days I traipsed through the colony, calling at houses and shopfronts in a desperate search for work. But a ticket of leave lass, I was quickly coming to learn, was no great commodity. Why would a man pay a woman to wash his laundry, clean his house, make his supper, when he could pull a lag from a prison ship and put her to work for far less cost? In a fleeting burst of optimism, I'd even called on a wealthy couple seeking a governess for their daughter. Outlined my education and my bank of unused knowledge. There had been enthusiasm in their eyes until I'd laid my ticket of leave on the table.

I slunk back to my room and perched on the bed, hands folded in my lap. My head and heart were thudding with anxiety. My coin pouch was close to empty, and I'd paid for just two more days at the Whaler's Arms. It felt like only a matter of time before I'd be on the floor of that kitchen beside Lottie.

I pulled the end from the loaf of bread I'd bought and chewed on it, short of anything else to do. I longed for a drink. Craved a few mouthfuls of the Rum Corps' dreadful liquor. When had I become a person who relied on moonshine to get me through the day?

I swallowed another mouthful of bread, trying to push the thought from my mind. Sashaying alone down to the tavern and ordering a glass of rum would be wildly inappropriate. I could barely believe I was even considering it.

But considering it I was, and before I could stop myself, I was tiptoeing down the stairs into the tavern. I peeked through the crack in the door that led to the bar. In the late afternoon the place was almost empty, just a couple of older men drinking by the window. I stepped inside before I changed my mind.

The innkeeper was leaning on the bar with account books opened in front of him. I hoped he would be too engrossed in his paperwork to judge me.

"Rum," I said, my voice impossibly small. "Or whisky, or… whatever it is you have." I dug a coin out of my pocket and sat it on the bar. A humoured smile flickered within his beard.

He filled a tin cup and sat it on the bar in front of me. "Only our finest for you, lass."

I snatched it up and scurried into a corner, trying to disappear into the long shadows that lay over the tavern. I took a gulp of the liquor. It was as dreadful as it had been in Parramatta, but I felt a hint of tension begin to slide from my shoulders. When I dared to look up, the barman was peering across the room at me.

"I don't bite," he chuckled, nodding to the rows of empty stools in front of him. I hesitated. I didn't want to be judged. But I was beginning to drown in my own chaotic thoughts. I knew the company would do me good. I carried my drink over to the bar and slid onto one of the stools.

The barman sat his pencil in the fold of his account book. "You find the fellow you were looking for then? Mr Owen?"

I sipped my drink. "I did. For all the good that did me."

"What you doing here?" he asked.

"Looking for work."

"His Majesty send you over?"

I felt my cheeks colour. I knew well I did not need to answer – what would I be doing in this place if I hadn't been hauled out on a prison ship? As a convict woman I was barely a novelty, of course. But I couldn't shake the shame of it.

Avoiding the barman's eyes, my gaze drifted over the scrawled numbers on his ledger. I pointed to one of the sums at the bottom of the page.

"That's wrong."

He chuckled. "You'll forgive me if I don't trust a lag to do my books."

I straightened my shoulders indignantly. "You've not

carried the two," I told him. "You're out by twenty pounds."

With a look of reluctance, he glanced down at the page. Irritation flickered across his eyes as he scrawled the correction on his ledger. "I was never one for arithmetic," he said, cheeks reddening beneath his beard.

I couldn't help a smile of self-satisfaction.

In the morning, he found me in the kitchen of the tavern. I was hovering by the fire, waiting for the kettle to boil.

He folded his thick arms across his chest. "Papers?"

I raised my eyebrows. "Pardon?"

"Your paperwork," he said impatiently. "I need to see it. Make sure you ain't a runaway."

I pulled out my ticket of leave and shoved it into his hand. "Why've you decided now that I'm a runaway?" I asked. "Because you're annoyed I corrected your arithmetic?"

He said nothing, just skimmed over my paperwork. He folded it messily and held it back out to me. Gave a half-satisfied grunt.

"Can you pour a drink?" he asked.

I hesitated. Was he offering me work? "I can do your books," I ventured boldly.

He snorted. "I already told you, I don't want no government lass rifling around in my accounts. I said, can you pour a drink?"

I allowed myself a smile. It had been worth a try. I thought of the woman from the factory who had poured drinks at the tavern in Parramatta. Never in my life had I imagined myself doing such a thing. But how hard could it be?

"Of course I can," I said.

The barman nodded. "Good," he said gruffly. "A lass behind the bar gets men through the door." He turned to leave, then looked back at me. "Name's Charlie," he said. "I don't like laziness and I keep things clean. And I don't need no help doing my books. You can start tonight."

I smiled to myself as I lifted the kettle. Hoped Charlie's accounting errors would fall in my favour.

CHAPTER TWENTY-THREE

"He is under no obligation to maintain her longer than she suits his inclination. There arises a very heavy national expense, as these women with their children are constantly likely to be turned out of doors; poor, friendless and forsaken."

Rev. Samuel Marsden
A Few Observations on the Situation of the Female Convict in New South Wales
1808-1817

The next morning, I went straight to the Rocks. I'd spent the evening behind the bar at the Whaler's Arms, learning my way around barrels of the Rum Corps' finest, and pouring ale that looked remarkably like dishwater. I'd not made it to bed until long after midnight.

But I'd woken with the dawn, eager to tell Lottie of the position I'd secured. To tell her she and Willie were welcome to stay with me for as long as they needed it. Tell her she had a chance at a life outside that filthy kitchen. Somehow, I would see to it that we both survived this place.

I found her on the street outside the kitchen, dunking her shift in a washtub. She was barefoot in dirt-streaked skirts, brown hair hanging loose on her shoulders. Willie was bleating in the basket beside her. At the sight of me, she stood up from the tub and wiped her hands on her apron.

"I've found work," I told her. "A place to stay. There's room enough for you and Willie. You ought to—"

"Don't be mad," she cut in. "I'll not think of it."

"Why not?" I'd not for a second imagined she might refuse.

She planted a hand on her hip. Her eyes held nothing but bitterness.

"What am I to do all day?" she demanded, swatting a platoon of flies away from her face. "Sit around in your room while you earn a living?" She shook her head. "No. I'm not a cause for your charity. However much you might think it."

I stood in the middle of the alley, clenching my teeth at her stubbornness. I debated whether to argue.

Think of your son, I wanted to say. But I held my words. In spite of, or perhaps because of all life had thrown at her, Lottie had a pride about her. A pride, I saw then, that would not let her accept charity from a *sasanaigh*. No matter how well meaning.

"And you'll not change your mind?"

"No, Nell," she said, hand on her hip. "I'll not change my mind."

Dejected as I was, a part of me understood. Being a cause for Blackwell's charity had stung. I'd not stopped to think I might be cutting Lottie as deeply. And what could I do but give a nod of understanding and head back towards the tavern?

Sydney Town was refreshing. In Parramatta, I'd seen the same stale faces walk the streets each day, added to only once or twice, when a new shipment of convicts had come crawling up the river.

But Sydney reminded me there was more to this world than the sand and stone of New South Wales. The Whaler's Arms was full of merchants, of sailors, of settlers with big dreams. They spoke of their new homes and their old, raged against the governor, the Rum Corps, the English, the Irish. I listened in on as many conversations as I could as I wiped tables and refilled glasses.

Did you hear young Bobby's been pardoned?
Can't get a thing to grow in this soil.
Bligh's behaving like God himself…

Soldiers and farmers, and emancipists celebrating with one too many ales. Sailors with hands that felt like tree bark when they pressed their coins into my palm.

I knew what the sailors were after, of course. Their eyes would gleam as they leaned across the bar to order their drinks, hands lingering against mine when I passed them their change. I was always quick to let them know I was no good for anything but putting a drink in their hands. But sometimes, when the tavern was quiet, I would listen to them speak. Hear them tell tale after tale of their travels. I needed to hear of that faraway world. Needed that reminder that we weren't all alone out here.

"London," I said to one. "Have you been to London?"

The sailor was older, with grey streaks dashed through his dark hair. Had a round, rough voice that spoke of coasts and cliffs and wrecks. He said:

"Aye. Of course. Was in London not a year ago."

"Tell me of it," I said wistfully, as though the place were paradise and not the hell I'd sailed out of with blood on my boots. I rested my chin in my palm and listened as he told me of strikes against the wars in Europe. Of the gas lights that had lit up Pall Mall as though it were morning.

"And this place?" I dared to ask. "What do they think of us back home?"

The sailor chuckled. "Every hot-blooded man has a mind to visit. They say them factory lasses are a good thing."

As I had learned in Parramatta, we lived in a deeply divided colony. The Whaler's Arms saw its fair share of croppies, who huddled in the back corners and murmured beneath clouds of pipe smoke. Though I never saw Owen or Brady among them, I was constantly on edge at the prospect of another uprising. I'd sidle past tables in hope of catching fragments of English. The murmured Gaelic made it all too easy to imagine them plotting their next rebellion. I felt a pang of shame as I thought back to the two croppies in Parramatta. Tied to the triangle for speaking their own tongue.

But while the croppies kept to themselves, the tension among the Englishmen was no less stark. Most evenings, the Whaler's rang with terse voices as the farmers and enlisted men argued the way forward.

"Would you listen to them?" Charlie snorted, passing a glass of rum to the older gentleman sitting at the bar. "Harping on like fishwives."

I peered over at the throng of men. Tonight there was plenty of them; half in their lobster coats, the others in the faded shirts and breeches of the men who worked the land. "What are they arguing about?"

"Love for Governor Bligh," said Charlie. "Or lack of it. Redcoats are losing their mind cos he's taking away their liquor stills." He looked over at the gentleman he had just served. "What do you make of all this, Flynn?"

The older man chuckled. "Heaven forbid we stop trading in liquor like savages and use the grain for bread instead."

I'd grown to like Arthur Flynn, with his neat frock coats and polished boots, a far cry from the mud-caked lags who usually tramped through this place. In the three weeks since I'd begun working at the Whaler's, he'd appeared on several occasions, always with a kind word for me.

Charlie nodded at the glass in Flynn's hand. "Didn't see you coming in here and ordering a loaf of bread."

Flynn chuckled. "Quite right. But all things in moderation."

"Get rid of the rum stills like Bligh wants and this place'll fall apart," said Charlie. "We're in a colony of drunkards."

Flynn lifted his glass. "Exactly. And if we're to flourish, then that must change. Bligh's done damn fine work here, if you ask me. Half of us holding land would have lost everything we had if it weren't for him. The Rum Corps would have bought our farms for pennies and ended up with this entire place to their name."

"My business is flourishing just nicely, thank you very

much," said Charlie. "It's all those fine drunkards that are keeping me in business."

I smiled.

Flynn turned, catching me listening. He gave me a warm smile. "Good evening, Miss Marling."

I'd never bothered to correct him; to tell him I was no *miss*; that I carried my dead husband's name, as well as his guilt. There seemed little point.

He nodded to the corner of the bar where one of the men was gesturing wildly. A fat cloud of cigar smoke hung over his head. "Have you ever seen such a pitiful display? Those men ought to be ashamed of themselves, behaving this way in front of a woman."

"I think she quite likes these pitiful displays," said Charlie. "Always with her ear to the ground, ain't you, Nell? Always keen to know what's happening." He winked at me. "She thinks we don't notice."

Flynn chuckled. "Is that so?"

"Here." Charlie took a fresh ash tray from beneath the counter and handed it to me. "You want to catch an earful you can take this over to them."

I took the ashtray and set it on the men's table, collecting the old one with its overflowing cigar butts, and as many empty cannikins as I could bundle into my arms. Oblivious to my arrival, the men continued talking over one another.

"Watch your damn mouth, boy," one of the soldiers was hissing. "Or you'll be at the coalmines before you know it and that farm of yours'll be nothing but dust."

"It's as it always is," I said, as I returned to the bar and dumped the empty cannikins in the trough. "The Rum Corps are the ones with the power. The rest of us just go where they lead us."

Flynn emptied his glass and took his top hat from the counter, pressing it on over his thick grey hair. "They'll be pulled into line soon enough. Bligh's cut from far too strong a cloth to let them keep up their run of the place." He bobbed his head at me as he made his way towards the door. "Take care, my dear. Keep that ear to the ground. You never know what you might hear."

I smiled, turning back to the trough to scrub out the empty glasses. The door creaked and thudded as several of the men left, a momentary quiet falling over the bar.

"I remember you," said a voice behind me. I whirled around to see a young soldier sliding onto a bar stool. "You're a Parramatta lass. Blackwell's lodger."

The words made heat blaze through me. I both did and didn't want to be Blackwell's.

"How d'you get down here then?" he asked.

"I have my paperwork." I reached into my pocket. "If you wish to see it, I—"

He waved a hand dismissively. "'S'all right. I was just making conversation." He slid off his jacket. "Ale, if you please."

I poured him a glass and sat it on the counter. The soldier's face had a faint familiarity to it. I remembered him standing on the edge of the green while the two Irishmen from the chain gang were flogged. "Lieutenant Harper," I said.

He nodded. "That's right."

"You're a long way from Parramatta."

"I've come downriver with the fishing party," he said. "We're to head back up north in the morning."

"And you managed a decent haul?"

"There's fine kingfish in Sydney Cove," he said, gulping down his ale. "Government stores'll be well stocked when we return."

There was far more I wanted to ask him about, of course. The rebels and their uprising. The rebuilding of the burned-out factory, and whether the women from the spinning wheels had roofs above their heads. Above all, I wanted to ask him about Blackwell.

My missing him was a deep ache inside me.

I opened my mouth to speak; nothing but casual questions of course. *Is he well? Will you pass on my regards?*

But it felt dangerous. Felt as though speaking of him would stoke a fire that needed to burn out. Perhaps even then, hidden somewhere at the back of my mind, I knew that having Blackwell in my life would destroy me.

Later that week I went back to the Rocks. It had been almost a fortnight since I'd last seen Lottie, and each night I fell asleep thinking of her crammed into that squalid kitchen with her baby in the basket beside her.

I made my way down the alley and peeked through the door into the kitchen. Lottie was sitting on the floor with her back to the wall, Willie held to her breast. Healthy, as far as I could tell. As safe as could be hoped for.

I hurried away before she could catch sight of me, and wove through the alleys towards the market. Carts were crammed into the streets, loaded with potatoes, with cabbages, with hessian bags of grain. An enormous brown horse nudged my shoulder as I passed.

I bought a loaf of bread and hunk of cheese, and tucked them into my basket.

A faint tug on my skirt. I whirled around and caught a small hand reaching into my pocket. I grabbed the wrist of the young, dark-haired girl. I guessed her no more than nine or ten. Her eyes widened as I tightened my grip.

"I didn't take nothing," she said hurriedly. "I swear it. Not a thing." She spoke with a forced confidence but I could see the fear in her wide blue eyes. I loosened my grip a little.

"What do you need the money for?" I asked. "Food?"

She nodded.

I let go of her wrist and reached into my coin pouch. Handed her a couple of shillings and a little of the bread.

She crammed the food into her pocket and tightened her fist around the coins. Gave me a tiny smile of thanks.

"Wait," I said, pressing a hand to her shoulder before she could dart away. "Do you have somewhere to sleep? Someone to take care of you?" I couldn't shake the fear that when night came, she would disappear into the maze of the Rocks with all the forgotten women.

She chewed her lip, as though debating whether to talk. Dark, tangled curls blew loose around her cheeks. "I lost my ma," she said.

"Where did you last see her?"

The girl didn't speak for a few moments. "Well," she said carefully. "I don't really remember." She looked down at her scuffed boots. "They took me to the Orphan School when I was little."

I let out my breath. I had heard far too many stories of the Orphan School around the spinning wheels.

I thought of the crying woman I had sat beside in my first week in Parramatta, tears falling for the child she would never see again. I thought of all the women in the factory sleeping beside their babies in the night, knowing it was only a matter of time before they were taken away. And I thought of the lifeless body I had found in the scrub on the side of the road. Because when I looked down at the young girl with my coins her hand, I saw Maggie Abbott's stark blue eyes staring back at me.

CHAPTER TWENTY-FOUR

This runaway from the Orphan School would not find her mother; of that I was certain.

I swallowed heavily. "What's your name?"

She looked over her shoulder, then back up at me. "Kate," she said finally. "Kate Abbott."

My heart was beating fast. "You've got to go back to the Orphan School, Kate. This is not a safe place to be."

She shook her head. "I finished at the school now. Got my Bible and everything. Only they sent me to work for some toff up in George Street. And he were real nasty… He… Well, he…" She faded out, her eyes back on the ground. "I don't want to say."

Something twisted in my chest. "You ran away?"

A faint nod.

My heart lurched then, for this child, traipsing through Sydney Town, looking for the mother she could barely have remembered. Walking the streets and waiting for a woman to claim her.

"All right," I said, churning through my mind for a way to tell her of Maggie's death. I had to take her back to the tavern with me. I could hardly tell her the truth standing here in the street with Sydney Town heaving around us. Who was I but a stranger with the worst of news to give her?

"Come with me," I said carefully. "I've a room at the Whaler's Arms. You can rest there. Have some food and—"

Kate whirled around suddenly and started to run. I looked over my shoulder to see what had startled her, coming face to face with a soldier. Kate's pockets, I guessed, were full of stolen coins.

I grabbed a handful of my skirts and ran in the direction she had disappeared. I wove past the market and into the narrow streets of the Rocks, my basket bumping against my hip.

I called after her, my voice bouncing between the walls of the alleys. I turned corners, climbed terraces, peered into shops and houses. But Maggie's daughter had disappeared.

By the time I made it back to the tavern, I was a dishevelled, sweaty mess. I was also late for work.

Charlie glared at me as he heaved a fresh rum barrel onto the shelf. "Don't make me regret hiring a lag."

"I'm sorry," I mumbled. I tossed my basket into the kitchen and hurried back to the bar. My stomach groaned loudly and I realised I hadn't managed to eat.

Charlie flung a dish cloth at me. "Get to work."

I poured ales and rum with my head full of Kate Abbott. I couldn't bear the thought of her roaming the streets of the Rocks, searching for her dead mother.

A part of me wished I could return to the state I had been in when I'd first been shipped out to this place; that state of pushing others' predicaments to the back of my mind. Of emptying myself of empathy.

But I couldn't do it. I ached for Lottie, for Willie, for Kate. I felt the weight of it all upon my shoulders. I felt the loneliness of the men and women shipped away from their loved ones; of men like Blackwell who had left their wives in the name of duty. I ached for the croppies tied to the triangle, and for the women sleeping between the spinning wheels on piles of tick-infested wool.

I felt suddenly exhausted. This was my life now, I realised. Even if I were somehow to obtain that magical pardon, and see the shores of England again, I knew I could never go back to my old ignorance. Couldn't turn my back while men were flogged and women died, and pretend the world was as it should be. I was powerless, yes, but I was no longer unaware. This place had changed me irrevocably.

I cringed at the sight of Arthur Flynn strolling into the bar in his top hat. I knew I looked a right mess, after tearing through the streets in search of Kate. Loose strands of hair clung to my cheeks, my plait hanging limply down my back. I knew my face had caught the sun. But at least with Flynn, I would be guaranteed an intelligent conversation, whether I looked a right mess or not. Something to take my mind off Kate and Lottie, and all the others who were pushing their way into my thoughts.

"This heat is quite dreadful, don't you think?" he said, as I poured him his customary liquor. "Although my farmhands tell me the corn crop is flourishing in this weather."

"Well," I said, pushing the cork back into the bottle. "Perhaps you ought to wish for more hot weather. I hear there are many farmers not lucky enough to have their crops flourishing."

"That's very true." He smiled. "You've a sharp mind. I like that." Flynn climbed awkwardly onto a stool at the bar. "Are you a free settler, Miss Marling?" he asked suddenly.

"No, sir," I said, cheeks colouring with shame. "I have my ticket of leave."

His gaze didn't falter. "I see." He slipped a tobacco box from his pocket and filled his pipe.

"I'm seeking a wife," he said matter-of-factly.

Short of a more astute response, I said, "Is that so?"

He used his little finger to tamp the tobacco into the pipe. "Perhaps you might consider it?"

That night, I found myself considering it.

I lay on my back, staring up at the crooked beams of the ceiling. The room was near lightless but I could hear laughter and the clop of horse hooves rising up from the street.

What would it mean for me, this elevation from concubine to wife? As I'd stood dazedly behind the bar, caught off guard by Flynn's proposal, he had outlined his credentials while puffing on his pipe. A house overlooking the sea. Fifty acres of farmland. A small household staff and eight convict workers.

I didn't love Arthur Flynn, of course. I barely knew the man. But who married for love in this place? Who married for love anywhere? Flynn was kind and studious, with a large property and a successful business. As a husband, he would be far more than I could ever have dared hope for when I'd been sent to the factory as one of the left-behind women.

As proud as I had been of finding work, I knew without a man beside me I had no security. No way of getting ahead in the world. Marrying was the only hope I had of a stable, protected life. It had been true in London and it was even more true here. Without a husband I had no way of getting ahead in the world, or of doing anything to help people like Lottie and Kate. Without a husband, I saw with grim certainty, I was nothing but a candle trying to outlast a gale.

CHAPTER TWENTY-FIVE

When Flynn returned to the Whaler's Arms two days later, I pulled my hands from the wash trough, wiped them on my apron and told him I would be most happy to become his wife. He took my water-creased hand in his, planting a small kiss on my knuckles.

"I'm very glad of it, my dear. I'm certain we will have a happy life together."

The following morning I met him outside the Whaler's, to begin a backwards courtship. Despite the heat, Flynn was dressed in a neat black frock coat, a pale blue scarf at his throat. Beneath his top hat, his grey hair was combed neatly.

Waiting beside him was an older woman in a dark dress and mobcap. She stood with her eyes down, hands folded in front of her. I smiled to myself that Flynn had thought to bring a chaperone. I had come to believe such traditions outdated after I'd been reduced to dressing under a blanket while lying on Blackwell's floor.

Though the woman's face was half hidden by her cap, I recognised her at once. Ann and I had made the journey to New South Wales together, crammed into the convict's quarters of the *Norfolk*. She'd been taken from the ship the day we arrived. Taken, I saw now, by Arthur Flynn.

Ann's eyes flickered with recognition. And resentment. She bobbed her head in greeting, but didn't say a word. I wondered if my husband-to-be knew he had walked right past me on the deck of the *Norfolk* and not looked twice.

Flynn smiled, broad and genuine, the creases beside his eyes deepening. "I'm very pleased to see you," he told me. "I thought perhaps a walk this morning? There are fine views to be had from Point Maskelyne." And off along the waterfront we went, my hand folded into my betrothed's arm, and Ann clomping along sulkily behind us.

We followed the curve of the sea up to a small stone structure on the headland. It looked out across the glistening puzzle of coves to where the Parramatta River spilled into the open ocean.

"Here now," said Flynn. "Dawes' observatory."

I peeked out from beneath my bonnet. "An observatory? How wonderful."

I thought of the astronomy lessons I'd had as a child, in which my tutor had painted a faraway world of comets and stars and planets that circled the sun. Against the limitlessness of the universe, England didn't feel quite so far away. I was surprised to find myself thinking such things. When I'd first climbed onto the *Norfolk*, New South Wales had felt more distant than the moon.

Flynn smiled as I shared my thoughts. "Well of course it feels that way," he said, as he squinted out over the ocean.

"After all, one can see the moon from the streets of London. But they cannot see New South Wales."

I felt comfortable with the man, I realised. Certainly more comfortable than I had when I'd first been betrothed to Jonathan as a mindless scrap of twenty. Back then, I'd been terrified of putting a foot wrong. I'd answered questions the way I thought he wanted them answered, and kept the less agreeable parts of my personality well hidden. But Arthur Flynn knew I had put enough feet wrong to be thrown onto a prison ship and he still wanted me as his wife.

"Where is home?" he asked me. And, "Have you ever been betrothed before?"

I told him then, in vague, broad strokes, about my marriage to Jonathan. About my inability to provide him with an heir.

Instead of the displeasure I was expecting, Flynn ventured a small smile. "Well," he said, with a shyness that was almost endearing, "perhaps you and I will have more luck."

I felt emboldened enough then to ask that that had been rolling around in the back of my mind since I'd agreed to become this man's wife.

"There's a woman I was at the factory with," I said carefully. "Her husband threw her out and she's fallen upon hard times. I wondered if perhaps there might be a position for her in your household."

A flicker of disappointment passed over Flynn's eyes. Disappointment that I'd brought my convict past to the table so early in our courtship.

He watched his feet as he walked. "I've no need for more staff."

"Please," I said, feeling my fingers tighten involuntarily around his arm. I knew, of course, that the hand I'd been dealt here in New South Wales, as in London, was better than most. And I needed to use that. But I knew Lottie was far more likely to take up my offer if it involved her working, rather than relying on charity. "She's sleeping on the floor of someone's kitchen, all crammed together with other women and children. She's—"

"You're not to go to such places," Flynn said, his voice hardening suddenly. "I'll not have my wife seen in such an area. Do you understand?"

I gritted my teeth. "Please. And I'll never ask anything of you again." I stopped walking and looked into his eyes. "It's very important to me. If you could find a way to do this one thing, I would be forever grateful."

Flynn rubbed his eyes, and for a moment, he looked an old man. He sighed, then finally gave a slight nod. "Very well. Just this once."

I slid my fingers down his arm to cover his leathery hand with mine. "Thank you."

He gave my hand a quick squeeze, managing something close to a smile.

Lottie was sleeping when I arrived at the kitchen that afternoon. She lay on her side, knees pulled to her chest and her body curled around Willie's basket. I rocked her shoulder gently.

She opened her eyes. "What are you doing here?" She got slowly to her feet, twisting the stiffness out of her shoulders.

"I'm to be married," I told her. I knew there was little point sidestepping the issue.

"Are you now?"

I pushed past her coldness. "There's a place for you," I said. "At my husband's farmhouse. Work. Shelter."

Lottie planted a hand on her hip. "I've told you before, Nell. I'm not one to accept charity. When are you going to get that into your head?"

"This is not charity," I argued. "There's work for you." I let out my breath in frustration. "I just want you and Willie to be safe."

"You got to prove yourself, don't you?" Lottie demanded. "You got to make sure everyone knows how well you've done for yourself."

"You truly think that's what this is about?"

"Isn't it?" A cold laugh. "You fell down to our level for a time, but you just got to show us all how much better than us you are." She stared at me for a long, wordless moment before turning away and shaking her head. Frustration burned through me.

"If you change your mind," I said tersely, "Mr Flynn's farm is at the top end of Bridge Street. Out behind the new Government House. We're to be married next Wednesday."

Lottie cut me with cold eyes.

I turned at the sound of footsteps behind me. Heard my sharp intake of breath. Patrick Owen stood in the doorway, arms folded across his chest. His sharp blue eyes bore into me.

"Well, well. Nellie *na sasanaigh*. Dan'll be pleased to hear you're floating around." He turned to Lottie. "What in hell is she doing here?"

"She's leaving," said Lottie, not looking at me.

Owen took a step towards me, without even a glance at his sleeping son. "How's Lieutenant Blackwell faring?"

"I've no idea," I said stiffly. I hated the sound of Blackwell's name on his lips. "I've had nothing to do with him since I left Parramatta."

Owen looked me up and down, as though trying to determine whether I was lying. I held his gaze, despite the hot shiver it sent through me.

"You've a new life here," I said. "Why not leave the past where it is?"

He took a step closer. "Is that all the lives of a few bog-trotters is worth to you, Nellie? You think we ought to just forget?"

I said nothing.

Finally, he turned away and spoke to Lottie in Irish. She picked up the baby and turned to follow Owen out of the kitchen. I grabbed her arm.

"Where is he taking you?"

"Back to his farm."

"He's taking you home?"

"For a time."

"What do you mean 'for a time'? What does he want?"

Lottie looked at me witheringly. "What do you think he wants?"

"And when he's finished with you? He sends you back here?"

Lottie didn't reply. Owen called her name.

"You can't go," I said, not releasing my grip on her wrist.

"Jesus Nell, would you mind your own damn business? What do you know about any of this?" She sighed, then lowered her voice. "He's the only chance I got of a little security. One day he's going to realise he was wrong to have let us go."

I could hear the uncertainty in her words.

"He is not your only chance," I hissed. "Flynn has work for you."

Her eyes flashed with impatience.

"All right," I said hurriedly, before she could speak. "Don't take the position. But please don't go with Owen."

"I have to," she said. "You wouldn't understand."

Lottie was wrong. I understood. I knew what it was to follow a man down the murkiest of paths for the sake of a little security.

And so, standing there in the kitchen, with Patrick Owen in the doorway, I told her of Jonathan's coining business and the way my desperate need to please my husband had almost led me to the gallows.

Something passed across Lottie's eyes. It was the first time I had told anyone I was not just a tale of stolen bread. The first time I had admitted I had been sent here for life.

Lottie's lips parted. The she looked up and down at my neatly stitched skirts. At the leather boots buckled at my ankles.

"Seven years," she said bitterly. "You told me you got seven years for thieving. And now I learn you're a lifer."

"I'm sorry," I said. I knew there was no excuse for my lies. I'd just been too embarrassed to tell the truth.

Lottie snorted. "And yet you seem to be doing just fine

for yourself now."

She pulled free of my grip and followed Owen down the alley, leaving me standing alone in the corner of the kitchen.

CHAPTER TWENTY-SIX

On our second tramp around the settlement, Flynn asked, "What was your crime?"

The question was put simply, as though he were asking about the weather. But there was enough forced casualness in it for me to know he had been trying to bring himself to spit out the words.

I couldn't blame him, of course. He was to sleep beside me in the night. For all he knew, I'd been shipped out here for murder.

As I told my sorry tale, I heard myself return to a victim, coerced into counterfeiting by my scheming husband. I felt oddly outside myself. When I'd first told this story to the magistrate in London, I'd clung to my victimhood, to my belief I'd been so grossly wronged by the world around me. Now the memory of my naivety just made me angry.

But I also knew what a precious thing it was to find a good man to marry here, and I felt instinctively that that naivety would tug at the sensibilities of fine upstanding Arthur Flynn. If I had to be a victim in order to please my betrothed, then that was what I would do.

I looked up at Flynn with wide eyes. "I was a fool," I told him. "And I was too afraid to turn my back on my husband."

He gave me a small smile. "We all make mistakes. Besides, what hope did you have with a man like that in your life?"

And I nodded along, *yes, indeed, a hardened criminal, the worst of men*, feeling more than a small pull of guilt for my murdered husband lying in his grave.

Flynn covered my hand with his. "I'd very much like you to see my property," he said, and I felt my shoulders sink with relief at the change of subject. "I could show you around the place. You could see your rooms. With Ann in attendance of course."

I smiled. "I'd like that very much."

Flynn beamed, patting my hand again. "Excellent. Tomorrow then. I'll have one of my workers come to collect you with the trap."

And he steered me back in the direction of the Whaler's Arms, Ann wheeling around to follow.

When I stepped through the door of the tavern, I froze. Lieutenant Blackwell was sitting at the table closest to the door. I felt a jolt in my chest. His hair was slightly overgrown beneath his cocked hat, the arctic blue of his eyes stark against his tanned skin.

At the sight of me, he stood, his face giving nothing away.

Flynn glanced at Blackwell, then back at me. "Is there

trouble?" he asked the lieutenant.

"There's no trouble," I garbled. "Lieutenant Blackwell is… He was kind enough to offer me lodgings in Parramatta." I felt my cheeks blaze. "Lieutenant, this is my betrothed, Arthur Flynn."

"You're to be married?" A flicker of surprise passed over Blackwell's eyes, but he blinked it away quickly.

"I am," I managed. "Yes." My mouth felt impossibly dry.

Blackwell's jaw tightened as the men shook hands. I could tell from Flynn's welcoming smile he had no thought of what a man usually demanded of his lodger in Parramatta.

Blackwell turned away from Flynn and looked me square in the eyes. "It's good to see you, Eleanor."

I tried to swallow. I wasn't sure the emotions roiling inside me could be described as good. "Lieutenant Harper told you how to find me?"

He nodded.

A stilted silence hung between us, punctuated by Charlie thumping a liquor barrel onto the shelf.

"Well then," Flynn said brassily. "A drink then perhaps? What do you say, Lieutenant?"

Before either of us could reply, Flynn was herding us towards a larger table in the centre of the tavern. Ann followed his lead, plopping neatly into a chair between Blackwell and I.

Flynn hovered over me. "Tea for you, my dear?"

"This is a tavern," I reminded him. "Tea isn't on offer." If I was going to stumble my way through this debacle I was going to need something far more mind-numbing than tea.

He waved a dismissive hand. "Nonsense. I'm sure Charlie will be quite happy to boil up a kettle for you. Won't you, Charlie?"

He grinned. "I've heard your wife-to-be has a liking for things a little stronger."

I shot him a glare.

Flynn smiled thinly at Charlie. "Tea will be just fine."

With my betrothed at the bar, I turned to Blackwell. "Why are you in Sydney?" My voice was low and far more conspiratorial than I had intended. Ann's eyes darted between us.

"I've completed my term of duty," he told me. "I'm entitled to a discharge."

In spite of myself, my stomach plunged. "You're going back to England."

He had brought me a sense of security, I realised then. Even with the Parramatta River between us, it had been reassuring to know Blackwell was in the colony with me. Reassuring to know I had the eye of such a powerful man.

I knew I was being foolish. I was to become another man's wife. Blackwell was another woman's husband. Neither of us had a place in the other's thoughts.

I forced a smile. "Your wife will be very pleased to see you, I'm sure."

No response.

"So you've come to say goodbye."

He looked at me with that infuriating expressionlessness I had come to know so well. I felt a flicker of annoyance. Why had he bothered coming to see me if he was to be so closed up?

"Yes," he said finally, as though sensing my irritation. "I suppose I have."

"When will you leave?" I tried to keep my voice light.

"I believe the next ship leaves in a fortnight."

"A fortnight?" I repeated. "And why did you come to see me now?"

His lips parted, as though caught off guard by my question. "Because I wished to see you," he said finally. "Forgive me. It was out of place. I—"

He stopped abruptly as Flynn reappeared at the table, two cannikins of rum in his hand. He set one in front of Blackwell, then slid into the chair beside me.

Flynn lifted his cup. "Well then, a toast perhaps? To this fair colony."

Blackwell smiled thinly. "And to your happy marriage." He gave me a sideways glance.

I suddenly had no idea what to do with my hands. I willed Charlie to hurry the hell up so I could at least hold my teacup.

Flynn beamed. "Indeed." He tossed back a mouthful of liquor.

Blackwell set his cannikin back on the table. His presence seemed to fill the room, and squeeze the air from my lungs.

"You're stationed in Parramatta then?" Flynn asked, crossing one leg over the other.

"I was," said Blackwell. "For the past five years."

"And do you have many women from the factory lodge with you?"

"No." Blackwell held his gaze. "Very few." He looked too tall for the chair.

Flynn took another mouthful. "I see."

"Lieutenant Blackwell is to return to England in a fortnight," I said, far too loudly.

Flynn's face lit up. "Really? How wonderful." I could tell his excitement came mostly from having found a conversation topic that did not revolve around my time in Parramatta. Out came a barrage of questions that felt as though he had prepared them in advance. Which ship was he travelling on? Which route was to be taken? Was he to be deployed to Europe on his return? Blackwell answered them all as though he were being quizzed by a magistrate.

"Tea for you, Nell," Charlie bellowed across the bar. Clumsily, I made to stand, but Flynn pressed a hand to my wrist, keeping me in place.

"Ann will fetch it," he said.

His housekeeper shuffled to the bar and returned with a tin cup filled with lukewarm tea. She slapped it down in front of me. I peered at it in disinterest.

"And you've a place to stay in the meantime, Lieutenant?" asked Flynn. "I assume you've somewhere more appropriate than this fine establishment."

Blackwell gave a thin smile. "I've lodgings at the home of a colleague. He and his wife are due to leave for Van Diemen's Land shortly."

"Ah," said Flynn, his face lighting with recognition. "Captain Grant's house perhaps?"

"That's right."

He chuckled. "I've been hearing about this little jaunt from Grant over cards for months now. At these very tables, in fact. He says the farmland's better down that way. I told him his wife would take one look at the settlement and curl up in horror. I've heard this place feels like Paris compared to how primitive things are down there."

I turned my teacup around in my hands. Ann shifted on her chair, making it squeak loudly. I wondered if I ought to offer her my tea.

"Give Captain Grant my regards," Flynn continued. "I regret that he's to miss our wedding celebrations."

"Of course." Blackwell tossed back the last of his liquor and stood a little too abruptly. "I'll not keep you. I only came to say goodbye." His eyes met mine. "And to wish you all the best."

My throat tightened.

What was I to say? How did you farewell a person you knew you were never going to see again? I couldn't bear the finality of it. I looked up at him. It felt as though Flynn and Ann were watching me; every nuance of my face under scrutiny.

"Have a safe journey home," I managed, my voice sounding hollow and completely unlike myself.

"Thank you." Blackwell opened his mouth to say more, then stopped. I could tell he too had no thought of how to proceed. "Take care."

I swallowed heavily, forcing down a sudden swell of tears. "And you."

Blackwell gave a short nod. And then he was gone.

The hollowness of it stayed with me into the afternoon. When Flynn and Ann returned to the farmhouse, I took a broom up to my room, biding time until work started that evening. I tried to focus on my cleaning, tried to let the rhythm of the sweeping still the commotion of my thoughts. I knew I was being foolish. How lucky I was to have a man like Arthur Flynn as my husband-to-be. But I couldn't help feeling empty.

I leant the broom up against the wall and picked up my empty wash basin for refilling. I trudged out of the tavern and headed for Tank Stream, waving wildly at the flies as they circled my face. The heat was making my skin itch beneath my stays and I felt inexplicably close to tears.

As I stepped onto the muddy bank of the stream, an arm grabbed me from behind. I thrashed against my captor and whirled around, coming face to face with Patrick Owen and Dan Brady. My washbin thudded dully into the mud.

I knew it no coincidence they had appeared the same day as Blackwell. Had they seen him at the tavern? Or had they simply caught word he was in Sydney? Assumed they might find him with me? I had little doubt Lottie had told Owen where I was living.

I knew what they wanted, of course. A chance to go after Blackwell without the rest of the Rum Corps around. A clean shot out of the confines of Parramatta. I was sure even Owen knew his immunity didn't stretch to the murder of an officer.

"He's not here," I said, before they could speak. Instantly, I regretted my words. I ought to have feigned ignorance, given them no hint that I knew anything of the lieutenant.

"Where is he?" asked Owen.

"Do you honestly imagine I would tell you?"

He took a step towards me and I stumbled back towards the water, the edge of the stream licking my boots. I forced myself to hold Owen's gaze. My heart was thundering. But I knew he intended to scare the information out of me and I refused to let him win.

"How dare you lay a hand on me," I hissed.

Owen gave a short chuckle. "Would you listen to her ordering us around?" He turned back to me, eyes close to mine. "Have you forgotten who you are, Nellie? You're nothing but a factory lag."

"Leave me alone," I said, my voice rattling.

Owen grabbed my arm again. I heard myself gasp as his fingers dug into my flesh.

"Blackwell does not just get to walk away," he hissed. "Not after what he did to my family. Tell me where he is."

I yanked out of his grip. "I've no idea where he is."

I grabbed my empty washbin and hurried back to the tavern.

Back in my room, I paced.

A fortnight until Blackwell's ship left. And the rebels knew he was here. In the anonymity of Sydney Town, it would be all too easy for Owen to pull the trigger. All too easy for him to emerged unscathed from yet another murder.

Lieutenant Blackwell does not just get to walk away.

I had to warn him.

CHAPTER TWENTY-SEVEN

"I snuck a little rum in that tea for you," said Charlie when I came down to the bar. "But you didn't even drink it. Highly ungrateful if you ask me."

"Do you know how to find Captain Grant?" I asked, pushing past his jibe. I prayed he hadn't overheard our conversation in the tavern earlier. Prayed he didn't know I was seeking out Blackwell.

Charlie frowned. "You all right, Nell? Something upset you?"

"Captain Grant," I pushed. "He plays cards here with Arthur Flynn. Do you know where he lives?"

"I know where everyone lives."

I raised my eyebrows. "Except Patrick Owen."

Charlie chuckled. "I know where everyone important lives."

I managed a small smile at that. Nodded impatiently as he rattled off directions, and then I was out of the tavern before he could ask questions.

Grant's property was not far from the Whaler's; the house guarded by a high wooden fence with a gate cut into one corner. I stood for a moment, hesitating. Would it be wildly inappropriate for me to just knock on the door? I was beginning to lose sense of what was right and wrong in this place. All the lines I knew had been blurred.

I clicked open the gate and stepped into a neatly manicured garden. Saplings surrounded a small, circular pond, grass hemmed with roses that had withered and browned in the heat.

And there was Blackwell, leaning against the house and lifting a pipe to his lips. He was without his jacket and waistcoat, shirtsleeves rolled to his elbows. His dark hair hung over one eye. He turned suddenly, catching sight of me. And at once he was striding towards me, the pipe left smoking on the garden path. The deliberateness of his movements made my heart jump into my throat.

"I know I shouldn't be here," I said. "I just—"

He grabbed my hand and led me around the side of the house, where the fence was covered with white-flowering vines. We slipped through the door and wove through empty servants' quarters, before climbing a wooden staircase to the second floor. Blackwell led me into the guestroom and locked the door behind us.

Before I could speak, he reached out and pulled me into a tight embrace. I felt myself sink against him, my arms sliding around his waist.

I stepped back, my hands tight around his bare forearms. "Captain Grant and his wife have left?"

"No. Not until tonight." His voice was low. "But they're

in the front wing. They needn't know you're here."

I nodded. Standing there before the tall, wide bulk of him, the idea that the rebels could touch him seemed almost laughable.

"Patrick Owen found me at Tank Stream," I said. "He must have caught word you'd visited me. Followed me from the tavern."

Blackwell's eyes darkened. "Did he hurt you?"

I shook my head. "No. But I'm worried he'll come after you." I swallowed. "I know he wants you dead." The words caught in my throat. Speaking them aloud made the brutality of it sting.

I needed to know the truth, I realised then. I needed to hear Blackwell's version of what had happened in that little hut near Squires' inn. In two weeks' time, he was to disappear on the sea, and all I would be left with would be Owen's tall tales.

"Patrick Owen says you killed his family," I said. "In their kitchen. After the uprising at Castle Hill."

I saw something pass over Blackwell's eyes.

"I told him I knew it was a lie."

But right then, I questioned it. Had I allowed myself to love a man who had done such things? For that was the other realisation that swung towards me as I stood there holding his gaze; that I was irrevocably in love with Adam Blackwell. I felt like a fool. I had no place to love such a man. All it would do was break me.

His lips parted. "You think it a lie?"

I stepped away from him, and stared at the polished floorboards. Blackwell moved towards the bed, the floorboards groaning loudly beneath his weight. He sat on the edge. Laced his fingers together and looked up to meet my eyes.

His story of the uprising was not the same as Owen's. There were no heroes; not the rebels, nor the Rum Corps. Just an impassive retelling of the rebels' attack on the government farm at Castle Hill, and of the way they had beaten down their overseers. Of their advance towards Parramatta, and the way the army had so quickly responded. A midnight march to meet the Irishmen. The surrounding of the rebels at nearby Rouse Hill. Firing lines formed to cut the croppies down.

His story emotionless, a thing of duty.

I thought of the rows of crosses in the clearing outside Parramatta. That day, I had seen emotion in Blackwell's eyes. When he had thought no one was looking, he had let it slip above the surface.

"And afterwards?" I asked.

"We were sent out to hunt down the rebels who got away." He spoke calmly, evenly. "We were told to find every one of them. Told that if we let them live, they'd overturn the order we'd created in this place. Undo everything we'd worked for.

"I found the Owens' hut out behind Squires' inn. Three of them were hiding there. I saw the stolen muskets up against the wall."

"You killed them."

"Yes," he said. "I did."

I closed my eyes for a moment. It was not surprise I was feeling. Not shock. Just a quiet acceptance that I had known this all along. I had seen the guilt within him the day I had followed him to the rebels' graveyard.

"You speak of it so calmly," I said finally.

Blackwell looked up at me. "How would you have me speak of it?"

I tilted my head, trying to see behind his eyes. "Do you regret what you did?"

"I was doing my job. Doing as I'd been instructed."

"That's not what I asked you."

For the first time, I understood Owen's hatred. But I also understood my own love. It was deep and unyielding. Unmoved by the blood on Blackwell's hands. And this, I realised, was my biggest betrayal of Lottie. I saw then how right she was to have refused to share things with me.

I would never see things from her point of view. How could I? Not only was I an Englishwoman of a far higher class, I would give my life for the man who had pulled the trigger.

There was regret in him; I could hear it in his voice, could see it in his eyes. But perhaps it showed too much weakness for him to speak of it, especially in front of a government lass. Perhaps it went against everything he had committed to when he had taken on his commission. Went against everything this place expected of him.

"I saw you at the graveyard outside Parramatta," I said. "Do you go there often?"

He let out his breath and ran his fingers through his hair. "You ask a lot of questions."

"What of the Owens' cottage? Do you ever go there? To pay your respects?"

Something flickered across Blackwell's face. The look in his eyes told me I was right; that he had returned to that cottage, as he had returned to the rebels' graves. Seeking what? Forgiveness? Absolution? The thought of it filled me with dread. If Owen or any of his remaining family were to discover the lieutenant alone at the cottage, he would likely not return.

I took a step towards him. Placed my hands on the broad plane of his shoulders and looked down to meet his eyes. He reached up, tracing gentle fingers along my bare forearm. I shivered.

"It's best that you leave," he said, but his hand slid around me as he spoke. Came to rest on the small of my back. A gentle pressure, guiding me closer.

His body felt heavy against mine, at once both weighted down and liberated at having spoken of the cottage. I wanted to give him a little in return.

I drew in a breath and sat beside him on the bed. "I was transported for high treason," I said. "I ran counterfeit coins across London."

I made no mention of Jonathan. I wanted to claim my crimes, just as Blackwell had done.

He said nothing. Just gave a nod that made my guilt fall away. He tucked a strand of hair behind my ear and ran his thumb along my cheek.

And then his lips were on mine. This was not what I had come for, I told myself. I had come to warn him about Owen. But a part of me knew that a lie. I had also come for that goodbye I had been deprived of at the tavern.

My mouth opened beneath his, deepening the kiss. My hands in his hair, pulling him towards me.

For all his urgency, Blackwell was hesitant, uncertain, his fingers sliding to the hooks at the front of my bodice, then pausing there, as if awaiting permission. I reached down to pull apart the first hook, sighing against his lips as his fingers slid beneath.

I pulled his shirt up over his head with a fervour I didn't recognise. Perhaps this place had corrupted me. Perhaps I had grown to fit the label the colony had saddled me with.

I didn't care. At least not there in the humid, sea-scented air, with Blackwell's breath on my skin.

It was me who loosened the last laces of my stays and let them ghost against the floor. Me who lay back on the bed, pulling him down over me. My hands slid up and down his back, over his shoulders, the backs of his thighs. I could feel the tension draining from his body; replaced with something far more urgent, more temporal.

"I missed you," he said, close to my ear. "I missed having you in my home. I missed seeing you each morning."

In the half-light, he pulled my shift up over my head, his lips moving over the pale skin of my shoulders, coarse fingers finding the warmth between my legs. I heard myself murmur, and pulled him down over me so he might trap the sound within his lips.

Was I marking myself as a loose woman? Perhaps. But the rest of the world couldn't see inside this room. The only man who knew this side of me was to disappear on the seas. I dug my fingers into the hot skin on the back of his neck, wanting to mark him as I was marking myself.

And his broad, tanned body was over mine; covering me, consuming me, filling me. I felt that barrier around him splinter as he groaned into my ear, worked his lips along my neck. Felt his control slipping and shattering as we moved together in the hatched sunlight spilling across the bed. The shame was there at the back of my mind. But I felt far too alive to care.

I lay in the shadows, feeling his heart beating against my ear. His arms were warm against my bare skin. I felt like all the things Reverend Marsden had accused us of being.

And I thought of her then, beautiful Sophia, with her doe eyes and her perfect curls, and I felt her husband's body shift beneath me.

Look what I had become.

I was always doomed to fail. I had been playing opposing games – on one hand, challenging myself not to give in, not to fall for him, not to succumb and be that weak, indecent concubine the female register had labelled me as. And at the same time, I had sought power. Tempted Blackwell to forget his wife, his God, his morality. Somewhere along the line I had fallen in love.

A losing game.

Blackwell's breathing grew steady and rhythmic, his chest rising and falling beneath my head.

I watched him in his sleep. I wanted to hold him, love him, take away the guilt and regret he refused to speak of. Take away the memories of that bloodstained cottage near Squire's inn. Perhaps that made me as bad as him. Perhaps those men who had fallen deserved more than for the memory of them to be taken away.

I climbed from the bed, careful not to wake him. I had to leave. I was due back at the tavern. And I needed to leave Grant's house before anyone realised I was here.

I took my shift from the floor and slid it over my head. I had left a thread of coppery hair on Blackwell's pillow. I stared at it as I laced my stays.

I felt an emptiness inside me. Now the line had been crossed, what did we have left for each other? He had Sophia, I had Arthur Flynn. I felt certain that when I stepped out of that room, I would never see him again.

I crossed the room, each step carefully placed to avoid the creak of the floorboards. I slipped out into the hall without looking back, that coil of red hair stark upon his pillow.

CHAPTER TWENTY-EIGHT

I crept down the stairs, each footstep carefully placed to avoid making a sound. Eyes down, I headed towards the empty servants' quarters. But as I stepped into the hallway, I came face to face with a tall, well-built man, whose grey eyes flickered in surprise. A regular fixture at the Whaler's Arms.

We stared at each other for a long second. I knew there was no need for questions. He had seen me come down from Blackwell's room.

There was a silent understanding between us that this was to remain wordless. Unspoken. I turned abruptly, and disappeared out of the house.

The shame gathered over me as I made my way back to the tavern. I had been caught as a concubine. Caught behaving as what Marsden's register had made me out to be.

But beneath the shame, there was a hint of relief. The afternoon I had spent with Blackwell would allow me to move on. Allow us both to. He, back to England where

Sophia was waiting. And I could marry Arthur Flynn, without feeling caught in an unfinished chapter. I knew such a marriage was the only way I would ever have a future.

The next afternoon, I went to see that future. Flynn had sent one of his farmhands to collect me in the trap and I sat in the back of the wagon, winding up towards the edge of Bridge Street where the colony met the wilderness.

Flynn's home was a great sandstone monolith that seemed to grow from the paddocks, the distant turquoise of the sea visible beyond the hill. Behind the house, a patchwork of fencing outlined the sheep-dotted farmland. There was a barren, eerie beauty to the place, with its oceanic fields glittering in the heat haze, gnarled skeletons of trees stark against the fierce blue of the sky. I felt a flicker of nerves at becoming the lady of such a vast and unfamiliar property. But for the first time since I had climbed off the *Norfolk*, I was able to see a future that did not make me cower at its misery.

The farmhand offered me his hand to help me out of the trap and I climbed down, my boots crunching on the brittle brown grass. Ann was waiting outside the house to meet me.

"Mr Flynn's asked me to bring you into the parlour."

I followed her across a wide veranda and across the dark polished floorboards of Flynn's entrance hall. She knocked lightly on the parlour door and I entered at Flynn's invitation. As I stepped into the room, he put down his teacup and rose from his armchair. He turned to look at Ann.

"Please leave us."

She bobbed a quick curtsey and pulled the door closed behind her. It clicked loudly in the stillness. My eyes pulled towards the vast stretch of glass that filled one wall of the parlour. I could see out to the rusty fields of the farm, and a landscape so predominantly sky.

I hesitated, waiting for the invitation to sit. The offer of tea. Perhaps Flynn wished to show me around the farm first. I wondered whether I ought to remove my bonnet. "The property is beautiful," I said. "This view is quite something."

"Yes. It is." He did not return my smile.

And as I looked in his eyes, I realised. He knew. There could be no doubt.

I felt something sink inside me.

Was I to speak first? Find some petty explanation? Assure him such a thing would never happen again?

"Captain Grant and I are good friends," said Flynn, before I could find the words.

At the back of my mind, I had known that, yes. Had known it when I had stared Grant down in the middle of his hallway. Foolishly, I had believed – or at least hoped – our meeting might go by unacknowledged.

Flynn rubbed his shorn chin and stared out the window. I wondered distantly if this was the end. I knew there were many men in this colony who would look past such things. But I felt instinctively that Arthur Flynn was not one of them.

He came towards me slowly, his boots clicking on the floorboards.

"I chose to look past what they say about your kind," he said. "Because I believed you were different. But I see now how wrong I was to do so."

"I'm sorry," I said. And I was; truly, deeply. Flynn had been achingly decent to me. He had been willing to see beyond my convict stain and make me *wife*. I felt a striking guilt at having hurt him. But I also knew that, had I the chance, I would do the same again and again.

My throat tightened. "I was a fool."

Flynn stood close. I could see the green flecks in his eyes. "No," he said. "I'm the one who has been a fool. To have let myself be shamed by a government lass. Any man with half a mind knows better than to try and find a little decency in a woman so unspeakably impure."

I waited for him to strike me. Closed my eyes and braced for the impact. But instead he swept a wild hand across the table, sending his teacup flying across the room. It shattered noisily against the hearth, making my heart leap into my throat.

Flynn turned away, folding his arms across his chest. "You need to leave."

I trudged back into town, having refused his stilted offer of the trap. This hot, dusty trek was what I deserved, I told myself, as I swatted furiously at the relentless onslaught of flies. Craving the bliss of drunkenness, I stopped at the first tavern I came to and bought a flask of the Rum Corps' finest. I didn't care who saw me. I had already been irretrievably shamed.

I carried the liquor up to my room and took a long mouthful. As it seared my throat, a barrage of tears spilled, and I pushed them away hurriedly. I couldn't bear to sit here in self-pity. Everything that had happened to me I had brought on myself.

I tucked the bottle beneath the bed and trudged down to the tavern with my apron in my hand. I wasn't due to start work for another hour.

"You're early," said Charlie, as he strode in from the kitchen.

"I know. I need the distraction. You don't have to pay me." I knotted my apron around my waist. I could smell the dust and sweat on my skin. Could feel my hair frizzing wildly around my cheeks. A lass behind the bar might bring men through the door, but one look at me and they'd walk right back out again.

"What's happened?" asked Charlie.

"Nothing." I couldn't bear to speak of it. Couldn't bear to think of it. Of any of it. I couldn't think of the hurt in Flynn's eyes, or of Blackwell sailing home to his wife. I couldn't think of Kate Abbott running through the streets picking pockets, or Lottie on the floor of that squalid kitchen. Couldn't think, couldn't think, couldn't think.

The tavern filled quickly and I was grateful for it. Exhaustion was pressing down on me, but I kept myself charging through the bar, wiping tables, and serving drinks.

When I knocked a glass of rum from the counter, sending it exploding on the floor, Charlie took the dish cloth from my hand.

"Go upstairs, Nell. Go and rest."

I shook my head. "I'm fine."

"You're not fine. Any fool can see that."

"I've got to clean it," I said, pointing to the shards of glass lying in the pool of liquor. Inexplicably, the sight of it made my tears spill.

Charlie pointed to the stairwell. "Upstairs," he said. "That's an order."

I trudged up to my room. Rain was beginning to patter against the windows. I sat on my bed, trying to swallow my tears.

I pulled the bottle out from under my bed and gulped

down a mouthful. And then another. And one more for good measure.

I had never felt more alone in my life. Never felt so directionless, or so empty. I stared at the window with glazed eyes, watching lines of water snake down the glass.

I knew that just a few blocks away, Blackwell would be alone in Captain Grant's house. I longed to go to him. To curl up against him and disappear from the world. But I couldn't do that to Sophia. Or to him.

And I couldn't do it to myself.

But nor could I stay here, drowning in rum and sadness. I got shakily to my feet and headed out towards the Rocks.

CHAPTER TWENTY-NINE

The sky ripped open as I walked, the drizzle growing into marbles of water that turned the roads to mud. The rain brought cool air with it, and I shivered as droplets ran down my bare arms. I put my head down and quickened my pace towards the kitchen.

I knew Lottie would not want a thing to do with me. Perhaps she would send me away. Or perhaps she would not even be here. Perhaps Owen had decided he wanted her for the night again.

The alleyways of the Rocks were near empty, rain pounding against roofs, and water trickling from the gutters. A few sailors were sheltering beneath dripping awnings with pipes in their hands. One of them called out to me as I stumbled past, but didn't bother following. I squinted in the darkness. Which way to Lottie?

I stumbled through the maze of cottages and shacks until I found the narrow door leading to the kitchen. I knocked loudly. Tripped slightly on the doorstep as an old woman let me inside. Lottie pushed her way towards me.

"Nell," she said. "What are you doing here?"

I felt myself swaying slightly. "I'm worried for you," I said. "I thought Owen…" The lie spilled out without me having a thought of it. Why couldn't I admit that I needed her? Why did I feel the urge to appear in control, even when I was soaked to the skin and my steps were crooked with liquor? Perhaps Lottie was right. Perhaps I did need to show her how well I'd done for myself.

"Are you drunk?" she demanded.

"A little." Water trickled down the back of my neck.

Her hand was suddenly around my arm, leading me to the corner of the room where Willie's basket was tucked away. Water dripped from the ceiling and ran down the wall, but the kitchen was marginally drier than the alley.

"Christ," Lottie said, unwrapping her shawl and draping it over my shoulders. "What happened to you?"

Suddenly, I wanted to tell her everything. The breaking of my betrothal, and being thrown from Flynn's house, and all that had happened between Blackwell and me. I wanted to tell her of the chaos of guilt and love that roiled inside me. But instead, I said:

"Has Owen been back for you?"

Lottie sighed. "Would you forget about Patrick for one damn minute? What's happened to you?" She slid an arm around my shoulder and I felt myself break. Deep sobs racked my body and I buried my head against her shoulder. She held me tightly.

My words came out in a tangle. "Flynn broke off our betrothal. I ruined everything. And Blackwell…" I knew I ought to stop; knew I shouldn't speak of him in front of Lottie. But I couldn't stop myself. "He's leaving," I sobbed. "Going back to England. To his wife."

Her arms tightened around me. "It's for the best, Nell. You know that. You know how the Rum Corps sees women like us. We're the lowest of the low. They can't look past our convict stain."

I wiped my eyes with the back of my hand. "Blackwell's in Sydney. Staying with a colleague. Flynn found out I went to him… To his room…" Perhaps it was a foolish confession. But with the words, I felt a weight lift from my chest.

"I see," Lottie said after a long silence. Outside the window, rain poured from the edge of the roof and thundered into the street.

A part of me wanted to tell her about the conversation I'd had with Blackwell about what had happened at the Owens' cottage after the rebellion. Tell her I understood her hatred, Owen's hatred. And I wanted to tell her of the remorse I could sense in Blackwell's words. Tell her of the way he saw the world through a guilty man's eyes.

But I did none of that. It felt like I conversation I was not permitted to have. She would know I still saw the story from Blackwell's side. How could she not, after all I'd just confessed?

I wiped my eyes. "I'm sorry," I coughed. "I didn't mean to burden you."

"Don't be a fool, Nell. You're not a burden." She leant her head against mine. I was so glad for her closeness, for the friendship I'd feared had been washed away completely.

In the basket beside us, Willie gave a weak cry. He

rubbed his eyes and squirmed beneath his blankets.

I frowned. "Is he unwell?"

"A fever," said Lottie, scooping him into her arms. "Came on last night. Neither of us have had a wink of sleep."

"Come back to the Whaler's with me," I said. "Stay in my room. It'll be quieter there. And drier." I could see her hesitation. "Please. I could use the company."

Lottie glanced at the baby, then back to me. "All right," she said finally. "But just for the night."

The rain was beginning to ease as we made our way back to the tavern. Lottie held Willie tightly to her chest, while I carried his empty basket, drawing in lungfuls of air to clear my liquored-up thoughts.

As we passed Captain Grant's house, I lowered my eyes and began to walk faster. Lottie jogged to keep up with me.

"What's this about then?"

"Nothing," I said. "I just—"

Oh." She peered up at the house with knowing eyes. "This where you paid the lieutenant a visit?"

I felt my cheeks burn with shame.

Lottie glanced back over her shoulder, then gave me a crooked smile. "House is dark," she said. "No need to rush by with your tail between your legs."

"The family's left for Van Diemen's Land," I mumbled. "But I'm sure Blackwell's still there." I turned the corner hurriedly, glad when the Whaler's Arms came into view. I stopped in surprise at the small figure standing outside the tavern. "Kate."

She offered me a sheepish smile, twisting a strand of dark hair around her finger. "You said you had a room here."

I smiled. "I do. Yes."

Her clothes were grimy and torn, her wet hair hanging loose on her shoulders. Had she been sleeping on the streets since I'd found her all those weeks ago?

"Where have you been?" I asked.

She chewed her lip, avoiding my eyes. "Just about."

I nodded. Wherever she'd been, whoever she'd been with, it didn't matter. I was just glad she was here now. I put a hand to her shoulder, ushering her inside. "Come on. Come and get yourself dry."

I led her and Lottie into the alley behind the tavern and used my key to unlock the back door. I ushered them up the stairs to my room.

As Kate hurried inside, Lottie reached for my arm, holding me back. "Who is she?"

I kept my voice low. "She's Maggie's daughter. I found her in the street."

Something flickered behind Lottie's eyes. "Does she know what happened to her mother?"

I shook my head. Kate turned back to us and I forced a smile, stepping inside and locking the door. I had no thought of where we would all sleep in my little snuff box of a room.

I went to the table by the bedside and lit the lamp. Lottie took the baby's basket from me and laid Willie inside it. She sat it on the floor and knelt beside him. I took my cloak from the hook beside the door and tucked it around the baby.

"He's sleeping at least," I said. "That's good. We can take him to the physician tomorrow."

Lottie gave an incredulous laugh. "You've no idea, do you, Nell? Two years in this place and you've not learned a thing. There's no physician who'll look at him once they learn he belongs to a factory lass."

"That's not true," I said. "It can't be."

Lottie looked at me witheringly, shaking her head. A reminder that my time at the spinning wheels had not washed away all my naivety.

She chewed her thumbnail. "He needs his father. Patrick would know what to do."

I glared at her. She couldn't speak his name. Not in front of Maggie's daughter.

Kate was hovering at the foot of the bed, chewing her hair and peering down at the baby.

"Is he going to die?" she asked.

"Of course not." I ushered her away from Willie's basket.

Lottie let out her breath. "I see she's got the same gift with words as her mother."

My stomach plunged. Kate's lips parted, and she looked up at me with wide eyes.

"Take off your dress and hang it up," I said hurriedly. "You'll catch a chill."

She slid her smock over her head, not taking her eyes off mine. "Do you know my mother?"

I glared at Lottie, willing her to speak. But she was kneeling over Willie with her head down, refusing to meet my eyes. Making it clear Kate was my responsibility. The girl was a fragile figure in her thin wet shift, with skeletal white arms and a face dwarfed by wild, wet curls.

"Your mother is dead, Kate," I said. "I'm sorry." I clenched my fist behind my back, trying to force away my anger at Lottie. A drop of water slid from the end of my hair and beaded on the floorboards.

Kate's mouth opened, then closed. She perched on the

bottom of the bed, her feet dangling inches from the floor. "Oh," she said. "Oh."

I sat beside her, my wet skirts tangling around my legs. "Lottie and I both knew her. At the factory in Parramatta." I opened my mouth to say more, but could find few words. My most vivid memories of Maggie were of her lying lifeless on the side of the road. But Kate was looking up at me, expectant. I knew I had to give her more. "She was a kind woman," I managed. "She always spoke her mind. And she loved you very much."

I remembered the tremor in Maggie's voice when she'd spoken of the Orphan School. I had no doubt her head had been full of her daughter at the time.

Kate began to gnaw on her thumbnail. I waited for her reaction. Tears? Anger? There was none of that. Just a silent acceptance. I put my hand to her shoulder and gave it a gentle squeeze.

"Come on. We ought to sleep. If we squeeze up we can all fit." I looked over at Lottie. She was sitting on her knees with her back to me, a protective hand on the edge of Willie's basket.

"Lottie," I said, "there's room for you on the bed." In spite of my anger, I hated the thought of her spending yet another night on the floor.

"There's no room for three," she said. "I'll stay here." The divide that had sprung up between us felt almost a physical thing.

Kate stayed planted on the edge of the bed, staring into the lamp. "How did she die?" she asked suddenly.

I hesitated. Was I to lie? Cobble together some more manageable version of the truth?

"She stopped breathing," I said finally. I stared at Lottie, willing her to turn around. Willing her to face the reality of who her husband was. What good would it do her; this blind hope that one day Owen would take her back? That impossible dream of having a family. I understood her need for security, of course. But surely she would do better if she let her faith in Owen die.

Kate stared at me with her mother's deep-set blue eyes. "What do you mean she stopped breathing? How?" I knew she'd spent too much time on the street for my all-too-gentle truths.

And I was thinking of Lottie and Owen when I said, "Someone killed her."

CHAPTER THIRTY

"Killed her?" Kate repeated. "Who killed her? Why?"

"She was killed by the savages," Lottie said, before I could answer. "She had too much to drink and wandered out into the bush." Her voice was cold. Empty of emotion. And suddenly she was on her feet, grabbing Willie's basket and making for the door.

I chased her out into the hallway, letting the door slam behind me. "Where are you going?"

"It was a mistake to come here." She strode towards the stairwell. I grabbed her arm.

"Please don't leave."

She pulled free of my grasp. "Instead I'm to stay here and listen to you spout lies about my husband?" She shook her head. "I ought to have known you'd do something like this. You turn up at my door, filthy drunk because you lifted your skirts to your lobster, and you're still doing all you can to show me how much better you've done than me."

"That's not what I'm trying to do," I hissed. "Kate deserves to know the truth."

"And that's what I told her. That Maggie was killed by the savages."

I let out my breath. "You can't truly believe that."

Lottie shook her head. "No," she said. "We're not going back here, Nell. Not after all this time. We're not having this conversation again."

I closed my eyes for a moment. "You're right." I dared to take a step towards her. Dared to press a hand to her forearm. I was relieved when she didn't pull away.

"I'm sorry," I said. "I never meant to look down on you. I just want you to be safe. That's all I've ever wanted."

Lottie sighed, but she didn't walk away. A burst of drunken laughter floated up from the tavern.

"We look out for each other," I said. "Isn't that what you always told me?" I squeezed her wrist. "And it goes both ways, Lottie. I need you to look out for me just as much. You saw the mess I was in tonight. I'm barely stumbling my way through this place."

Finally, she looked up to meet my eyes.

"Please come inside," I said. "Willie needs to be warm and dry. You know that." I flashed her a tentative smile. "I'll not speak of Owen again. I promise."

When I woke, I was alone in the bed. Pale dawn light was filtering into the room. Kate was at the window, peering through the curtains. I sat up, frowning. "Where's Lottie?"

Kate looked back over her shoulder at me, a thread of dark hair clinging to her lip. "She left."

"What do you mean? Where did she go?"

She shrugged. "I just saw her leave."

"When?" I tried to rein in my impatience.

"Don't know. But it was still dark. And then I went back to sleep."

A knot of panic tightened in my stomach. Had something happened to Willie in the night? Or had Lottie gone to Owen? Was she making another attempt at getting him to take her back?

If she had, who was I to stop her? Perhaps I had done all I could. Perhaps the time had come for me to accept that. To let her live her own life and make her own mistakes.

I pushed the thought aside. I knew I would never be able to do such a thing. Owen had wrung Maggie's throat and left her body at the side of the road. I would fight until I died to stop the same thing happening to Lottie.

I grabbed my damp dress from the chair and slid it over my head. "Stay here," I told Kate, fastening the hooks with unsteady fingers. "There's bread on the shelf. And you can go to the kitchen and make some tea. Charlie will help you."

"Where are you going?"

"I need to find Lottie."

I climbed downstairs and out through the empty tavern, locking the door behind me. In the early morning, the air was cool and still. Empty barrels were stacked up against the wall of the tavern, flies swarming and the smell of stale liquor thick in the air.

I began to walk. I would go to Owen's farm first, and if

there was no sign of Lottie, I would try at the Rocks. The streets were close to empty, just a few sailors stumbling from the taverns. At least if Lottie was roaming the alleys, I would have a chance of finding her.

I passed the Dog and Duck tavern, and hurried along the street that wound around past Captain Grant's house. Kept my eyes firmly on the ground.

The sound of footsteps made me look up. There was Lottie, rounding the bend, flanked by Owen and Brady. Willie was strapped to her chest. They were striding down the narrow street from the direction of Owen's farm, heading for Captain Grant's house. A pistol peeked out of Brady's fist.

At once I knew exactly why Lottie had left the tavern in the night. To lead Patrick Owen to the man he despised. To give him a chance at Blackwell without the Rum Corps watching.

Heat flooded me. Lottie's betrayal burned under my skin. But it was the fear that caused my heart to race. Fear that Blackwell would never set foot on that ship back to England. That he might die by the rebels' bullet and never again see his wife.

I darted down the side of a neighbouring house and stood with my back pressed against the wall. By now, Grant and his family would have left for Van Diemen's Land. The house would be near empty. If Owen and Brady made it inside, they would have a clear shot at Blackwell, with not a single witness.

I would not make it to the Grants' without being seen. But I had to warn Blackwell the men were coming.

At the sound of my footfalls, Lottie turned to look behind her. Our eyes met. I stared at her, hot with fury. I'd never felt more betrayed. I knew, of course, that at its core, this conflict was about Owen and Blackwell and all that had happened in that cottage after the uprising. But at that moment, it felt intensely personal. Felt as though it were between she and I alone.

The baby whined against her chest. She turned away, refusing to hold my gaze. And I saw the end. Saw that, for all I had tried to make it otherwise, the two of us were to go no further. Saw that an Irishwoman and a *sasaniagh* could not build a friendship strong enough to withstand what a woman would do to survive this place.

Owen turned, catching sight of me, and I raced towards the Grants' gate, calling Blackwell's name. A firm hand grabbed my arm, yanking me backwards. Brady clamped his grimy hand over my mouth.

"Let her go," said Owen on a laugh. "Let her bring him out here. Save us from breaking in."

I shook free of Brady's grasp and whirled around for something to use as a weapon. I grabbed a scrap of wood lying on the side of the road. I held it out in front of me, backing towards the gate.

"Get out of the way, Nell," said Lottie, a waver in her voice.

I didn't look at her. She had no say in this.

I heard a movement in the Grants' garden behind me, and felt a sudden weakness in my legs. I wished I hadn't called for Blackwell. For all I ached for him to run and hide, I knew he would come for me, come for the rebels; come to see an end to this thing that had poisoned both he and Owen for the past four years. If Owen got through this gate, there would be shots fired. And someone would die.

Suddenly Brady was coming at me, wrestling the wood from my hand. He flung it onto the ground. I kicked hard, connecting with his shins. He slammed me back against the gate. My vision swam and pain jolted down my spine.

"Please, Nell," I heard Lottie say again, "just get out of the way. Please." Her voice was tearful.

Brady came at me again and I drove my knee upward into his groin. I was dimly aware of Owen reaching for the plank of wood. Dimly aware of Lottie shrieking.

As Brady stumbled backwards, I lurched at him, my fingers grazing the cold metal of the pistol in his hands. I wrenched hard, trying to seize the weapon. A sudden pain to the side of my head and the world around me was gone.

When I opened my eyes, I was alone. The back of my head was thumping, the ground rough and cold beneath my cheek. I tried to sit, but dizziness was pressing down on me. And then I remembered. Owen. Brady. Lottie.

Blackwell.

Everything was quiet. Too quiet.

A pistol was lying beside my head. And as I looked past it, I saw the Grants' gate swinging open. Panic overtook me, pushing through the dizziness. I climbed to my feet, swallowing a violent wave of nausea. I swiped at the thin line of blood trickling down the side of my face. I turned. I stepped. And then I saw it.

The body lay just a few feet in front of me, a pool of

blood creeping steadily towards my boots.

I stumbled, terrified to approach.

I took one step. Then another. Horror welled up inside me.

I had been expecting a gunshot wound, but the entire figure was a mess of crimson. The limbs were thrashed and misshapen, the face a chaos of slashes. The red coat was blackened with blood, buttons opened to reveal a maze of knife wounds. And there, below the ribs, the entry point of a single ball. I stared at it for several moments, my vision swimming. Flies darted around the wounds. My gaze drifted up to the neat white braiding on the jacket, the stark yellow facings. And to the glimmer of gold poking from the coat pocket. I bent, breathless, and looped a finger around the chain of the pocket watch. It thudded dully into mud, a drop of blood sliding over Sophia's engraved dedication. I stumbled, landing heavily on my knees, and vomited beside the body.

CHAPTER THIRTY-ONE

I stayed on my hands and knees, gulping down my breath. My body began to shake. A desperate sob escaped me.

And so Patrick Owen had gotten what he wanted, in the most vicious way imaginable. Repayment for that blood-streaked shack in the bush behind the Squires' inn. Repayment for the lives taken in the aftermath of the uprising.

Had the rebels killed Blackwell inside the house, and then brought his body down into the alley? Laid him here beside me so I might see what my actions had brought about? Or had the lieutenant heard me calling him? Had he come down to help me? Had my own actions led to his death? The thought brought another sob from deep inside me.

I stared at the blood seeping into the gaps between the cobbles. Tears blurred my vision and I let them slide unhindered from my cheeks. I couldn't bear to look at Blackwell's body. And I couldn't bear to look away.

I was distantly aware of footsteps coming towards me. Distantly aware of soldiers approaching. Standing over the body. Standing over me.

I looked down. My floral dress was covered in blood. So were my hands. A pistol on the ground beside me. And as they hauled me to my feet, I couldn't find a single word.

My thoughts were blank as they shoved me into the back of the police wagon. We began to rattle along the streets, the wheels sighing as they slid through the remnants of the downpour.

The journey was a short one, and I wondered distantly why they had felt the need to put me in the carriage. Hands around the tops of my arms, and I was led into a vast sandstone building. Led down a narrow corridor into an empty room. A table with three stools sat in the middle. A tiny window above the table let in a spear of sunlight. The soldiers shoved me onto a stool. And there I sat in my bloodstained skirts, clasping my bloodstained hands.

For a long time, I was left alone on that stool, in front of that table, with the morning light building as it streamed through that tiny window. A guard stood at the door, rifle across his chest, not saying a word. I felt an old terror. The terror I had felt when I had heard *high treason* and *death by hanging*.

Finally; two marines. A captain. An ensign. They asked me my name. Asked me my status. I pulled my ticket of leave from the pocket of my dress, and sat it on the table. The edges were stained in blood.

The captain leant forward and placed the pocket watch on the table. "Who does this belong to?"

I swallowed hard. "It belongs to Adam Blackwell." I looked down at the blood on my hands, feeling sickness rise in my throat. Feeling a little hysteria rise with it. "Let me wash. Please. I need to wash."

"You're not going anywhere."

I squeezed my eyes closed and tried to breathe deeply. I felt as though I were trapped in the worst of my nightmares. "I didn't kill him," I said. "It was Patrick Owen."

A moment of silence. I kept my eyes on my knotted fingers. I couldn't look at that watch. Couldn't look at the stains on the edge of my ticket of leave. I thought of Blackwell handing it to me as smoke poured from the factory above the jail. Thought of the fleeting kiss he had pressed into my neck. I blinked back my tears.

"Tell me what happened," said the captain.

But of course, I knew nothing of what had happened. Nothing beyond the moment Owen had struck me with the plank of wood.

I garbled through a tangled tale of finding the rebels outside Captain Grant's house. Of my altercation with Brady. Of Lottie's cries and Owen's laughter and the blow to my head that had left me unconscious in the street. "The next I knew," I said, "Lieutenant Blackwell's body was beside me."

"You did not see Mr Owen kill Lieutenant Blackwell."

A question? Or was he painting a picture of my guilt?

And then I told them, as slowly and calmly as I could, of the way I had taken Lottie back to my room at the Whaler's Arms. Of the way she had disappeared in the night and gone for Owen. Told him of the lieutenant's whereabouts.

I spoke of the events that had taken place at the Owens' cottage after the Castle Hill rebellion. And I spoke of Patrick

Owen's need for revenge.

"How did you come to know Lieutenant Blackwell?" asked the captain.

I knotted my fingers together. "I met him in Parramatta. He… offered me a bed."

"Ah." And that one word was all it took for me to know my story had been taken for fiction. I was a concubine from the factory above the jail. As striking an admission of guilt as there could ever be.

Do you know why Lieutenant Blackwell was in Sydney?

Yes. He was returning to England to see his wife.

That must have angered you I'm sure. Perhaps enough to kill?

My body shook with anger, fear, grief. But I clenched my fists and pressed my shoulders back. I would not fit neatly into their story. I was not a jealous government lass driven to murder.

I used a clean patch of skin on my wrist to wipe my eyes. "It was Patrick Owen," I said again. But I had no proof. I could not even claim to be a witness. "The body," I coughed. "It was… defaced. How do you imagine I might have done such a thing? With what weapon?"

But the look the captain gave me said he knew the weapon would be found. And he knew that I was capable.

The guard led me down the passage and unlocked the door to a narrow stone cell. He followed me inside and locked the door behind us. Shoved me hard against the cold stone wall. Pain jolted down my spine.

"Blackwell was a friend," he said. "A schoolmate."

I heard a sudden, hysterical laugh escape me. Because of course he was. Because this place was ruled by redcoats who had studied together, trained together, fought together. And they would band together to see that everyone below them fell into line.

And when I laughed, I also cried; sobs that came from deep inside me and stole my breath. I turned away from the guard and crumpled to the floor, my head pressed to my knees.

I waited to be thrown against the wall again. Waited to be struck, or for some fierce interrogation. But the guard didn't speak again. Engulfed in tears, I did not hear him leave. Did not hear the door open, or close, or lock. All I knew was when I finally looked up in an attempt to catch my breath, the dark was thick and I was alone.

That night, I huddled in the corner of the cell, shivering in spite of the thick, wet heat. In fleeting moments of clarity, I told myself I would fight. I would make sure the world knew Patrick Owen had been the one to pull the trigger. But my resolve was without determination. My will to fight was swamped by grief.

Every time I closed my eyes, I saw Blackwell's beaten body, stained in blood, his face unrecognisable, the uniform he had always worn so neatly hanging open at his sides.

I heard myself inhale.

The jacket unbuttoned.

In all the time I had known him, Blackwell had never worn his jacket unbuttoned.

I hugged my legs, pressing my eyes hard against my knees. A trivial detail. Owen had likely caught Blackwell unaware. Or he had heard me calling for him. Had raced out of the house to help me.

But the thought gnawed at the back of my mind.

The jacket unbuttoned.

And in the darkness I was back there again; in the street outside the Grants' house, with Brady's hands on my shoulders and my fingers reaching for his pistol. I felt the metal, felt my hand slide around the stock. And then? I dug into my memories, into that fragment of a second before I had been struck. Had there been the sound of a gunshot? Had I pulled the trigger?

I heard myself breathe louder, faster. Dan Brady, lurching in front of me as I thrust my knee into his groin. Dan Brady stumbling, my hand on his weapon. Had I put a bullet in his chest?

Brady was tall like Blackwell. Dark-haired and broad-shouldered. The two men could easily be mistaken from a distance.

And at once I was on my feet, pacing back and forth across the lightless cell, my feverish mind grappling at the possibility. Was it was Dan Brady's body that had been lying at my feet?

I knew I was walking a straighter path to the hangman. But the next morning, I told the captain I had pulled the trigger on Dan Brady. Told him the body had been defaced. Made to look like Blackwell.

I knew the bloodstained ticket of leave in my pocket would send me to the gallows, no matter what I said in that interrogation room. But I needed the truth to be known.

Was Owen seeking to punish me? Had he broken into the house and gone to Blackwell's room to find it empty but for his belongings? Had he defaced Brady's body to disguise his identity? Put him in Blackwell's uniform and left him lying at my feet?

I felt deathly certain of it. Knew Owen had done this so I might believe he had killed the man I loved.

I told my story again, of the altercation outside the tavern, ending with my new and firm belief that I had pulled the trigger on Brady before I had been knocked out. But there was nothing but my word to support my story. Nothing beyond my desperate belief to suggest the body did not belong to Blackwell.

"If the lieutenant was not killed, as you claim, why has he not come forward?"

I closed my eyes. It almost felt as though the soldiers wanted the dead man to be Blackwell. What an example they could make of me then; the factory lass who had murdered a soldier. My body would hang in a gibbet over Pinchgut Island, to greet the ships as they bucked their way into the harbour.

"Perhaps Owen found him," I said. "Perhaps he's harmed him." This, of course, was the other reason I was so adamant that the body was proven to be Brady's. Because I knew there was every chance Blackwell was in danger. And I needed him to be found.

The captain was quick to remind me there were no witnesses to the shooting. Nothing but my word to go on. The rest did not need to be said. *The word of a factory lass found covered in blood with a pistol beside her.*

"What of Dan Brady?" I asked. "You've not found him,

have you." But I knew hunting down Brady, an emancipist with no fixed address, was not something the redcoats were willing to entertain.

Back in my cell, I paced. My heart was racing and my skin was damp with sweat. I was overflowing with fear. But the fear, I realised, was no longer for myself. I was a factory lass with blood on my hands. I'd escaped the hangman once, but I knew I would not do so again. Somehow, knowing I had no chance to win made it easier to push away the terror.

But my fear for Blackwell was consuming. Now I had let myself believe he was alive, I couldn't bear to go back to the alternative. But there had been no sign of him since the morning of Brady's death. Had he fallen into the hands of the rebels? If he were still in Sydney Town, he would surely have been sighted. I would not be being held for his murder.

I had no answers, of course. Just a desperate hope he still lived. The optimism felt dangerous. A thing that could all too easily be torn away.

Two and a half years ago I had stood in a courtroom dock at the Old Bailey and listened to the judge sentence me to a lifetime in New South Wales.

It had felt like a reprieve. I had been expecting a walk to the gallows.

I'd learned later that a literate, well-mannered woman like me was never destined for the hangman. I was a desirable thing for this new colony.

Now here I was with the murder of a soldier to my name. I knew well my education would not save me.

The trial was short. A foregone conclusion. Beside me, the other prisoners shifted in the dock; sent to the coalmines, sent to Toongabbie. Two hundred lashes, three days on Pinchgut Island.

I let my mind escape. I thought of birdsong and pearly light and the distant sigh of the sea. Thought of the rugged beauty of this place I had not learned to truly appreciate until now, when it was far too late.

Though I could not claim to be surprised by it, the verdict still weakened my knees.

"For the murder of Adam Blackwell, you are sentenced to hang by the neck until you are dead."

PART FOUR

CHAPTER THIRTY-TWO

And so tomorrow morning I am to die in the orange light of New South Wales. I had always known, as I had felt the ship buck its way down the Thames, that I would never be returning to the land of my birth. But I had not expected the end to come so abruptly. I will not see my thirtieth birthday.

In the dim light of my cell, I look down at my hands. I can still see the bloodstains; can still see where the skin is discoloured, darker than the rest. For all my astronomy lessons and garden parties, for all the scales my fingers have churned through on the piano, I will go to my death with blood on my hands.

I don't sleep. Though I want to escape the violent chaos of my thoughts, I know I will have this escape soon enough. The darkness is almost impenetrable, and the hours are blank. At once both interminably long and painfully fast.

I am terrified for Blackwell. Wherever he is, I know he is

not safe. Perhaps Owen has already killed him. Perhaps the rebel leader has gotten the revenge he so desperately sought. And I am the one who will swing for Blackwell's death.

Untouchable Owen.

Faint birdsong breaks through the dark and it makes sickness rise in my throat. Throughout the night, I had felt a sense of cold resignation, but with the light, I am terrified. Today I am to die.

The sunlight comes, brighter and brighter, straining beneath the door, through the keyhole. My entire body shakes as I wait for the footsteps of the men who will take me to my death.

I wait.

And I wait. I alternate between pacing the cell and huddling in the corner with my knees to my chest. At times I want this horror to be over; I crave stillness in my pounding chest. The next moment, I want time to freeze, so I might catch hold of every last thread of my waning life.

I hear footsteps, murmurs, but they do not come to my cell.

And then it is afternoon. And then the pink light of evening. My thoughts knock together, jumping around my memories. Twelfth night balls, the stained bulkheads of the *Norfolk*. Counterfeit coins in my reticule, Blackwell's hands in my hair.

Another night comes and I am still alive. I am dizzy, sweat-soaked, disoriented. I don't know what to do. I was not supposed to be here, not supposed to see this hour. And so I keep sitting. Keep pacing. Keep waiting.

It is the next morning when the footsteps finally come. I

am unprepared. I had readied myself for my death and the moment had passed. I had even fallen into an exhausted sleep.

The door clicks open and I hear a cry of fear escape me.

"This way," says the guard. His voice is cold and empty.

My legs feel weak beneath me. The world swims and my mouth goes dry. I grapple at the stone wall, searching for something to steady myself. My legs give way and I fall to my knees.

The guard looks at me with something close to pity, and for some reason, this is worse than his coldness.

I follow him out of my cell and down a long stone corridor. We stop in front of the door leading to the room I had first been interrogated in. The guard knocks.

"Enter," says the voice on the other side.

When we step into the room, I see the captain and ensign who had placed this murder at my feet. They gesture to a chair in front of the table.

I crumple into the seat, my legs barely able to hold me. My vision is swimming. I don't understand what is happening. I was expecting to be led to the gallows.

The captain folds his hands on the table in front of him. He says:

"Another woman has come forth and confessed to the murder."

For a long time, I don't speak. There is so much wrong with this. I had been the one to pull the trigger. The memories are there; hazy, but they are there. I had made myself certain of them. But if I am wrong about this, perhaps I am also wrong about the body being Dan Brady's.

"No," I hear myself say.

They tell me of a trial that took place while I was waiting out my last day on earth. They tell me of the woman who came forth and spoke of the altercation outside Captain Grant's home. Spoke of the ball she had put in the chest of Dan Brady.

Dan Brady, says the voice in my head.

Dan Brady.

Dan Brady.

I don't understand why Lottie has done this; I only know it can be no one else.

I don't move. I don't speak. I can't deny this story, of course. I was unconscious at the time.

Even if I could deny it, the trial has taken place. Lottie has already condemned herself to the hangman. And in doing so, she has freed me.

"Please," I say. "Let me see her."

The guard takes me to Lottie's cell, two doors down from where I had been held for the past five days. She is sitting in the corner with her knees to her chest. She barely looks up as I enter. I glance over my shoulder at the guard.

"Will you let us speak?"

A faint nod. He pulls the door closed, locking us in.

I kneel beside Lottie in the filthy straw and press my hand to her arm. Her skin is cold. I am still blazing from my aborted date with the hangman. Even at the touch of my hand, she doesn't shift her gaze.

"Lottie," I say. Finally, she looks up at me. Her eyes are dry, almost expressionless. Her hair hangs in pieces around her hollow cheeks.

"Why are you doing this?" I ask.

"Because I was the one who killed Dan Brady."

"No. You're lying."

Lottie looks at me squarely. "Why would I do that?"

"Why would you kill Brady?"

"Because you were struggling with him. He was going to shoot you."

She is lying. I remember the feel of my finger on the trigger. Don't I?

"How did you kill him?" I ask.

"With the pistol I stole from Patrick. The one I kept in Willie's basket. I took it with me everywhere."

I shake my head. "Owen would have killed you for it."

"For harming Brady?" She lets out a cold laugh. "Patrick don't care what happens to anyone but himself. All he cares about is his revenge."

I wrap my arms around myself, suddenly cold. "What about Willie?" I ask. "What is he to do without you, if—"

I stop speaking as Lottie shakes her head. And then her tears come. "The fever," she says, "he couldn't fight it off. He was too weak. Too small."

I let out my breath, pulling her into me "I'm sorry," I cough. "I'm so sorry." She feels limp and fragile in my arms, as though all the fight has drained out of her. After a moment, I sit back, trying to find her eyes. "Is that why you're doing this? Because you lost Willie?"

She winds her bootlace listlessly around her finger. I hear the guard's footsteps thud back and forth outside the door.

"The whole of it was my fault," she says after a while. "I was the one who brought Patrick to the house. I thought if I led him to Blackwell he might see I was worth something. See I was of use." She swipes at her tears. "I thought he might take me and Willie back to the farm. For good this time. Not just for the night. I thought we could make another go of things. Be a family."

My throat tightens, my own tears threatening. I want to feel anger, but all I feel is sorrow.

"Where is Blackwell?" I dare to ask.

Lottie sniffs. "I don't know. After Dan... was killed, Patrick broke into the house looking for the lieutenant. He came back with his coat. Said the whole place was empty. He was furious about it."

"You've not seen Blackwell since?"

She shakes her head.

My thoughts race. And they go to a tiny hut near Squires' inn where Patrick Owen's family had died.

Has Blackwell been driven there by the ghosts he is haunted by? The ghosts he refuses to speak of?

I want to go to him. But I don't want to leave Lottie.

"Was it Owen's idea to do what he did to the body? To make me think it were Blackwell?"

Lottie nods faintly. "He took the coat from Blackwell's room. Defaced Dan's body so you'd think..." She coughs down her tears. "That was it for me, Nell. When I saw him do that to Dan... His friend... Just to punish you for prying into our business... I couldn't have nothing more to do with him."

I swallow hard. Her realisation has come far too late.

"I asked him why he killed Maggie," Lottie says suddenly.

For a moment I don't speak. "I thought you believed him innocent."

"That's what I needed to believe."

I nod slowly. I understand, of course. How many times

had I told myself Blackwell had not pulled the trigger on Owen's family? In the end, the truth had not mattered for me. But I knew it mattered to Lottie.

"He was my way out of the factory," she says, looking at her hands. "I couldn't have managed three more years of weaving cloth and lying with old Bert. I had to get out. You must think me such a fool."

I shake my head faintly. "I understand," I say. "I know you don't believe it, but I do. I know how desperate the factory can make you."

Lottie wipes her eyes with the back of her hand. "Phil Cunningham was the leader of the croppies before they rose up at Castle Hill," she told me. "He'd come to Parramatta sometimes and drink with us at the river. Tell us of how things would be different after the Irish were in charge. We all believed him. He gave us hope. There weren't one of us who thought things would end like they did. There weren't one of us who thought Phil wouldn't come back that day." She stares blankly ahead, her eyes glazed.

"After Castle Hill, Patrick took his place. Tried to keep our spirits high. I was so taken by him, Nell. I was drawn to him right from the day I first met him. But he were a different kind of man to Phil. He weren't interested in freedom. Not once did he ever try and rouse the croppies to rise up again. He were only interested in revenge. In making Blackwell pay for what he did to his family.

"I'd convinced myself it were the savages that killed Maggie," she says. "But after I saw Patrick do what he did to Dan's body… I weren't so sure." She turns to face me then, her eyes round and glistening. "He couldn't even find a reason. Just told me she had it coming." She takes a deep breath. "I know that being Irish makes him feel weak. Powerless. He needs to prove how strong he is."

A knot tightens in my stomach. Killing a mere factory lass will not have given Owen the power he craves. That will only come with killing Blackwell.

"Does he know you've turned yourself in?" I ask.

Lottie shakes her head, tears sliding down her cheeks. "The day Dan died," she says, "Patrick sent me back to the Rocks. But I didn't go. I went to his farmhouse and I stood there with his pistol in my hand." She looks me in the eye. "I wanted to do it, Nell. I wanted to break back into the house and kill him. Retribution for Maggie. And Dan. And you. But I couldn't do it." For a long time, she doesn't speak. "He needs to be stopped," she says. "The Rum Corps won't do it. They had the chance after Maggie, but they're too afraid of another uprising."

I nod silently.

"And the croppies," she says, "they're blinded by him. They can't see the kind of man he truly is. The colony would be better off without him. And the Irish need to follow a better man." Her eyes plead with mine. "He needs to be stopped," she says again.

I open my mouth to speak, but can't find the words. "I couldn't," I say finally.

"Of course you could. You despise him. And he wants Blackwell dead. You're strong enough to do it, Nell. I'm not."

I think of myself, tearful and pleading when I'd first been hauled away by the thief-takers in London. How have I become the strong one?

I think of the night I had stood outside Owen's hut with the knife in my hand. And I think of Dan Brady's body, lying lifeless in the alley. I have already become a killer. Or is Lottie telling the truth? I have no thought of it. All I know is that now she is the one who will be taken to the gallows. And I am the one who is to live.

"You must," says Lottie. "Or else more of us will die. More croppies. And more of the factory lasses."

She has given her life for me. And so what can I do but agree?

The guard escorts me down the corridor, towards the heavy wooden doors that lead to the outside world. A part of me is oddly reluctant to step through them; to do so is acknowledge completely this sacrifice Lottie has made for me. Acknowledge she will be sent to the scaffold in my place. And acknowledge that she is sending me out into the world to end Patrick Owen's life.

Before I step into the street, I look back at the guard. "Lieutenant Blackwell's family," I say. "Have there been letters sent informing them of his death?"

I think of Blackwell's father. I think of Sophia. The next ship to England leaves in days' time. And I have no idea whether Blackwell will be aboard. But word of his death must not leave the harbour. If news of the murder is sent on the ship, it could be years before his family learns the truth.

"The situation has been rectified," says the guard. He has been stiltedly polite to me since he has learned I did not kill his schoolmate. "The letter informing his father of the murder has been recalled."

"And his wife?" I ask.

"The lieutenant has no wife."

"He does," I say. "Sophia."

The guard looks at me curiously. "Sophia died years ago in London. Long before Blackwell came out here."

I feel suddenly hot and unsteady. "Are you certain?"

"Certain as anything," says the guard. "I was at her burial."

CHAPTER THIRTY-THREE

The weight of it all cows me. Sophia's burial and Lottie's sacrifice and this great overwhelming relief that I am standing here; living, breathing. Sydney Town is searing in its brightness and I hunch for long moments in the street outside the jail, wearing the grey flannel smock I had expected to die in. My heart is thundering in my chest, a stark reminder that I have survived.

I fill my lungs with air, trying to steady myself. I was not supposed to see this world again. I have no idea how to act within it.

My head is full of Lottie, of Owen, of Blackwell. Of beautiful curly-haired Sophia lying lifeless in her grave.

I push the thought of her away. There is no room in my mind to grapple with the reason for Blackwell's lies.

I know he has gone to the Owens' cottage. I know he is in danger. And I know that, for all his painful untruths, I have no choice but to find him.

By afternoon, I am walking a narrow track out of Sydney Town, following the river into tangled wilderness. One pocket is stuffed with bread, the other with an apple I had taken from the Whaler's kitchen.

"You sure about this, Nell?" Charlie had asked, when I'd gone to him for directions. Kate clung to my wrist as I filled a flask of water. "It's a hell of a walk."

I am terrified, but sure. I know this is where I must go to find Blackwell. And only once I have done such a thing can I turn my thoughts to what Lottie has asked of me.

I trudge along the riverbank, following the narrow path along the water. Trees hang low, trying to reclaim the wilderness. Thin walking tracks are beaten into the bush, interlocking paths carved by the boots of twenty years of settlers. Flies swarm about my face, clouds of mosquitoes rising from the mangroves.

I keep walking, my skirts in my fist and my eyes darting. My shift is damp with sweat, and my hair curls and clings to my cheeks.

I will see James Squires' inn at Kissing Point, Charlie has told me. And from there I must turn in towards the forest to find that hut belonging to the Owens.

I feel certain Blackwell will not find the absolution he is looking for. Instead, he will stand on that doorstep and make himself a target. If he comes face to face with the woman who watched him kill her family, it will not be forgiveness he receives. It will likely be a ball to the chest.

As I walk and walk, my thoughts turn to Sophia. To all the lies Blackwell had told me. Lies, I see clearly, that were constructed to keep me at a distance.

I understand. I despise it, but I understand. For all my

twelfth night balls and worsted gowns, I am still a convict woman. It is a stain I will never wash away. I understand the great shame it would bring to a military officer; a man of God, to give his heart to a factory lass. A concubine.

A part of me loathes myself for this unshakable love I feel, after all the lies he has told. I want to turn my back. But I know I will never be able to. Because as hard as I had tried to be the one with the power, I am well aware of the pull he has over me. Instead of the anger I want to feel, I am gripped with terror that I will find him dead.

There is Squires' inn; square and white at the water's edge. Row boats are tied to the jetty, men sitting on the riverbank with pipes in their hands. The sinking sun sears off the water.

I turn away from the river to face the thick wall of bushland. I push my way through branches and step over tangled knots of ferns.

Is that an overgrown path beneath my feet? Impossible to tell. I follow it anyway, deeper into the shadowed wilderness, pushing away thoughts of natives' spears, and of the monsters that hide in the bush. Ancient trees reach forever upwards, barely moved by a breath of hot wind.

And then I stop walking. Because I see a crooked stone chimney peering out from between the trees.

The thin path leading up to the cottage is almost lost beneath the undergrowth. Exhaustion pressing down on me, I take slow, careful steps, holding my skirts above my ankles. With each step, the twigs beneath my feet crackle loudly. Birds flee as I approach; flashes of colour in the fading light.

I can tell from a distance the place is abandoned. The bush has started to reclaim the house; vines growing up one wall and a tree branch curling through a window. The door hangs open on its hinges.

I step inside. Remnants of old lives are still here; the table in the corner, the iron fingers of the grate, jar lids scattered between fallen leaves. And there on the wooden walls are the bloodstains; wine-dark shadows that have barely begun to fade. But at the back of the house, a rotting patch of wall has been replaced, the new planks of wood stark and white against the old. They seem out of place, out of time.

I stare at the bloodstains. And I imagine Blackwell pulling the trigger. Imagine Owen's cousins falling. The images don't make sense to me; they don't feel right. A part of my brain refuses to accept that Blackwell is capable of doing such a thing. But I have learnt better than to succumb to my naivety.

He has killed. And he has lied. But none of that changes the worry that is heaving in my chest.

I call his name. It feels wrong to do so; to disrupt this silence with the name of the man who had pulled the trigger. My voice vanishes. And I turn abruptly, unable to bear being in the place any longer.

I call again.

Still, there is silence. I keep walking.

A hundred yards from the hut, I see a swathe of grey fabric hanging from a tree. Old curtains, I realise. Taken from the cottage. They have been hung from low branches to create a crude shelter.

In front of the tent is a burned-out campfire, and beside it, a pile of tools; a hammer and saw, a wood plane lying on its side. I walk towards them, holding my breath.

Blackwell steps out from beneath the shelter.

A sob of relief escapes me and I throw my arms around him. For a fleeting moment, I don't care about his lies, or the blood staining the wall of the cottage. I am just glad he is alive. Glad I am alive. The odds of us both standing here breathing seem impossibly high.

I feel his arms slide around me. And I could break. But I step back, out of his embrace. He grips my shoulders, eyes full of questions.

"What are you doing here, Eleanor?"

"I came to find you. I was worried for you. I was so afraid that…" I glance around. "Are you alone? You've not been followed? Owen…"

"Owen's not here," he says. "No one is here."

That doesn't feel true. There are ghosts from the past here. Spectres of Owen's family, of Blackwell's unspoken guilt.

"Why have you come out here?" I ask, though I feel I already know the answer. If he leaves this place without absolution, those ghosts will follow him all the way to England.

"When I came to this cottage after the uprising," he says, "there was a woman here. One of the men's wives perhaps. She was hiding in the bush outside the house. She must have seen me coming." He sighs deeply. "I didn't see her until after the men were dead. I looked into her eyes and all I saw was hate.

"I came back here to tell her how much I regret what I did." His voice is low, and as unsteady as I've ever heard it. "But she's gone. There's no one left."

I stare through the trees at the outline of the house. Look back at the makeshift shelter he has erected. A cockatoo swoops; a ghostly flash of white.

"Why such guilt over this above all the other conflict you've seen?" I don't mean to excuse this bloodstained cottage. Just to understand.

"Because this was no battlefield," says Blackwell. "This was a man's home."

"You were doing as you were instructed."

"Yes. Without question." I hear that expressionlessness I had seen so often in that hut in Parramatta. An emptiness, I see now, for his guilt to hide behind. Is this the cost of power, I wonder? A haunting guilt? Perhaps power is something that ought not be so fiercely sought.

"You must have been here for days," I say, thinking of all the blurred sunrises and sunsets I had been locked in my prison cell. My eyes drift to the tools scattered beside the firepit. And I think back to the day we had sat beside the Parramatta River and stared up at the towering redgums.

I learned a little construction when I was at school, he had said. *A way of leaving your mark on a place.*

"You're the one who made the repairs to the house," I say. "A way of leaving your mark."

He doesn't speak at once, just turns to look at the cottage, silhouetted in the twilight. "Well," he says finally, "perhaps in this case it is more about undoing the mark I have left on the place."

"The cottage is empty. Why have you continued? Fixing the house will not change what happened inside it."

"No," he says. "It won't. But mending this cottage was to be an act of decency. Perhaps in some small way it still can."

I hear the fragility in his voice; the guilt hiding beneath

the surface that is pushing its way out.

"Maggie's trial?" I say huskily. "Is that why you let Owen walk free? Because of all that happened at this cottage?"

Blackwell's eyes are on the cracked windows of the house. "How could I send another member of this family to his death?"

I let out my breath in a sharp exhalation. I need to walk away. I can't stand here speaking to the man who has lied to me from the beginning. The man who let Maggie's killer walk free.

I stride out past the tent, past the cottage, past the remains of the campfire, yanking on my skirts as they entangle themselves on branches. I have no thought of which direction I'm walking, or what I will find. A part of me wants to walk all the way back to Sydney Town, but if I set out in the dark, the forest will swallow me. I turn in a circle. I cannot have walked more than a mile from Squires' inn. But in which direction?

I hear footsteps behind me, the undergrowth crackling. Blackwell calls my name. I hear confusion in his voice. Why am I running away?

He reaches for my arm, but I yank away.

"You lied," I say. "About your wife."

Something passes across his eyes. What is he to attempt? An apology? An explanation? How can any of that be sufficient?

"Yes," he says finally. "I did."

A part of me is glad for his bluntness – glad he has attempted neither apology nor explanation. I don't need him to explain. I know what I am. I know why he did what he did. I had arrived on his doorstep in blue striped skirts.

Wind rustles the bush, making me shiver. The light is draining quickly. The shadows are thickening and the birds shrieking in the trees.

"You can't stay out here," Blackwell says finally. "It's getting dark." He turns back to look at the tent. "I have shelter."

I let out a humourless laugh, because at those words I am back on the streets of Parramatta, standing in the rain outside Reverend Marsden's church. Where would I be right now if I had chosen not to follow Blackwell back to his hut? A pointless question, of course. Because we both know well there can be no changing the past.

And just like I did that stormy night, I walk with him back to his shelter, because I have no place else to go.

I take the food from my pockets and sit it on the edge of the blanket. Despite all the walking, I'm not hungry. All I want is to sleep. To forget this most confronting, draining of days; a day I was never supposed to even see.

I curl up on the edge of the blanket Blackwell has laid across the ground. The wool smells stale and damp. And I watch the last of the light give way to the dark. My thoughts are churning. I think of Lottie alone in her cell, awaiting death. Waiting for me to take Owen's life; to bring about the justice I have been so desperately craving since I found Maggie's body on the side of the road. I think of Blackwell's lies and the ghosts in the cottage that have kept him unable to leave this place.

I lie there in the dark, listening to him breathe. I know he is awake. I imagine he is staring into the darkness, eyes open, thoughts whirring as quickly as my own.

I feel his hand slide over my shoulder. I can't bring

myself to look at him, even through the thick dark. Moonlight shafts through the trees, painting shadows on the roof of the tent.

"A God-fearing soldier like you is not supposed to love a woman who sits at the spinning wheels in the factory," I say. "That's why you lied, isn't it." It is not a question.

He lets out a deep breath. "I was led to believe certain things about this place. About the Irish. And about the convicts. Especially the women. And I never questioned any of it.

"I was taught to think of the Irish as animals. I didn't question that before I came out here to the Owens' cottage. And I pulled the trigger on innocent men." His fingers tighten around the top of my arm. "And when I took in a factory lass from the street, I was not expecting you. I was expecting what I had been told I would see."

"Immorality," I say. "A loose woman."

I know that, had I not been the one in convict slops, I would have seen this place in the same way. I would have watched the women from the factory crawl into bed with their settlers and soldiers, and I would have called them whores.

"And so? Your lie was protection against temptation?"

"Yes," he says. "I suppose that's what it was."

Protection against the shame of falling for a factory lass.

I can't bring myself to speak – to do so would be to either voice my anger or relinquish it. And I can do neither.

The silence between us is thick; heavier than it had been the night I'd first lain beside him in the night. Had he decided then to lie to me about his wife? Erect that barrier that would keep me distanced? Or had that decision come later?

"For whatever it's worth," he says, "I feel a great anger at myself."

"Because of me? Because I caused you to sin?" I hear my own bitterness.

"Because of you," he says. "But not because you caused me to sin. Because I lost you. To my own foolishness. And my own lies."

I roll over. I can barely see more than his outline, but I know I am looking into his eyes.

"You're a good person, Eleanor," he says. "You deserve far better than what you've been given in this place."

I let out a cold laugh. I'm unsure if his words are an understatement, or the greatest of untruths. I don't feel like a good person. I'm not sure I ever have.

"Captain Grant told Flynn you and I were together," I tell him. "He broke off our betrothal."

For a long time, Blackwell doesn't speak. "I'm sorry," he says finally. "I truly am."

His words have left an ache inside me. For the first time, there is no barrier between us; no Flynn, no Sophia, no colony watching. No barrier but my own anger, my own reluctance to let him near me after all he has done.

His hand tightens around my arm. Does he mean to hold on to me? Do so and he will likely drown. I am barely able to hold my head above water.

"My entire world," he says finally, "it's been upturned since I came to this place. I've found myself questioning everything I thought I knew. And that has shown me very clearly that I should not have blindly accepted the things I was taught. I ought to have thought for myself."

How well I know that feeling. *I ought to have thought for*

myself, as I had carted counterfeit coins around the city. *I ought to have thought for myself* as the thief-takers had led me from Jonathan's townhouse.

"This place changes you," I say.

"No. Not the place. The people in it." His thumb moves against my shoulder.

"I was to die," I say. "For your murder."

He sits up suddenly. "What?"

And I tell him it all; of the rebels coming to the Grants', and the body in the street. I tell him of how I slid out of the hangman's grasp and how Lottie is to die.

Blackwell lets out his breath. He shuffles across the blanket, pressing his forehead against mine. His hands are tangled tightly in my hair. He pulls me hard against him, his nose brushing against mine. "I'm sorry," he breathes. "I'm sorry I wasn't there. I'm sorry for everything."

I let him hold me. I need him to do it. My anger has not faded, but I need something to steady myself. The relief of escaping the gallows is so fierce I can barely fathom it. Coupled with grief over Lottie and the pain of Blackwell's betrayal, I feel as though I am falling.

"In the morning," I say, "we go back to Sydney. You've only days until your ship leaves. And nothing you do here is going to change the past."

Each of us here must live with our mistakes; live with the crimes that sent us into this new world. Why should Blackwell be any different? But in spite of myself I curl up against his chest, trying to memorise the feel of him beneath my fingers before he disappears from my life forever.

I hear noise outside and sit up quickly. A crackle of twigs. It is not the sound of an animal. It is the sound of footsteps.

Natives? My heart speeds.

Blackwell climbs out from beneath the shelter. On my knees behind him, I look into the darkness. I can make out the shapes of the trees in the moonlight.

"Who's there?" says Blackwell. The old authority is back in his voice. The sound of it is swallowed quickly by the dark. He reaches for the tinderbox and lights the lamp. He holds it up, shining it over the thick pillars of the trees. The orange glow picks out a small face between the gnarled trunks.

"Kate?" I can't make sense of her being here.

Blackwell looks at me for an explanation, but I just stumble through the darkness towards the girl.

"What are you doing here? You came all this way on your own?"

She throws her arms around my waist. "A man came to the tavern," she coughs. "He made me tell him where you were." Her voice is wavering, cheeks stained with tears.

My stomach tightens. "Did he hurt you?"

She shakes her head, but keeps it pressed hard against my chest. "He's here," she says. "He came for you." She looks past me at Blackwell. "And him."

I catch Blackwell's glance, then look hurriedly back at Kate. "Did he force you to come out here?"

She shakes her head. "I followed him." Her voice is trembling. "I thought he was going to hurt you. I had to find you. Tell you he was coming."

I close my eyes and pull Kate close again. "You must be exhausted." I feel a tug in my chest that she might put herself in danger on my account. "Where is Owen now?" I whisper. And her gaze drifts past me to the inky outline of the cottage.

Blackwell steps out into the night.

"No," I say. "Please don't."

I know that somehow, this has to end. But Blackwell is walking towards Owen without a weapon. And I see that this can only end one way.

CHAPTER THIRTY-FOUR

"Now my boys, liberty or death."

Philip Cunningham,
Leader of Castle Hill rebellion
Sunday 4 March 1804

Faint light appears in the window of the cottage. Blackwell walks towards it, his steps almost soundless against the undergrowth.

I crawl back into the shelter, feeling my way through the flickering light for his pack. A water flask. A husk of bread. Jar of potted meat. I find no weapon.

I let out my breath in frustration and crawl back out of the shelter. Hand the lamp to Kate.

"Stay here," I tell her, putting my hand to her back to usher her inside. She crawls onto the blanket and sits up on her knees. "Rest," I say, though her eyes are wide and bright. Lamplight flickers on her cheeks, and for a second I see her mother.

The cottage door is hanging open. I can see Owen at the table. Blackwell sits opposite him, on chairs they have reclaimed from the wilderness. There is a pistol in the centre of the table, Owen's hand splayed over it.

"You're not welcome in this place, Lieutenant," he is saying. "You shouldn't have come." He shifts in his chair, making it creak loudly.

Blackwell nods slowly. "I understand. And if you wish to kill me now, I understand that too."

Owen falters. A response he was not expecting. He glances out the door. "Where's Nell? I know she's here."

"Your business is with me," says Blackwell. "Not with her."

But Blackwell knows nothing of the silent promise I made to Lottie as we knelt together in her jail cell. My business with Patrick Owen goes far deeper than either of these men know.

You're strong enough to do it, Nell. I hadn't believed her words then and I don't believe them now. But I want to.

Owen's hand tightens around the pistol and I clench my teeth to keep from crying out. If I force myself to look at this from his perspective, I can see the perfection of Blackwell dying in this place. Of catching him here so his blood might be added to that he had spilled.

Owen turns the pistol over and shuffles in his chair. It scrapes noisily against the earthen floor. Opposite him, Blackwell is motionless. His hands are curled around his knees, chest open as though awaiting the shot. Taller, broader; he is the more dominant of the men, without even trying.

He faces Owen, waiting. Waiting for him to do as he has been invited, and pull the trigger.

I see then that Blackwell's invitation has taken the power out of this moment. Maggie's murder had been a way for Owen to prove his dominance, Lottie had said. He kills to be powerful, to be strong. But where is the power in this?

"Where is Nell?" he asks again.

"I'm here," I say, stepping inside the hut. Blackwell glances at me. My eyes go to the pistol on the table, then I look back at Owen, expectant.

"The girl," he says. "Who is she?"

"You know who she is."

His jaw tightens.

What does he see when he looks at Kate? Does he see her mother writhing beneath his hands as he crushed the life from her? Or does he just see something to be discarded, like Maggie, like Lottie, like his son?

His breathing grows louder. Is he rattled by the sight of Kate Abbott, with her mother's eyes, her mother's face? Is he haunted by his own ghosts, just as Blackwell is? Have the women of the factory somehow crawled beneath his skin?

"Does she make you feel guilty, Owen?" I ask. "Does she make you think of her mother?"

"Guilty?" he repeats, his humourless laugh sounding hollow in the stillness. "Why would I feel guilty? They're just worthless lags."

In a flash of rage, I snatch the gun from the table. Hold it out, Owen in my line of sight. And in a second, Blackwell is on his feet. I feel his hands on my shoulders, easing my arms down. And then he stops. Steps back.

He is giving me the choice, I realise. He is letting me make my own decision.

Untouchable Owen. If I pull the trigger here, with only Blackwell as a witness, I know I would avoid the hangman. My thoughts are far clearer than they were the night I had walked towards Owen's hut with a kitchen knife in my hand.

I couldn't do it then, but perhaps I can do it now.

For a moment, I see it; Owen's body slumping as I fire into his chest. The look of shock on his face as he falls; surprise that he might be taken out by a factory lass. I imagine the sense of satisfaction I will feel to know I have done as Lottie had asked. To know there is some tiny flicker of justice in this place.

And then I see the Irish rebels, gathering, rising at the death of their leader, inspired to seek revenge. Placing the blame for Owen's murder at Lieutenant Blackwell's feet.

And it won't be satisfaction I feel; not really. It will be that awful sickness I felt when I saw Dan Brady's body sprawled across the alley. And it will be terror at the thought that there are still days until Blackwell's ship leaves for England and the croppies may ensure he does not see them out.

I keep the pistol held out in front of me. Still, I don't know what my decision will be. Perhaps Owen's death will let me feel some hollow sense of justice. Perhaps it will still the constant churning in my chest. Or perhaps taking his life will haunt me forever.

Owen's eyes meet mine for a moment. In the flickering lamplight, they are glazed and expectant. Fearful. The sight of his terror brings a rush of satisfaction.

I hear my heart thudding in my ears. An animal shrieks in the bush beyond the hut. The sound seems both close and far away. The world feels unsteady, as though I am being tossed upon the seas.

The next sound I hear is footsteps. Soft footfalls against the floor of the cottage. Owen is walking. He has decided I will not shoot. Has decided I am too weak.

I tighten my hands around the stock of the pistol, feeling my finger on the trigger. And then I feel Blackwell's hand against my shoulder. I lower the pistol and set it on the table as I hear Owen's footsteps disappearing into the bush. Let him walk, I think, as he is swallowed by the darkness. Let him carry his guilt, and his shame, just as the rest of us must.

CHAPTER THIRTY-FIVE

A swarm of people has gathered in George Street, waiting for the gates of the jail yard to open. A woman's execution always draws a crowd.

People are chatting excitedly, laughing, children leaping over puddles. I want to scream; want to shake them. How can there be chatter, laughter, leaping, when Lottie is to die?

My eyes dart, searching for Owen. I pray he will stay away. I don't want Lottie to know I have failed to do as she has asked. And I don't want him to be the last thing she sees before she dies.

I don't see Owen, but I do see Blackwell. As the gates creak open and the crowd funnels through, our eyes meet. I look away quickly.

At the sight of the hangman standing upon the gallows, I am breathless. I have never seen a person put to death. And just a few days earlier the noose had been tied for me. I want to rush from the jail yard. Close my eyes and pretend this isn't happening. Pretend that when I next step into the Rocks I will find Lottie in the kitchen with a baby's basket at her feet. I try to breathe. And against every thread of instinct I have, I push my way to the front of the crowd. I need Lottie to see me. I need her to know that today she is not alone.

Though my eyes are on the noose dancing in the hot wind, I'm aware of Blackwell making his way towards me. Always, I'm aware of him.

He pushes his way through the crowd and stands behind me. Puts a hand to my shoulder. And yes, this simple gesture is a big thing, a part of me sees that. Him with his red coat and me with my convict stain, and anyone in the colony who could see us. But it is not enough to undo two years of lies.

In spite of myself, a part of me wants to step closer. Let him hold me while I watch Lottie die. But I don't want to be comforted by him. I don't want to need him. I've already needed him far too much. I take a step away.

Out Lottie comes from the jail; a soldier in front of her, behind her; a rifle at her back. Her chin is lifted defiantly, and her eyes are sharp. She has conjured up her pride, her confidence, her brassiness, and I am glad of it. This is the way I want to remember her; not as the tearful mess she had been the last time we had spoken. She looks strikingly, painfully alive.

I think of that tiny smile she had given me the day I had first arrived in Parramatta; a smile that had done so much to calm me, to reassure me, to show me this place had some humanity in it.

I think of drinking with her by the river, and of dancing on Christmas night. And I think of standing outside her hut the day she had been betrothed to Owen, begging her to stay.

What if I had found kinder words? Or had not turned away from her when she'd had the men tell me of Blackwell's crimes? Could I have tried harder to keep her from marrying? Tears well up behind my eyes – I know it is far too late for any of these questions.

She climbs the scaffold on steady legs. My throat is tight and my heart is fast. I look up at her. I want her to see how grateful I am that she came forward, gave herself up to save me. Still, I have no thought of whether she is telling the truth about Dan Brady's death. Perhaps I never will. There are no more words I can say to her, of course, but I meet her gaze; thank her, forgive her for leading Owen to Blackwell. Hope the look in my eyes tells her how much I love her.

As the hangman slides the noose over her head, I feel my body grow hot, begin to shake. I keep my feet planted in the dust of the jail yard, praying my legs will support me. I hold my breath and clench my jaw, as though trying to preserve this last fleeting second of Lottie's life.

A knock of the trapdoor and she is gone. A quick death, but one that feels all too easy. As though it is nothing but a trifle to take a factory lass from the world.

I stumble out of the jail. There is a strange energy to the place. Perhaps it's just my imagination; I am dizzy and unsettled as I try to navigate this world of which Lottie is no longer a part.

Soldiers are gathering in the street, murmuring among themselves. Blackwell passes me and his eyes meet mine. Then he leaves the jail with the other soldiers. Crunch and thud go the boots, in flawless formation.

For a moment, I stand motionless, watching after them;

that vibrant wash of colour against the muted earth and sandstone of Sydney Town. The Rum Corps dominates this land in every way.

On my walk back to the tavern, a dam opens inside me. The tears I have been holding back cascade down my cheeks. I cry messy, racking sobs as I walk, ignoring the stares of passers-by. I cry for Lottie, for Willie, for both my inability to kill Owen and out of gratitude for the fact I found the strength to let him go free. I cry over Blackwell's lies, and for the convict stain I will never wash away. I cry because tomorrow he will be gone.

When I get back to the Whaler's, my eyes are swollen and my cheeks are hot.

Charlie goes to the counter and pours a shallow cannikin of rum. Presses it into my hand without a word.

I manage a faint smile. "Thank you, Charlie. You're good to me."

"Ain't hard," he says with a smile. "Mouthful of liquor and you're tame as a kitten." He nods to the cup. "Drink up. It'll help."

I toss back the rum, relishing the warmth in my throat. "Where's Kate?"

"Upstairs. Sweeping the hallway." He gives me a pointed look. "She's a good worker. But I can't spare another room."

I nod. "She can stay with me."

"You sure?"

"Of course." It feels like the least I can do for Maggie, and for all the women still weaving cloth in Parramatta.

Charlie takes a glass from the shelf and pours his own drink. "How was it?" he asks, elbows on the counter. "It happen quickly?"

I nod, my throat tightening. Two fresh tears slide down my face.

He reaches across the bar and squeezes my shoulder. "That's all you can hope for."

I turn the cannikin around in my hands. "It ought to have been me."

Charlie tosses back his drink in one mouthful. "You remember killing that man?"

I shake my head. "I don't remember anything except—"

"Well then," he cuts in, "how do you know it ought to have been you?"

I appreciate his attempt to relieve me of my guilt. But I know the sight of Dan Brady with a bullet in his chest will haunt me until I die.

By evening, the tavern is busy, full of curious chatter. Soldiers march past the windows, people clustered to the sides of the street, cheering, hooting, booing as they pass.

Kate stands with her forehead pressed to the glass. "What's happening, Nell?"

"I don't know." I look over her shoulder. A military band struts past the window, the pompous brass melody muted behind the glass. I usher Kate away. "Go and wipe those tables in the back."

The gossip filters in later in the evening, the story told by men with shining eyes, the tale growing more theatrical with each cannikin of rum.

Captain Macarthur, the governor's most prominent opponent, had refused to stand trial over unpaid fines.

"They say the judge owed Macarthur money," one man tells me, jabbing his pipe in my face for emphasis. "Can't hardly blame him for not wanting to be tried by such a man, now can you."

Macarthur, another man announces, had been supported by the Corps officers presiding over the trial. And in response Governor Bligh had brought charges of treason upon the soldiers. Demanded they present themselves at Government House.

"Them officers, they didn't go to Bligh," says the man with the pipe. "They went to Johnson, their commanding officer. Then they all marched their way to Government House and overthrew the governor." He slams his empty cup on the bar. "Another, lass. Fill it to the top this time."

The conversation in the tavern becomes louder, more heated. There are those who support the Rum Corps' coup. Others who are wary of the military's power.

"They say Macarthur planned the whole thing from his prison cell."

"Heard Bligh was hiding under his bed when the redcoats came."

"What hope we got now the lobsters are in charge?"

And so this is the rebellion that has been brewing throughout my time in New South Wales. I'd imagined it would be the croppies who would rise up. Had imagined the Irish rebels would be the ones to turn this place on its head. But I can't be surprised by this. Can't be surprised it is the Rum Corps that has marched forth with guns out to take what they want. The power has been with them all along.

Much later, when the tales have become muted and all heard before, Blackwell slips into the tavern. His uniform makes him a beacon, and men and women surround him, asking questions, demanding answers. I can tell from his flushed cheeks and slightly dishevelled hair that there is liquor in him. Can tell he was among the men who had descended on Governor Bligh. Though the tavern is heaving, the patrons clear a table for him to sit at in the corner of the room. One man, who's already told five conflicting stories, waves a hand in the air, trying to get my attention.

"A drink for the lieutenant, lass! Quick now!"

I can feel Blackwell trying to catch my eye through the crowd. I turn away, filling a glass and handing it to Kate.

"Take this to the lieutenant."

She weaves her way through the people, returning with a sassy smile on her lips that makes me think of Maggie. "He wants to speak with you."

"I'm busy," I say, well aware of my own pettiness. And I sail up and down the bar, finding glasses to polish and shelves to tidy. But I am acutely aware of his presence. Unable to keep from looking at him. And finally, I give in, taking his empty glass from his table with as much nonchalance as I can muster.

He holds out a penny. "May I have another?"

I take the money and slide it into my apron. "Two in an hour. That's not like you."

"Well," he says, eyes meeting mine, "I've to do something while I sit here hoping you'll eventually speak to me."

I say nothing. I want him to leave. But I also want him to stay. Stay in the tavern. Stay in the colony. But it's far too late for any of that.

"I was a fool," he says. His words should feel like a victory, but they don't. Because I know he had not been a fool. He had been acting in line with beliefs that had been ingrained in him since he had first pulled on his uniform.

I shake my head. "You're no fool. You knew exactly what you were doing."

"Yes," he says. "I knew what I was doing. I was doing as I was taught to do. And that's what makes me a fool."

I close my eyes for a moment. A dark strand of hair hangs over his cheek and it takes all my resolve not to reach out and touch it.

"Meet me at the wharf tomorrow morning," he says. "Please. Nine o'clock."

I fold my arms; a gesture of self-preservation. "Your ship is due to leave tomorrow."

"Yes," says Blackwell. "In the evening. So give me the day. And then you never need have anything to do with me again."

I hesitate. But then I find myself nodding.

I see the faintest of smiles on Blackwell's lips. "Thank you," he says. He stands. "I don't need that second drink."

He is out the door before I can give him back his penny.

CHAPTER THIRTY-SIX

In the morning, I sit at a table in the corner of the tavern and write a carefully worded letter. I fold it, seal it and slip it into my pocket. And then I make my way to the wharf.

Blackwell is waiting for me on the edge of the water, coat buttoned to his neck and boots gleaming. At the sight of me, a tentative smile breaks across his face. "I'm glad to see you. I wasn't sure you'd come."

A small, single-masted boat is bobbing on the swell, its sail furled against the hot wind. A seaman sits by the tiller, legs stretched out in front of him, awaiting our arrival.

I raise my eyebrows. "Where are we going?"

"You'll see."

Blackwell offers me his hand and helps me step into the boat. I fold myself neatly onto the bench seat and look out over the glittering sea. An enormous three-masted ship lies at anchor beside the dock, men swarming up the gangway with crates in their arms. Tonight it will set sail for England.

Soon, our boat is flying down the river, the hot wind billowing the sail. When last I made this journey, from the silver swell of Sydney Harbour, inland towards Parramatta, I was bound for the factory above the jail. The enormous shadows of the trees, the animal shrieks within the bush, the inky darkness that had cloaked the land; every part of it had filled me with terror. But today the golden water feels different. I lift my face upwards, enjoying the warmth on my cheeks. This sun-bleached land will be my life forever, but I am achingly grateful to be living it.

For a moment I imagine I am the one with the ticket for England in my hand. The one with the freedom to leave this place at will. Would I climb onto that ship if I had the chance? The woman I am now has no place in London.

And is there a place for me here, on the edge of this vast wilderness? I have been gifted the life I thought I was to lose, and I want to believe there is something for me in it beyond the misery of the factory. A purpose beyond mere survival.

I can feel Blackwell's eyes on me. He peers beneath the brim of my straw bonnet, trying to catch my gaze. I'm acutely aware I've barely spoken a word to him as the hot morning has stretched towards afternoon.

I reach into my pocket for the letter. Hold it out to him. "When you go back to England, I need you to deliver this."

He frowns. "What is it?"

That morning, I had penned a letter to the magistrate who had sent me across the seas. I had outlined the role Henry Wilder had played in my husband's coining venture. And I had outlined my firm belief that he had murdered Jonathan Marling in order to keep his own involvement a secret.

Perhaps Wilder will not be found guilty. Perhaps I am too late in finding my voice. But I can no longer stay silent. There is already far too much injustice in the world.

Blackwell slides the letter into his pocket. "Is this the reason you came today? To see that the letter got back to London?"

I hesitate. Would I be here otherwise? I don't know. But here I am.

The boat knocks against a narrow jetty. Ahead of us, the trees part to reveal manicured farmland, the outline of a large brick cottage in the distance. I frown.

"Who lives here?"

"Captain Macarthur and his wife." Blackwell climbs to his feet, helping me out of the boat. I stay planted on the jetty, swatting at the flies that are circling my face.

"Why have you brought me here?"

"I'll show you." He puts a gentle hand to my elbow, ushering me up the path from the jetty and across a wide brown lawn towards the house. Fledgling trees waver on either side of the path.

My nerves are roiling. Once upon a time I could have held my own against people like this. Dined on jellies and drunk champagne. But I am wearing threadbare skirts from Parramatta market, my stained convict papers tucked in my pocket. I don't belong in this world any longer.

I look edgily at Blackwell. Is this an attempt to parade me on his arm? To show me he has found a way past his shame?

But then I see it is more than that. Because after stilted introductions, Mrs Macarthur leads me into a drawing room where a fortepiano is sitting against one wall.

"Lieutenant Blackwell tells me you play," she says.

I stare at the piano, hardly able to believe the sight of it pressed up against the wall. "Yes," I manage. "At least, I used to."

"A surgeon on the First Fleet brought it over with him," says Mrs Macarthur. "When he returned to England he had no mind to take it back. The dear man left it for me." She gestures to the instrument. "Please."

For a long time, I don't play. I just sit at the bench and stare down at the keys. I have left behind so much of who I once was, a part of me feels lost and unsure. I was a lady when I last sat at the keyboard. I don't want my skills to have left me.

From somewhere deep in the house, I hear the ringing of servants' bells, footsteps, children's laughter. I feel almost unbearably small. I know well that following last night's coup, Captain Macarthur has taken joint control of the colony. I am a factory lass sitting in the drawing room of the most powerful man in New South Wales.

I bring my hands to the keys. Lower my fingers into a deep, resonant chord. The sound feels oddly out of place with the forest encroaching on the window. But it brings a smile to my face. Brings a warmth to my entire body.

My fingers move, uncertain and imprecise, as they begin to remember this part of me. Faster they go, churning through preludes and fugues, and neat, rippling sonatas. And then a freeing improvisation that goes some way to easing the grief pressing down on my chest.

Blackwell enters the room. He sits beside me on the piano bench and watches my fingers move.

I stop playing, letting the silence settle. And I turn to face him. "Thank you. This means more to me than you could know."

A nod. "Of course." He puts a hand to my wrist. "We ought to leave if I'm to get this letter back to the ship in time."

When we are gliding back down the river, I say, "Are you not to leave New South Wales?" Blackwell's farewell with Mrs Macarthur had been casual, brief. Not the farewell of a man leaving for the other side of the world.

His eyes drift towards the bushland on the edge of the river. The Owens' hut is there somewhere with its bloodstained walls, being slowly devoured by the forest. Then he looks back to face me.

"Eleanor," he says carefully, "I didn't come to Sydney to find a ship back to England. I came to find you. To tell you the truth about Sophia. In hope that you might find some way to forgive me."

I open my mouth to speak, but find nothing but silence. I had never questioned the fact that Blackwell was to leave. But had he ever said as much? Or had I drawn the conclusion on my own?

"That day at the Whaler's Arms, you told me your ship was leaving in a fortnight."

He looks at me pointedly. "And you told me you were to be married."

"Oh," I say. "I…" My unformed sentence trails off. The sailor leans on the tiller, easing the boat through the mangroves encroaching on the centre of the river. If he has heard our murmured conversation, his face gives nothing away.

Blackwell shifts forward on the bench, so his knees are inches from mine. "I know I will never make things right with

Owen. It's something I must live with." He looks up to meet my gaze. "But perhaps I might begin to make things right with you?"

There is apprehension in his eyes; a certain shyness completely mismatched with the ruby gold brilliance of his uniform. That shyness makes my breath catch. Because for the first time, I see without doubt that I matter. That a factory lass with a bloodstained ticket of leave might be the difference between this officer staying in this place or sailing away.

But I also realise that I do not want that power.

I feel an unbidden happiness at the thought of him staying. But the lies he had told me are still there, not so far beneath the surface. Still I don't know if I will be able to look past them.

"That choice must be yours," I tell him. "I can make no promises."

He nods. "Of course." But the tiny smile that passes between us makes something warm in my chest.

Last night, I had trudged upstairs long after midnight. Crawled into bed beside Kate and stared out into the darkness. Something felt different about the place; an energy in the air, brought about by the governor's demise.

I know that, in the aftermath of the Rum Corps' coup, little will change for those of us at the bottom of the pile. The overthrowing of the governor was all for the benefit of the men at the top.

But things have been shaken, tipped from their axis. And if things can change at the top, perhaps one day they might also change at the bottom. Perhaps an officer and a factory lass might find a way to share a life.

And perhaps when the next barge of women comes gliding up the Parramatta River, they might find a safe place to sleep. Perhaps the next Irish lag to open his mouth will not be tied to the triangle and flogged until his back is raw.

Perhaps if we continue to speak, one day we may be heard.

HISTORICAL NOTE

Reverend Samuel Marsden's "female register" was created in 1806, classing all women in the colony, with the exception of some widows, as either "wife" or "concubine". Only Church of England marriages were recognised as legitimate; any woman married in Catholic or Jewish services was automatically considered a concubine. The document reached influential circles in London and led to the perception of Australian women being sexually immoral; a view which survived long into the 20th century.

But the female register was not entirely without benefit. Samuel Marsden was acutely conscious of overcrowding at the "factory above the jail", and well aware that many women were turning to prostitution in order to secure lodgings, particularly after the fire that destroyed much of the factory in December 1807. The register was part of Marsden's ongoing attempt to have suitable housing built for the ever-growing number of female convicts. In 1818, he was finally successful, with work beginning on the colony's second female factory, which would operate from 1821 to 1848. While overcrowding, limited rations, and an unsanitary work environment were still major problems at the new Parramatta factory, the women were at least provided with a place to sleep each night.

***

The Castle Hill Irish rebellion became known as "Australia's Vinegar Hill", named after a major battle in the 1798 rebellion in Ireland. While the Castle Hill uprising of 1804 was swiftly quashed by the Rum Corps, its ideals of freedom and justice later served as inspiration for one of Australia's most famous rebellions. In the Eureka Stockade of 1854, in which gold miners protested against over-policing and unfair laws, rebels used the password "Vinegar Hill".

***

In 1793, the trading vessel *Hope* arrived in New South Wales from America carrying much-needed supplies – along with 7,500 gallons of rum. The *Hope's* captain stubbornly announced that he would not sell a scrap of his supplies until every ounce of liquor was first purchased. A group of officers from the New South Wales Corps banded together to purchase all the *Hope's* cargo without competition. New

South Wales, like many British colonies, was short on coins, and rum (a catch-all term for all liquor) soon became an accepted form of currency, with its value largely controlled by the military. The newly nicknamed Rum Corps soon began importing stills, exchanging the liquor produced for food and labour at extremely favourable rates.

In 1806, William Bligh became governor of New South Wales. He found himself in charge of a colony with a severe shortage of food, largely due to the fact that so much of the grain produced was being used to make liquor, rather than bread.

Bligh had been ordered to control the use of alcohol as currency, and put an end to the Rum Corps' monopoly on trade. Almost immediately upon his arrival in New South Wales, Bligh clashed with Captain John Macarthur, a prominent landowner, politician and former military officer who held great sway over both the Rum Corps and the colony at large. Bligh was an iron-willed disciplinarian, a trait that had contributed to his infamous mutiny on the *Bounty,* and was again to be his undoing in New South Wales.

In January 1808, Macarthur was due to face trial over an unpaid fine, however refused to be tried by the judge, Richard Atkins, on the basis that Atkins owed him money. Macarthur received the support of the six Rum Corps officers presiding over the trial.

The following morning, Bligh requested the officers present themselves at Government House to face charges of treason. Rather than doing so, the soldiers called for their commanding officer, Major George Johnson. After almost two years of tension between Bligh and the military, Major Johnson appointed himself lieutenant governor of New

South Wales, despite there being no legal grounds for him to do so.

On the evening of the 26th of January 1808, the twentieth anniversary of the First Fleet's arrival in Sydney Cove, almost the entire New South Wales Corps marched on Government House to arrest Bligh. He and his daughter remained under house arrest for more than a year, with Major Johnson and Captain Macarthur taking control of the colony. The rumour that Bligh was cowering under the bed when the soldiers arrived was almost certainly started by the Rum Corps themselves.

***

The colony's first piano was brought to New South Wales by First Fleet surgeon George Wogan, and gifted to Elizabeth Macarthur several years later. After many years in the custody of Edith Cowan University in Perth, Western Australia, the piano was returned to the UK in 2019, to be restored in Bath.

ABOUT THE AUTHOR

Johanna Craven is an Australian-born author, composer, pianist and terrible folk fiddler. She currently divides her time between London and Melbourne. Her more questionable hobbies include ghost hunting, meditative dance and pretending to be a competitor on The Amazing Race when travelling abroad.

Find out more at www.johannacraven.com.

Lightning Source UK Ltd.
Milton Keynes UK
UKHW010808010721
386460UK00002B/230